LATE in the DAY

Also by Tessa Hadley

PRAISE FOR *LATE IN THE DAY*

"Brilliant. . . . In the hands of a lesser novelist, the intricate tangle of lives at the center of *Late in the Day* would feel like just such a self-satisfied riddle or, at best, like sly narrative machinations. Because this is Tessa Hadley, it instead feels earned and real and, even in its smallest nuances, important. . . . Hadley manages to be old-fashioned and modern and brilliantly postmodern all at once. . . . We've seen this before, and we've never seen this before, and it's spectacular."

—Rebecca Makkai, *New York Times Book Review*

"With each new book by Tessa Hadley, I grow more convinced that she's one of the greatest stylists alive. . . . To read Hadley's fiction is to grow self-conscious in the best way: to recognize with astonishment the emotions playing behind our own expressions, to hear articulated our own inchoate anxieties. . . . The whole grief-steeped story should be as fun as a dirge, but instead it feels effervescent—lit not with mockery but with the energy of Hadley's attention, her sensitivity to the abiding comedy of human desire. . . . Extraordinary."

—Ron Charles, *Washington Post*

"[Hadley] is a gifted anatomist of human relationships, with those among family members being her specialty. Her particular genius lies in the elegance and precision with which she captures the fleeting emotion, the passing, indefinable perception or tiny epiphany."

—Katherine Powers, *Wall Street Journal*

"Gorgeous, utterly absorbing. . . . More than many of her contemporaries, the British writer Tessa Hadley understands that life is full of moments when the past presses up against the present, and when the present transforms the past. Her brilliant new novel, *Late in the Day*, explores both with equal urgency."

—Margot Livesey, *Boston Globe*

"Sumptuous. . . . Hadley's fiction—both long and short—has, with a delicious, detached clarity, observed the shape of relationships: their unconventionality, their transgressions. She is a superb stylist, with none of the pretensions that have latterly been attached to such a term: dispassionate, yet voluptuous in her prose."   —Catherine Taylor, *Financial Times*

"Strange, unsettling—eerily beautiful, discomfiting, stay-up-late-addictive, sometimes hair-raising. . . . Always, it's Hadley's high-res magnification on the interplay of marital (and friendship, and parental) dynamics that supplies her work's steady gold."
                                      —Joan Frank, *San Francisco Chronicle*

"[A] splendid, perceptive book. . . . Hadley has expertly examined the complications and intimacies of marriage and family in such novels as *The Past*, *The Master Bedroom* and *Clever Girl*. In *Late in the Day* she continues her persistent exploration of human frailty and resilience, moving easily between the present and the past to reveal the hard edges and silent compromises that shape all relationships."
                                      —Connie Ogle, *Minneapolis Star Tribune*

"An immersive tale of two intertwined couples. . . . Hadley tells a juicy story in the voice of a poet."   —*People*, Best New Books

"Tessa Hadley is well-known for her inimitable portrayal of character and her latest effort, *Late in the Day*, is no disappointment. . . . A smart exploration of human nature, desire, and friendship."
                                      —*Vanity Fair*

"Her prose has the penetrating quality of Henry James at his most accessible . . . and is alert, as Virginia Woolf and Elizabeth Bowen were, to how time sculpts, warps, or casually destroys us. . . . A quiet triumph."
                                      —Michael Upchurch, *Seattle Times*

LATE

in the

DAY

A NOVEL

Tessa Hadley

HARPER ● PERENNIAL

NEW YORK ● LONDON ● TORONTO ● SYDNEY ● NEW DELHI ● AUCKLAND

HARPER ● PERENNIAL

First published in the United Kingdom in 2019 by Jonathan Cape, an imprint of Vintage Publishing.

A hardcover edition of this book was published in 2019 by HarperCollins Publishers.

P.S.™ is a trademark of HarperCollins Publishers.

Designed by Bonni Leon-Berman

Library of Congress Cataloging-in-Publication Data has been applied for.

ISBN 978-0-06-247670-8 (pbk.)

20 21 22 23 24 OFF/LSC 10 9 8 7 6 5 4 3 2 1

For Mum and Dad

ONE

THEY WERE LISTENING TO MUSIC when the telephone rang. It was a summer's evening, nine o'clock. They had finished supper and Christine was listening with intensity, sitting with her feet tucked under her in the armchair; she recognised the music although she didn't know what it was. Alex had chosen it, he hadn't consulted her and now she stubbornly wouldn't ask – he took too much pleasure in knowing what she didn't know. He lay on the sofa in the bay window with a book open in his hand, not reading it, the book dropped across his chest; he was watching the sky outside. Their flat was on the first floor and the sitting-room window looked out over a wide street lined with plane trees. A gang of parakeets zipped across from the park, and the purple-brown darkness of the copper beech next door fumed against the turquoise sky, swallowing the last light. A blackbird silhouetted with open beak on a branch must be singing, but the recorded music overrode it.

It was the landline ringing. Christine was dragged away from the music; she stood up and looked around her, to see where they'd put the handset down when they last finished with it – probably somewhere here, among the piles of books and papers. Or in the kitchen with the washing-up? Alex ignored the ringing, or only showed he was aware of it by a little irritable tension in his face – always liquidly expressive, foreign, because the eyes were so dark, outlined as if they were painted. This effect was more striking as he was growing older and brightness was leaching out of his hair, which used to be the colour of tarnished dark gold.

It was more likely to be her mother on the phone than his – or it might be their daughter Isobel, and Christine wanted to talk to her. Giving up on the handset, not bothering to fish in her bare feet for her espadrilles, she hurried up the stairs, taking them two at a time – she could still do it – to where the phone extension was, in their bedroom in the attic. The music carried on without her in the room behind, Schubert or something, and as Christine dropped onto the side of the bed and answered the phone breathlessly she was aware of the sweetness of a tumbling succession of descending notes. This room they had made under the sharp angles of the roof held in all the heat of the day and was thick with smells – traffic fumes, honeysuckle from the garden below, dusty carpet, books, her perfume and face cream, the faint body-staleness of their sheets. The prints and photographs and drawings on the walls – her own work, some of it – had sunk into the shadows, obliterated, and only the pattern of their framed shapes showed against the white paint. Through the open skylight she could hear the blackbird now.

Sweetness.

— Yes?

There was some confusion of noises at the other end of the line, as if the call was coming from a public place like a station, where it was difficult to speak. Intently someone was asking for her. — Can you hear me?

— Is it you, Lyd? Christine felt herself smiling pleasantly, sociable even though she couldn't be seen, sitting on the low bed with her knees pressed together. She thought that Lydia must have been drinking, which wasn't unheard of. Her voice was heavy, slurring as if something in it had come loose. — What are you up to?

— I'm at the hospital, Lydia shouted. — Something's happened.

— What's happened?

— It's Zachary. He was taken ill at work.

The room quaked and its stillness adjusted, a few dust motes came spiralling down from the ceiling. Unheard of for anything to harm Zachary. He was a rock, he was never ill. No, nothing so numb as a rock: a striding cheerful giant with torrents of energy. Christine said she would call a cab at once, be with Lydia in half an hour at the most. — Which hospital? Which ward should I come to? What's the matter with him?

— It's his heart.

— He's had a heart attack?

— They don't know really, Lydia said. — But they think it's his heart. One minute apparently he was in the office at the gallery, perfectly fine, talking to Jane Ogden about a new show, the next minute he keeled over. Hit the desk, everything went flying. Maybe he hit his head when he hit the desk.

3

— And what's happening now? Are they going to operate?

— Why aren't you listening, Christine? I told you, he's dead.

On her way to tell Alex, Christine paused outside the open door of her studio, where the shapes of her work waited faithfully for her in the dusk: bottles of ink, twisted tubes of paint, the Chinese porcelain pot with her pens and brushes, the pinboard stuck with postcards and pictures torn from magazines, feathers, stained cloth, scraps of weathered plastic. Creamy sheets of thick paper, laid out on her desk, waited for her mark; primed canvases were stacked against the wall, pieces in progress were on the easel or pinned onto boards. She came to this scene of her labours each morning like coming to a religious observance, performing little rituals she had never mentioned to anyone. Her strongest desire these days was to be at work in there – standing up at the easel, or head and shoulders bowed over the paper on her desk in concentration, absorbed in her imitation of forms, her inventions. But now the idea of this work – the fixed point by which she steered – was sickening. It seemed fraudulent, the sticky project of her own vanity: she closed the door on it quickly. Then she opened it again – there was a key in the lock which she turned sometimes when she didn't want to be interrupted. She took out this key and locked the studio from the outside, put the key in her jeans pocket.

The music was still playing in the front room.

— Was it your mother? Alex asked.

Her heart lunged in thick beats in her chest, she didn't know if she could speak. It was terrible to have to ruin his happiness with this news, standing over him where he lay propped up on cushions on the sofa, untroubled – or no more troubled than usual. — It was Lydia.

— What did she want?

— Alex, I have to tell you. Zachary has had a heart attack. It sounds as if it was a heart attack.

— No.

— He's dead, he's gone.

For a moment Alex was exposed to his wife in his raw shock, vivid against the brilliant red of the cushions. — Oh no, you're kidding. No.

Usually he seemed so completed and impervious, with his springy compact energy and pugnacious sharp jaw, shapely head alert and sensuous like an emperor's.

— She rang me from the hospital, UCH. I'm going to her now. I've called a cab.

His book fell to the floor and he stood up in the darkening room. — It can't be true. What happened?

— One minute he was at his desk in the office at the gallery, talking to Jane Ogden, perfectly fine, the next he keeled over, hit his head perhaps, everything went flying. Hannah tried CPR, the paramedics tried everything. Before they got him to the hospital, he was dead. Jane had to phone Lydia, she was out shopping.

— What time was this?

Christine wasn't sure, some time in the late afternoon or early evening.

5

— I can't believe it, Alex said. — No, it's impossible. When I saw him at the weekend he was fine.

— I know. It's impossible.

When Christine moved to stop the music on the CD player he told her to wait, it had almost finished. — Let it end.

He put his hands on her shoulders, detaining her, comforting her. His touch was kind, only she couldn't let herself feel it. They stood confronted. Alex was stocky, medium height – she was probably an inch or so taller than him, even in her bare feet, only he'd never believe it. At first she chafed in his grip. — I have to hurry. I don't know if she's at the hospital alone.

— The cab's not here yet, wait. Listen.

It seemed artificial and forced, waiting until the music was over. Her thoughts were racing and she couldn't hear it, hated its offer of complexity and beauty. Then she began to yield, under the steady weight of his hands, to the violin and piano and cello as they went hastening to their finish. They unlocked something clenched inside her. She realised that her arms were hugged across her chest as if she were protecting herself, or holding herself tightly shut; at least they hadn't put on the lamps in the room. They held each other. There were tears on Alex's face, he cried easily. He had a gift for ceremonies which she didn't have, they embarrassed her. Now this moment felt ceremonial, and her consciousness hushed and paused. She thought directly about Zachary for the first time, the reality of him. But that wasn't bearable.

— Let me come with you to the hospital, Alex said. — I'll drive you.

Christine thought about it. — No, it's best if I go alone. If it's just the two of us, at first. I'll bring her here. You could make up the bed for her.

She had imagined herself hurrying up and down hospital corridors in search of Lydia, who might be with Zach's body behind drawn curtains, or might have been ushered into some room set aside for the newly bereaved. But as soon as Christine came in through the glass doors of the main entrance of the hospital, Lydia stood up from one of the blue plastic chairs set out in rows in front of the reception desk, where she had been sitting among the others waiting. She had her air of a disgruntled queen, haughty and exceptional in a sky-blue velvet jacket with a fake leopard-skin collar; when Christine hurried to embrace her, people turned their heads to stare. Lydia was often mistaken for someone famous. Voluptuous, with coiling honey-coloured hair and a swollen, pouting lower lip, she devoted serious attention to her make-up and clothes to achieve this arty, sexy, theatrical look. Her pale skin was blue with shadows, like skimmed milk.

— Where have you been? I've been waiting forever!

— Only half an hour. I had to call a cab.

Christine realised that she had dreaded this meeting, imagining Lydia would be made more domineering somehow by the blow of Zachary's death: now she was ashamed and stabbed with pity, because Lydia only looked displaced and lost. Putting her arms round her friend she felt how she held herself rigidly, as if she were hurt; Lydia's hands, stiff with rings, were cold and inert. It would be her task, Christine thought, to surround her with care from now on, not to fail her. — I can't believe they've left you here alone!

— I wanted to be alone. I sent everyone away. I can't stand Jane Ogden anyway. You could see how she couldn't wait to tell the story to everyone, with her at the centre of it all, naturally. I said I only wanted you and Alex. Where's Alex?

— He's at home, making up a bed for you.

Christine had been crying in the taxi; she had been determined not to cry when she was with Lydia, in case she seemed to usurp Lydia's grief, which had priority. But now she began again, mopping her face with a wet tissue from her sleeve, knowing how ugly and foolish she looked in front of all these strangers watching – her face flushed red, mouth working helplessly open, dragged down like a baby's. — I can't believe this. It can't be true. Are you sure?

— Of course it's true. The shittiest thing is always true.

— Lyd, where is Zachary? Have you seen him? Was he still alive when you got here?

— No, and I don't want to see him. It's not him, is it? So what's the point?

She said this rather loudly and people turned to look at her. Christine reassured her, she didn't have to do anything if she didn't want to. She knew that Lydia was afraid of Zachary's body, shying away from the idea of it with an animal revulsion. And it was terrible, imagining him lying somewhere alone in this eerie impersonal building, which was lit up in the night like a ship at sea. Christine was afraid of Zachary's body too. The idea of it made her sick with dread. Yet in Lydia's place she'd probably have chosen to see it, to give a form to her fear – or at least, she'd have been even more afraid of regretting not doing it afterwards. This was one of the differences between them: Lydia acted superstitiously and followed her instincts, while Christine tried to bargain with them.

— Let's get out of this place, Lydia said.

— Don't you have to sign forms or something?

She'd signed the forms. There had to be an autopsy, she said.

— And does Grace know? Where is she?

The idea of her daughter made Lydia panic. — I've tried to ring her but she doesn't answer. She's somewhere in Glasgow, I suppose, doing whatever it is students do. Of course she'll blame me, you know how she adores her father. Everything's always my fault.

She looked challengingly at Christine, to see if her selfishness was shocking. And Christine was shocked: she was sure that her own first thought in such circumstances would have been for Isobel, protective of her, dreading Isobel's loss even more than her own. But things had been raw recently between Lydia and Grace; and Lydia had always complained, half-joking, that she was left out because her husband and her daughter were so perfectly attuned. She couldn't reinvent herself and her relationships in one instant of change.

— I thought that perhaps you could tell her, Lydia said. — You're better at that sort of thing.

Christine was about to protest, *but you're her mother*, then she stopped. Who knows: if anything had happened to Alex, she might have found herself behaving just as selfishly –

towards Sandy, for instance, Alex's son by his first wife, Christine's stepson, whom she struggled to love. Everything is provisional, she warned herself. In the next hours our perceptions will change over and over in a speeded-up evolution, as we adapt to this new torn-off shape of our lives. At every point our duty is to watch out for these stricken ones, for Lydia and Grace, not to say or do anything to hurt them. Then she thought, but I am stricken too. We're all stricken, Alex and Isobel and I, even Sandy – and all the people at the gallery. Without Zachary, our lives are thrown into disorder. Of all of us, he's the one we couldn't afford to lose.

In the back of the taxi the women hardly spoke. They didn't want the driver to know what had happened; their news wasn't ready to go into the world yet, it was still inside them, hard as stones. Seizing Christine's hand in the darkness, Lydia pressed it into her velvet jacket against her stomach, bending double over it, crushing Christine's fingers against the metal buckle of her wide belt; Christine smelled the musky, wood-notes perfume her friend always wore. — Do you have a pain? she whispered. Lydia nodded, not letting go. They were vaguely aware of the driver's apprehension, thinking she was drunk and might throw up.

The lights were on in the windows at home, and Alex was standing looking out for them. By the time they got upstairs, he had the front door of the flat held open. He opened his arms to Lydia and she stumbled into them.

— It can't be true, it can't be true, he cried. He stood

stroking her hair for a long time, in the same absorbed way he used to stroke Isobel's when she was a child, and he reached out his other hand for Christine. — But it is true, Lydia said flatly, eventually, pulling herself away.

Then she searched for her lipstick, checked her eyes in her handbag mirror. — Am I grotesque? I look such a fright. She waved a twenty-pound note. — Here's what I need, Alex darling. Buy me twenty Bensons.

He protested. — Lydia, cigarettes aren't what you need. You don't want to start that slavery again after all these years.

— You don't know what I need, you're the famous puritan. Anyway Jane Ogden gave me hers, I just remembered. They're in here somewhere.

— We need a drink, Christine said.

They poured out vodka from a bottle in the freezer; in a broken voice Alex toasted their dear friend. Dearly loved, he said and couldn't finish.

— Shut up, Alex, Christine said shakily. — You sound like a headmaster.

He couldn't sit down, he wouldn't, as if something were burning him up, keeping him on his feet. Lydia lit up a cigarette with hands that trembled. She complained that the vodka tasted like poison. Didn't they have any red wine? Alex found wine for her, poured it solicitously. When she wanted to try Grace's phone again, saying she wished Christine would talk to her, he was horrified. He insisted they couldn't announce her father's death just like that, over a mobile phone.

Lydia submitted bleakly. — You're right of course.

He would drive up to Glasgow to find Grace, and tell her

himself. Wasn't he her godfather? Her unofficial godfather, it wasn't a church thing. If he set out now he'd be there by early morning. — Zach will have her address written down somewhere, Lydia said. — I don't know where. He's always the one who knows.

Alex phoned Hannah, the gallery administrator, who'd gone to the hospital with Zachary in the ambulance. She said she'd call in to the gallery, the address must be somewhere in Zachary's desk or on his phone, she'd text it to Alex in half an hour. Hannah's voice was thick with crying. Alex asked her to contact everyone who knew, get them to keep it under wraps until he'd found Grace and told her. — Imagine if she found out on Facebook.

— *Keep it under wraps,* Christine murmured. — I can't believe he really said that.

He paced around forcefully between the lamps, making these arrangements; the women, dazed and collapsed, were grateful to him really. He was fearless and competent, he knew what to do. He told Christine to telephone the school where he worked in the morning, explain why he wouldn't be in. Before he left he kissed both the women, touching their faces with his fingertips in that intimate way he had. But they also knew that he was craving movement, couldn't bear the idea of staying there in the flat with them while they mulled over this sorrow, fermenting it.

Alex had actually been a headmaster – in a local primary school, where the kids spoke thirty-two languages between them and forty-eight per cent were on free meals. When he got the headmaster's job it had seemed like the inevitable destination of his career as an inspiring, progressive teacher, adored by the children. But in fact it had made him unhappy, and after three years he'd returned to being a classroom teacher with a class of nine-year-olds, never regretted it. Under his urbane, appealing surface, Alex wasn't really a public man as Zachary was. He was too intolerant when he was thwarted, driving his enemies into bitter opposition. Really he was a solitary thinker, not interested in most of his colleagues. The vision he had for the school – with children as thinkers and artists at its core – went needless to say against the grain of public policy on education. It went against the way the world worked. And unlike Zachary, Alex had no conviction that progress was possible, or that you could build any institution into a power for good. There was a contradiction, Christine thought, between his passionate scepticism and his commitment to the children's education. He didn't believe that anything could get better, and was often despairing – yet he dedicated himself to building and nourishing their imaginations, as if hope depended on it. She also sometimes thought, when she was angry with him, that when they left his class he forgot them.

Lydia always took up the same position when she was in their flat, at one end of the sofa where Alex had been reading his book earlier. In the pink light of the lamp she leaned back against the cushions, her sultry beauty in relief. Zachary had said that she posed like an odalisque. Christine wanted to sit close beside her, touching her, but couldn't: something warned her off. Because Lydia was desperate, she was putting on a performance of exaggerated calm. — Is this going to be the end of me? she said, lighting up another cigarette. — Did Zachary define me, who I am? I didn't think he did. But perhaps I'll have to change my mind. I've never taken the trouble to imagine myself without him. I've never done anything without him, not for years. I'm not even competent. I don't know how to pay my taxes. I can't drive.

— Oh, Lyd, don't worry about that now, Christine said. — Of course you're competent. It won't be the end of you.

— Why not now? We should talk about everything now. I suspect this moment doesn't come round again. What happens next is that everything hardens into its final form. We forget what he was really like.

— We won't forget.

— I'm forgetting him already. Something else is taking his place: the whole idea of his death, which is so improbable. He wasn't the dying type. Death is crowding out the real sensations of what he was. I'm trying to remember him at breakfast today, for instance. What did he eat?

— What did he usually eat?

— By the time I came downstairs, still in my dressing gown, he had been round to the bagel shop already, probably done a hundred things. You know he just sort of bursts out of bed energetically in the mornings, it's so exhausting. He wakes up singing. If you're not like that, if you're a night person, it can be trying. We had fresh bagels with our coffee. He slathered on that special Brittany butter he buys with the salt crystals in it, then piled it up with home-made jam from the farmers' market, ate it standing up, gulping down his coffee, always in a rush. No wonder he had a heart attack. I did warn him, I was always warning him.

Their eyes met, they were horrified by the lost innocence of that breakfast, imagining the reality of his body now.

— Chris, he was so strong. How could this happen?

— Oh I know, I know how strong he was.

As if to hold off finality, they began listing all Zachary's faults. — He wasn't perfect, Lydia said. — We mustn't forget that he was just really himself, not a dream.

— Nobody's perfect.

— He was so noisy, and he talked a lot as if he knew everything – but really he was bluffing half the time. He drank too much and then he was a bore, when he was drunk he didn't make sense.

— He papered over bad things, Christine said. — Sometimes he was sentimental, he wanted to be too hopeful about everything.

Lydia sat very still, her face was white. — I found that difficult, you know. Because sometimes he was lazy, he didn't want to face the truth.

— But that's why you two balance out so perfectly! Christine insisted fervently – as if she were trying to save their marriage, not console her friend for her loss. Then she realised this was the last day, ever, that Zachary would have been alive in, and she didn't want it to end. But when she looked at her watch it was past midnight already.

— Tell me when you want to sleep, she said gently to Lydia.

— The bed is all made up ready. I'll sit with you if you like.

— I can't! Lydia shuddered. — Imagine waking up, to this.

I can cope with it now because I'm all screwed up to it, but I don't think I can bear to let it all go and then have to start again from the beginning. Anyway, I'm waiting for Grace. I ought to be awake for her. I know I'm such a rotten mother. I have to be better from now on.

— But she won't be here until tomorrow lunchtime, at the earliest.

Lydia smoked one cigarette after another, staring at the lit ends between puffs, coughing. — I'm not really going to take up smoking again. I only really did it to annoy Alex.

They opened another bottle and soon Lydia's lips and teeth were blue from the red wine. She did sleep eventually and in the early morning Christine heard her crying, and went into the spare room in her nightdress, sat beside her on the bed. Lydia grabbed her hand, dragging it under the bedclothes to hold it again against her stomach which was hot and tensed and hard. — I feel it in here, she said. — It's a pain, a terrible pain. But it's not love. I have to tell the truth to you, no one else. Otherwise I can't bear it. You know it isn't love, don't you?

Grace was finishing her third year as an art student, very talented, a sculptor in stone and wood. Alex drove all night and arrived in Glasgow at dawn. He slept for an hour in the car, and then he searched in the early morning light until he found the address Hannah had given him. The city seemed like an underworld – a Victorian necropolis towered behind the blackened cathedral, the lights were all on in a vast hospital. Grace was sharing a house with other students, in the south side of the city, above a shop; metal shutters were pulled down across all the shop windows. By this time it was seven o'clock. The front door was beside the shop entrance and the bell didn't work; Alex hammered on it with his fist, not loudly but insistently, not giving up; after a while he heard footsteps on the stairs inside and a boy came down to the door, prepared to be aggrieved. Alex said he needed to talk to Grace, it was important, a family illness. Grace wasn't there, the boy didn't think: he would check her room. No, she'd been out to a party the night before, hadn't come home.

— What party? Where?

Then Alex drove to where the party had taken place – Grace wasn't there either. He picked his way across an apocalyptic scene, bodies curled in sleeping bags among the party debris; a girl in the kitchen, cooking eggs, remembered that Grace had left the party with somebody. She looked cautiously at Alex before she would tell him any more. — Why don't you try her phone? she said. He explained that someone in Grace's family had been taken ill and she needed to know at once, he'd driven all the way from London to tell her in person. Then he made his way to another house, someone let him in and called to Grace, who was sleeping upstairs. Alex went up to look for her. He didn't care what he saw, although at any other time he'd have respected Grace's privacy. She was asleep on a mattress on the floor in a little cramped room, with the duvet pulled over her head; the thick mop of her black curls gave her away. She and her boyfriend from the night before were sleeping without touching, backs turned to each other, the boy's back raw with acne. The room stank oppressively of their bodies and of cigarette smoke and sex. A thick curtain was pulled across the closed window; Alex opened the window, then sat on the floor beside the bed to wait until Grace woke. She opened her eyes into his gaze, her breath sour with sleep. When she recognised him she sat up abruptly. — What are you doing here? Alex?

Scrambling up on all fours, backing away from him, she retreated against the wall as if she were poised for flight; she looked so like her father that he almost couldn't speak. The dirty white T-shirt didn't cover her nakedness: her flanks were lean as a boy's and the bristling, dark pubic hair was just like Zachary's. Her beauty wasn't the type Alex desired in women, too forceful; she'd had this force ever since she was a tiny girl, and it had always roused some pain of protection in him, afraid for the consequences of her bluntness and lack of inhibition. He was relieved that his own daughter Isobel was reserved and feminine, knew how to take care of herself. Grace was tall and sturdily built, muscular from her work with hard materials; her slight breasts were the merest points under the T-shirt and her head was shapely, proportionate like a classical ideal, almost androgynous; her wiry hair grew out in a dense mass of black. Under ordinary circumstances, she was drily humorous. She and Alex were famous jokers usually, when they got together.

— Who is this? the boy said, putting a hand out to Grace supportively, but she shook him off, smacking out at him, so that Alex saw he wasn't important. He was clearly a mistake, with his whiskery gingery beard, blundering out of his depth.

18

— Would you mind leaving us? Alex said. — I have something I have to tell her.

Grace put her hands over her ears. — No, no, don't tell me. I don't want to know! I don't want to hear it!

The boy was bemused. — What's going on?

— I'm so sorry, my beloved Grace, Alex said.

— Don't tell me! she cried.

Afterwards she said she'd known, as soon as she opened her eyes and saw his face. — You should see your face, Alex. It's a giveaway. And of course if anyone else had died, Dad would have come to tell me.

In the car on the way home, she kept her little rucksack on her knee and was distinctively herself: looking round her out the window, taking everything in, questioning him sensibly about what had happened. He repeated to her all the detail that was becoming mythic, about Jane Ogden's new show, Zachary keeling over in the gallery, hitting his head on the desk. — But why, but why? Grace said, staring straight ahead through the windscreen, rocking backwards and forwards just perceptibly in a childish rhythm, hugging the rucksack that she wouldn't put down on the back seat, or on the floor. At some point she announced that she was starving, and they stopped at a motorway service station. She ate something disgusting, with every sign of hearty appetite – a full English breakfast; and then shortly afterwards, when they were on the motorway again, he had to pull over quickly onto the hard shoulder. She jumped out of the car and vomited into the tall grass full of daisies, which was blowing in sensuous long ripples in the wind.

— That was melodramatic, she said when she sat beside him again, wiping her mouth. — Sorry.

— It's a time for melodrama, he said. — You do whatever you need to.

The journey seemed twice as far as when he'd driven up to fetch her. Grace fiddled with the radio, found some pop music which Alex tolerated because he understood it was difficult for her to speak. Then she got out her phone and began sending texts. — So is that your new boyfriend? he asked.

— Jesus, no, she said. — Just some guy I met at a party.

He wanted to warn her to hold herself back from the guys she met at parties, to keep herself aloof in the upper sphere where she belonged, because she was an exceptional, rare being. But it wasn't the moment for that. He talked to her instead about his own father, who had died when he was about the same age as she was now. Grace listened attentively, rocking in her seat, although he guessed she could hardly make any connection between what was happening to her, tearing up her life, and his old story worn smooth in history.

Parking at last outside the flat, he saw how she was tensed in anticipation of meeting her mother, or meeting anyone. The knot of muscles in her neck was hard as iron when he touched her. Upstairs it was as if the women hadn't moved since he left: Lydia was in her usual place on the sofa, Christine – who had changed into a dark navy dress, choosing mourning colours perhaps unconsciously – was in the big armchair. She glanced away from him evasively – she preferred to conceal herself, in extreme situations, behind her habitual irony. Against the dark dress her face looked haggard, flesh slack on her bones: probably she hadn't slept. They were drinking coffee instead of alcohol, that was the only change – and Isobel had joined them, she was standing beside the mantelpiece with her back to her reflection in the gilt mirror, waiting calmly and sorrowfully. When Grace came in, still hugging her rucksack, she went straight to Isobel, who opened her arms to her. The two young friends were so spontaneous in their sorrow that their mothers looked frozen beside them.

There was something intolerable in the expectation in that room, strained around Zachary's absence, which could not be filled. The time when they might have been waiting for him to walk through the door was so recent, so close at hand, that it seemed vividly possible; they could imagine how he'd make his entrance, noisy with reassurances, full of jokes, puzzled by their glum faces. He was always so up to date on everything, so full of news. It seemed impossible he didn't know this latest fact, his own death.

— Where is Dad? Grace asked. — I want to see him.

Lydia tried to dissuade her. — It's only his empty body, darling, he won't be there.

— I love his body. I want to say goodbye to it.

Then Grace announced that she wanted to make a death mask, so that later she could carve her father's face in stone. — I was planning it all the way from Glasgow, she said. - I know where I can find out how to do it properly. I know someone I can ask.

— As if things weren't grotesque enough, Lydia said, shuddering.

— Let's take our time, Alex said, placating them. — Let's think about it.

He supposed there would have to be an autopsy.

— I'd like to be present at the autopsy, Grace volunteered promptly.

— That's not possible, my sweet girl, he said flatly. — Not possible or desirable.

Christine put out food on the kitchen table, but all anyone wanted was coffee, which they drank until it tasted poisonous. The phone began to ring in the afternoon and didn't stop: friends who'd heard something, or artists Zachary had worked with, who'd got hold of their number. Lydia had spoken already to Zachary's brother, but there were so many other people who needed to know what had happened. Alex took the phone into the study next door; again and again, patient with each new shock, he had to tell the story of Zachary's keeling over in the office, Jane Ogden and Hannah going with him to the hospital. They could all hear him from the sitting room. While he was speaking they sat in silence, as if they needed to hear the story over and over, experience the fresh astonishment with every caller. Grace sat on the floor with her forehead dropped against her knees; Isobel was on the sofa close beside her, her hand on Grace's hair. The girls had been very close since they were children, although they were opposite types: Grace so abrasive and rash, with her spectacular boyish beauty, Isobel distinctively poised and reserved. She worked as a civil servant, fast-track entrance, in housing; her green eyes were set wide apart, her skin was clear, her light brown hair pinned up in a smooth knot.

— I did ask about the mask, Alex said, crouching in front of Grace, taking her hands in his. — Not sure it's a good idea. Wait and see how you feel about it in the morning.

— Most of it's on the internet, Grace said. — But there's someone I need to talk to about sourcing the right kind of plaster.

— Don't I have any say in this? Lydia asked.

— Wait and see, wait and see, Christine soothed them.

Lydia wanted to talk about money. Had Zachary had life insurance? She had no idea, he took care of all that side of things. — How can you? Grace said. When Lydia had retired to her bed in the spare room with a sleeping pill, Christine tried to explain to Grace why her mother was behaving so clumsily. — You don't need to tell me, Grace said, pushing her springy hair back from her forehead under both palms as if it helped her to think, her face stark in its severe lines. — I get it. I understand.

Grace and Isobel went over to Isobel's flat in Queens Park, where Grace would sleep – it was only twenty minutes on the bus, they insisted they didn't want a lift, or a cab. — I want to be normal, Grace said. They would come back in the evening to eat, so they could all be together again. When they'd gone, Christine took a lasagne out of the freezer. Then she stood for a few minutes alone under the sloping roof in her bedroom. It wasn't like a stone after all, this intrusion of grief: a stone was cold and still, you could surround it, but this swelled inside her and receded then swelled again uncontrollably; she felt helpless against its violence, her usual self wrecked and lost, turned inside out. She called out subduedly to Alex, to come upstairs. They spoke in low voices. — Do you mind if I go out just for half an hour while Lydia sleeps? Will you keep an eye on her? I need to walk.

He touched her face sympathetically; the flesh under her eyes was swollen with crying and fatigue. In a crisis Alex was strong and she leaned on him: it was a form of laziness, a convenience between them. And it suited him too, she thought, to play the role of her protector from time to time. Neither she nor Lydia were conventional in their personalities, they called themselves feminists, yet both had chosen patterns of relationship with men which looked almost like their mothers' marriages, dependent and sheltered; they lived their secret lives inside the strong shell of their husbands' worldliness and competence. Now Lydia's shell had been broken open and she was exposed, alone.

Christine didn't often wear make-up but felt the need to put it on today, before she could show her face outside. When the drawer in her dressing table jammed she was flooded with rage and tugged so hard that it came flying out, scattering its stupid contents. She stared at the mess, then crouched to pick up the eye-pencils, hair grips, eyeshadow, tubes of face cream, sachets of depilatory cream, indigestion pills, contraceptives she no longer needed – even a couple of ancient Tampax from the past, their paper wrappings tatty and grubby. A film of dirty, greasy powder from the bottom of the drawer settled on the wool carpet.

In the street things were better. She gulped down the tarry, tainted city air, felt the heat of the car engines on her legs and the paving stones hard under her feet, took in the shopfronts one after another in all their vivid detail: the bolts of African fabrics, rows of bottles of coloured varnish in the nail parlour, jars of vermilion peppers lined up on the shelves of the Polish delicatessen. All this was a relief: the impersonal solid forms of the world which would persist without Zachary, without happiness, without her.

— I fucked someone really unsuitable, Grace confessed to Isobel on the bus.

— Who?

— This dirty guy, Dan, friend of a friend, met him at a party. By the time we got back to his place I'd sobered up and I didn't even fancy him, but I couldn't be arsed by then, going all the way home. Guess where Alex found me when he came to tell me? Isn't that glorious? Heard the news of my dad's death in the bed of a dirty guy I didn't even want to fuck.

Isobel didn't falter, the whole of her composure was dedicated to sustaining Grace, balancing her thoughts, making them all right – though she did wonder how many passengers on the bus were listening. — When you say dirty ...

— I don't mean dirty sex. The sex wasn't anything special, as far as I can remember. I mean actual dirt, actually on his body. He smelled like he hadn't washed for a while.

— In time you'll come to see it's funny.

— Oh yes, hilarious. Don't ever tell Sandy, will you?

— I don't tell Sandy anything.

— I don't want him to know that I'm so gross.

— You're not gross, you're the least gross person I've ever known. You're just – Isobel cast around for the right word – an adventurer. Everything you do is like an explorer, venturing into new territory. I wish I was more like you. I wish I wasn't so cautious.

Tears squeezed from under Grace's eyelids as she turned away to stare out of the bus window; she looked desperate. — Does Sandy know? she persisted. — I mean, does he know about Dad? Has anyone told him? Is he still seeing that Italian girl?

Isobel said that her mother had called Sandy; he might be coming round that evening. As far as she knew the thing with the Italian was off. — Do you think he'll come? Grace said. — Why don't we phone him to make sure?

— If he can come, he'll be there.

Isobel understood that Grace was opening up this well-worn old story – of her long-time, devouring, unslaked passion for Sandy, Isobel's half-brother – mostly as a distraction from thinking about her father. When they arrived at the flat Grace went around exclaiming over everything that was new – Isobel had painted the kitchen, bought an Ercol sofa on eBay. The little flat wasn't really anything special – the ceilings were low and the kitchen an awkward galley shape – but the way Isobel had things arranged was airy and tranquil. The sofa which was her spare bed was heaped with pretty cushions. Grace opened up the fridge – packed with vegetables from the farmers' market

– and then the wardrobe, as if she were searching for something. Isobel loved buying clothes but her taste was cautious, she dressed in skirts and cardigans and flat shoes. Grace wore vintage or scruffy combats or dramatic satin, changing her look often, as if her appearance were a perpetual art show.

— Everything's so calm here. Flowers for the table. It's calming me, she said, touching the petals of the blue scabious. — It's such a change after my grotty student life.

— Too calm, Isobel said. — I could do with a man, messing things up.

— A dirty man.

— A really dirty one. Gracie, are you actually going to make a mask?

— Is it too weird? It's macabre, isn't it? I'm going to look up death masks on your laptop.

— Be careful, please be careful. You don't know what you'll see.

Isobel hovered anxiously, looking over Grace's shoulder while she found some actual masks – Oliver Cromwell's, and Pascal's – and then some funeral directors' websites, and then a photograph from the end of the nineteenth century of a death mask being made, in some place that looked almost like a barber's shop. The living men's own faces, in the lovely silvery old print, were distinctive and mournful, exalted in their dedication to their work. — You see, Grace said. — It's quite a beautiful process. It's solemn.

Isobel hesitated still. — But I don't think you could do it though, not to your own father. I think it has to be impersonal.

— Strange, isn't it, to think that these men are long, long dead too: the mask-takers? The photograph is a kind of death mask in itself. I could take a photograph of Dad, I suppose. A photograph of him, dead. That would be easier. It wouldn't drive my mother so berserk. I could take it on my phone. Then show it to the dirty guys at parties, see if it creeps them out. *Hey fellas, think you can live up to this?*

— Pretty creepy.

Isobel made tea in the kitchen and when she came out carrying two mugs, Grace had dumped the cushions on the floor and was lying on the sofa with her back turned, face to the wall. Putting down the tea, Isobel slipped off her shoes and lay behind her. She knew that her friend had her eyes open, staring at nothing. When she touched her she seemed to feel a blockage in her turned back, between her shoulder blades, like a dam; some force that ought to be flowing through Grace couldn't escape and was building up inside. Isobel massaged her gently, trying to conjure away the pain.

Before they began to eat that evening, Alex again poured glasses of the Stará myslivecká vodka which had been Zachary's favourite, and spoke briefly. Christine stared at her plate, the others followed Alex with their eyes, willing him to find words for what had happened. He said that Zachary was a man who knew how to do everything the right way, and now he was gone, so they had to do this clumsily without him, as best they could. Zachary had loved art, art that wasn't stupid or spurious. He'd been exceptional in his insight, and he'd had a singular vision, with the remarkable Garret's Lane gallery at its centre, of an art radically open to its community. — But for us, Alex said, — his family and close friends, gathered round this table, the loss is so much more, we can't even begin to measure it. I would be inclined personally to take his death as yet more evidence of the supreme shitty law of life that takes away the best and lifts up the worst. Yet somehow because it's Zachary, he won't let me do that. I keep on feeling his resistance, and his force for good, and his belief in it. And yet I don't know how I'm feeling it, because he's gone.

Isobel covered her face with her napkin to cry, Sandy wiped his eyes on his sleeve. Lydia touched Alex's arm in appreciation, briefly she buried her face against his shirt – though when she looked up again her eyes were still dry, watchful and glittering. Hannah from the gallery was with them that evening too, and Zachary's younger brother Max, and Nathan Kearney, Zachary and Alex's old friend from university days. The presence among them of Max and Grace felt uncanny, because they both looked so like Zachary: with his rosy high colouring and wiry black hair, his bright red mouth and big voice, his air of benevolence and force. Max even ate greedily like his brother, pushing his bread in his mouth while he helped himself to salad; and recently he had grown a stiff beard like Zachary's, a prophet's strong beard – although in fact Max didn't have his brother's determination; he was anxiously touchy, not decisive.

They all ate something of the lasagne on their plates, they

were actually hungry. The noise of their forks scraping against the china and their glasses chiming was like familiar life returning to their circle, however bruised and subdued, and they began to talk. Nathan Kearney, who'd known them all forever – he reviewed films and was sometimes on telly – was usually unstoppable, but couldn't speak about Zachary. He bent his big head low over his plate, lank hair hanging down like a curtain, concealing his expression, and could only join in with the talk when they were safely on the dry ground of art and politics.

Lydia pushed the rest of her food aside.

— You have to eat, Alex said, concerned and gentle. He had been round to her place earlier, to pick up a change of clothes and her wash things.

— I know I do. I'll eat tomorrow.

He put his arm around Lydia, pulling her close, managing his lasagne with his other hand, waving his fork around when he spoke. Christine was grateful to him, for taking charge of the occasion. Grace had done something extraordinary while she was away at Isobel's: she had chopped off all her thick curls – in mourning for Zachary, she said – so that the silky under-hair was exposed, curled close to her skull, like a shorn lamb's. Isobel defended Grace's action stoutly, said it was a beautiful idea. — Anyway, I couldn't stop her.

Lydia said drily that it didn't look too bad. — Luckily her head is a good shape.

Now Grace was questioning Sandy about his music, flirting feverishly with hot spots of red in her cheeks, embarrassing him because he was so sorry for her. He was shocked out of his usual charmed self-belief by what had happened, and by her naked head. He didn't want to be holding forth, at that moment, about his own successes; his glance kept slipping away from her uneasily, he laughed self-deprecatingly as she tried to draw him out. Grace was too much for Sandy. He was fond of her but wrong-footed by her crush on him, because she wasn't his type: he thought of her as an honorary boy, masculine in her assertiveness, and preferred women who were polished and self-possessed. Sandy's own good looks were sinuous and sulky, evasive as if he were keeping something back – perhaps for when he was on stage. He was in a band, they were big. Sandy was famous. It was only in his own family that he wasn't treated with adulation, as a star.

After Sandy had gone, Grace's animation sank to nothing. Lydia called for her in a plaintive voice and patted a place beside her on the sofa, then Grace lay with her head in her mother's lap. Someone turned on the television news. — I don't know if I can bear to watch this, Christine said, but she stayed, standing up by the door as if she was on her way out. Alex always watched the news; there was this cold anger ready in him, leaping up to meet whatever new outrage presented itself. They saw footage of events at Calais, where desperate migrants who wanted to enter the UK were trying to board lorries or break into the tunnels under cover of darkness; one man lay spread-eagled on top of a train. Watching this scalded Christine, the horror of that inky starfish shape, dark against the darkness – who was he, what became of him? – mingled in her awareness with her own suffering. Yet she knew it was indecent to make any connection between their private loss and this public shame. Their world was privileged even in its grieving; there wasn't any moral meaning to Zachary's death, it wasn't an injustice. And yet it undid them all.

It seemed airless in their bedroom while Christine undressed; she pushed the Velux skylight open to its furthest extent and the hot night rolled in from outside, tainted and gritty. She was tensely aware of the others sleeping or not sleeping below her in the crowded flat: Lydia in the spare room, Max on the sofa. The girls had gone back to Isobel's in a cab. Alex had wanted to put Max on the pull-out bed in Christine's studio, he'd been surprised to find the door locked. She'd shaken her head at him when he asked if she knew where the key was. — Just put him on the sofa in the front.

She and Alex lay side by side in bed in the dark like effigies, on their backs in their nightclothes, with their legs stretched out and their feet sticking up, staring up at nothing, not touching – yet she felt the heat of his skin, scorching hers. Sleep seemed very remote. — Was it strange to be in their home? she asked. — When you went round for Lydia's clothes. Zachary's things must have been lying round everywhere.

Lydia and Zachary lived in converted parish rooms attached to the chapel which was now an art gallery. Christine had envied them the austere high ceilings and high arched windows of imperfect greenish glass, the old tiles and brass tap in the kitchen, the stylish ultra-modern conversion. She and Alex couldn't have afforded to live anywhere so distinguished.

— I was preoccupied, Alex said, — finding all the bits and pieces Lydia asked for. Then there were voices outside and without thinking I was so sure that it was Zachary coming home. Until I remembered that it couldn't be.

She felt for his hand which lay between them on the sheet, he grasped hers strongly in his hot dry grip. They didn't often hold hands. Christine wasn't easily demonstrative; Alex thought that holding hands was for children, not for men touching women. They didn't often talk, for that matter – not any longer – with this confessional closeness. Christine felt sometimes as though the long years of their familiarity had grown across her throat like a membrane, so that she couldn't easily speak to him, and kept herself hidden. Now, though, they must be kind to each other at all costs. — You did well driving up to Glasgow to tell Grace, she said. — That was a good thing to do.

— What was Lydia thinking!

She whispered to him to be careful, Lydia might hear them, she was only downstairs. Alex lowered his voice hoarsely. — To imagine giving her daughter the news so casually, on her mobile phone!

— Lydia isn't thinking straight, of course.

— She's dangerous when she doesn't think.

This was another old pattern between them, his criticism of Lydia, Christine's defence of her friend. Alex had sometimes, in the past, implied that Lydia was too shallow to make Zachary happy as he deserved. — This is a catastrophe for her. It's our business to take care of her, Christine said.

— I want to take care of her.

— I know, she feels it. She appreciates it.

Alex turned on his side, to face her in the dark; he put his hand on her pyjama top, onto her breast. Christine was shocked by the violence of her reluctance to make love to him. She knew they ought to be opened up to each other: Alex was right, his instincts were always good, more generous than hers. She half longed for the comfort he wanted to give her, and to comfort him. It was the same as when he'd made her listen right through to the end of the music, the day before. In her mind she understood how sex and death were both part of the mystery of entrances and exits, both opening onto this same strange place where they all belonged now, in the sudden shadow of Zachary's death. But her body contracted against him in spite of her mind, she felt withdrawn inside her flesh, concealed in its sealed chamber, fierce against its violation. She wanted to try to explain to him that she couldn't bear to be touched, not now, not yet: but she couldn't, the words seized up in her chest, they wouldn't come out. She pushed his hand away without a word, turned over with her back to him and pretended to sleep.

In the middle of the night, Lydia came into their room. They woke confusedly to see her standing up at the end of the bed in her white nightdress, looking taller than she actually was against the faint light from the Velux, with her hair hanging down like a figure from a melodramatic play or an opera.

— Lydia, can't you sleep? Christine said.

— I'm too frightened to sleep. And my feet are cold.

Christine jumped up, she went rummaging in the chest of drawers for a pair of socks for her friend. — Get in under the duvet, she said. — Keep warm.

When Lydia climbed into the bed, her movements were stiff-backed as an old woman; she did actually seem to be shuddering with cold, in spite of the warm night. Alex said nothing at first, lay turned away although he must have been awake. — I'm frightened, Lydia said. — Jane Ogden told me that Zachary vomited black blood.

— Now, why did she have to tell you that? Christine said soothingly. — Why did you need to know?

— I feel safer in here, between you two.

Christine felt for her friend's icy feet under the duvet. Tenderly she put on the woollen socks, then got back into bed beside her, putting an arm around her where she lay between them, against Alex's turned back. Then he turned around and embraced her too. — Poor Lydia, he said.

— Oh Alex. I wish that I had died instead, and he was still here.

— Don't be silly. You're what we have left, you're all the more precious to us.

At first Christine thought that Lydia would never sleep: she could feel the panic racing in her friend's body like an animal's fast metabolism. But very quickly Lydia's breathing changed and grew shallow, she began twitching and jerking unconsciously. It was Christine's turn to lie aridly awake. She was too hot, Lydia's feverish dreams seemed to be burning her up. Christine couldn't tell whether Alex was also awake. She half expected him to slip out of bed, go down to sleep more comfortably in the spare room. But he didn't move.

TWO

WHEN THEY WERE ALL IN their twenties and getting to know one another, it was Lydia Smith who was in love first with Alexandr. He was married at that time, in the mid-eighties, to his first wife Juliet. Sandy was three or four years old. Lydia and Christine had only just graduated, they were still living in a shared house with a couple of other student friends; Christine had embarked on the PhD in literature which she never actually finished, Lydia was working part-time in a bar. Alexandr Klimec was a few years older, he seemed properly grown-up to them, with a real life. They had met him when he taught French classes at their university; in those days you still had to do some French, as part of an English degree. Probably he'd hardly noticed them, two girls in a mixed group of students – although men usually noticed Lydia. Anyhow Alex had seemed entrancing to the girls, with his foreign handsomeness so exact and polished, his peculiar hazel eyes like cat's eyes, his intelligence harsh as a knife, his disdain for their ignorance, his slightly guttural French accent.

He hadn't even taken the trouble to flirt with them, as other male teachers did. They had felt exquisitely crushed.

When the French classes ended, Christine hardly thought about him again – she only remembered *Hypocrite lecteur, mon semblable, mon frère!* But in the autumn after they'd graduated, Lydia confessed that she had found out where Alex lived, and that he was married with a child. She had introduced herself to Juliet as one of Alex's students, said that she was looking for babysitting work. Juliet had taken her number, and had already called her.

— I want you to come with me the first couple of times, Lydia said to Christine. — So they don't think it's anything sinister. Although it is, of course.

— But you don't even like children!

— I'm not doing it to get close to his child. Chris, I'm desperate about this man. I've let him into my dreams – I don't mean daydreams, I mean actual dreams in my sleep at night. In these dreams I'm always stumbling after him, and then he turns around and doesn't even know me, or looks right through me. Or I've got blood on my skirt or something, or I've done my homework for him but it's dirty because I've dropped the pages in the street.

— This is awful though, Lyd, snooping around his home.

— I have to *know,* if I've got any chance. I swear, if we find out they're contentedly, blissfully married, I'll abandon the whole thing. I'll tell Juliet I've given up babysitting because a dog bit me or something. Or a baby. I won't mention the name Klimec to you ever again. I'll retire to a nunnery.

They were drinking China tea with lemon, in Lydia's room;

sitting cross-legged on her unmade bed, in a crumpled scarlet silk kimono, her eyes painted with kohl, she waved a cigarette about between her fingertips in the affected way she had, puffing at it superficially. Lydia could make Christine feel very unworldly. She was unworldly in those days: tall and thin and oblivious, with a rope of light brown hair coiled round her head like a caricature of an old-fashioned lady scholar, though she was only twenty-two; she rode an old bicycle round everywhere, with her books in the front basket, kicking off with one foot from the pavement then sitting very upright on the saddle, almost comically upright, in the dense London traffic. Christine had grown up in London, she was perfectly at ease in the city, yet she lived there somehow as if she were in exile from a more stately, slower world. There was something virginal about her, although she wasn't literally a virgin. Lydia envied her friend's calm self-possession: she couldn't ride a bike, couldn't imagine ever making her way so unprotected and trusting through the city traffic.

— So what's his wife like? Christine asked, concerned.

— One of those miniature doll-bodies, dyed black hair, parchment skin, nervous. I should think she was a child-bride. Juliet by name, Juliet by nature. Apparently she's an actress. Going out of her mind looking after the kid all day while Alex writes his poetry.

— Does he write poetry?

— He has a book of poems coming out. He's a genius of course.

Lydia never hesitated when she was pronouncing judgements in her flat, hard little girl's voice – though afterwards she would laugh at herself, at her own excesses. The friends had felt such relief at finding each other's irony when they first met at their girls' grammar school – each had feared she was the only unbeliever. Lydia doubted everything. It was almost a disappointment to Christine that Lydia had fallen heavily in love at last: it had always been the boys who pursued her, while she kept aloof. And Alex wasn't supposed to be Lydia's type – she had claimed that she hated intellectuals, so awkward and so self-important. Her boyfriends until now had been the pretty boys she met in clubs, or at the bar where she worked: lithe and skinny, with bleached hair or wearing eye make-up, hard and dangerous. When these boys took furtive calls on the house phone, monosyllabic or coaxing, Christine thought they might be dealing drugs. She had kept herself apart from this aspect of Lydia's life – not because she disapproved of it, but because she was shy, and afraid that the boys would despise her plummy accent, her good manners.

Lydia felt herself at some crisis, now they'd arrived at the end of their formal education. Dissent and scepticism had been easy while they were held tight inside its frame – now something more was called for, and she dreaded testing her reserves of imagination and energy, finding them empty. At first she had played at falling in love with Alex because it gave a shape to her days, and a motivation: then her obsession had swallowed up its original purpose. Her lack of him gnawed at her, making her incomplete; she thought fatalistically that if she had any talent it was probably for this, for a destructive passion. Lydia had the biggest room in the shared house, with the biggest bed – where she slept sprawling luxuriantly in dirty sheets, rarely getting up before midday. Her room was chaotically untidy, with clothes heaped on every piece of furniture, or dropped on the floor where she'd taken them off. She had a gift for finding treasures – old couture silks and satins, stiff net petticoats – among the dross in junk shops; everything smelled of mothballs, or of beer and cigarette smoke from the bar.

The whole house was a semi-ruin and they lived in it like children camping, playing at grown-up life. Christine's room on the ground floor was half the size of Lydia's and chilly, with a greenish light she loved: its French windows opened onto a ruined conservatory and overgrown garden. It was in this green-lit room that Christine pored over her books of poetry, making notes, working in the evenings in the light from her desk lamp, hearing the subdued frisson of rain on the leaves in the garden at her back. Her PhD was on Christina Rossetti. The male teachers at university had tried to dissuade her, saying Rossetti's verse was too flimsy, wouldn't bear up under that level of sustained attention. She persevered, but not without self-doubt. If Lydia had a night off from bar-work, then Christine would take a tray of tea things up to her room at the end of the evening. Lydia would have been reading too: the whole house would seem charged with their separate concentration, their silence. But Lydia read so differently: always novels, not poetry, devouring them one after another, classics and contemporary fiction and thrillers muddled in together, opening up something new almost as soon as she'd finished reading the last words of the previous one. While she read she was utterly absorbed, then she closed the books mostly without comment, or with a snap judgement uttered with finality: *dull,* or *excellent.* Christine would pick up the book and puzzle into its pages, worrying over so many words. — But *why* is it dull?

— The heroine had such a silly name.

As soon as she'd finished her last university exam, Lydia had stopped thinking about books in the critical language she'd had to learn for her degree; yet in her exams she'd done very well, almost as well as Christine. She spoke about that critical analysis as if it was a trick you could put on and off, for strategic purposes; this was bruising to Christine, who was betting her future on analysis. But then she was used to being bruised by Lydia, she didn't mind. Christine had had such a happy childhood, she'd been so encouraged, she had a lot to make up for. Lydia's family were perfectly all right too: her parents ran a pub. Only they weren't very interested in their daughter's cleverness, and wondered why she didn't get a proper job. When she won a free place at the grammar school they'd supposed she might become a businesswoman, or a lawyer. Christine was in awe of Lydia's parents because in those days she romanticised the working classes, so they thought that Lydia's inseparable friend was stand-offish. And certainly didn't think of themselves as working class.

The friends had met in a long look of shared incredulity at their first school Founder's Commemoration Day, across so many submissive heads bowed in prayer, the muddy tide of voices obediently murmuring forms of words learned by rote. It wasn't that they were naughty: other girls who believed everything the school told them were far naughtier. Christine Drinkwater and Lydia Smith had the subversive earnestness of true dissenters. They pinned on the noticeboard newspaper articles denouncing the evils of private education, they boycotted the Form Charity – which was always for animals. Christine was drawn to Lydia's concentrated energy, which wasn't turned outward but was like something unrealised, burning with a slow heat inside her. Her daring negativity opened up possibilities, promised adventures.

Christine was bemused now by the long days when she had nothing to do except study in the university library, or at her desk at home. She didn't need a job because she had a full grant for her PhD – and she hadn't embarked yet on any university teaching. She was diligent, and liked her work, but it couldn't really fill all the hours of her day, or all the space inside her. And so she too, like Lydia, lived in a suspended state, expecting to discover something more serious to be the business of her life. Perhaps it would be motherhood, Christine sometimes thought. Her own mother spoke significantly about the happiness that came with children, and Christine believed in it – and yet that possibility seemed remote, so she waited patiently.

She was overcome with sleep sometimes, while she sat poring over her texts. And sometimes she lay down on her bed in the middle of the afternoon, guiltily but deliciously, relinquishing responsibility. Then she woke up to the green light of the room in a strange mood, exempted from all the solid pressures of her usual nature and her obligations. Sometimes on these lost afternoons she drew, and while she was drawing she turned the face of her alarm clock away so that she couldn't see how time was passing. She had done well in art classes at school, she had a gift for catching the likeness of things, but no one had ever suggested she should continue with her art, it had never seriously occurred to her. She and her brothers had all aimed at university; art school could only have been seen as a compensation for failing to get in anywhere worthwhile. Her family put a high value on the visual arts, and went to all the exhibitions, but would have found it presumptuous to dream of being an actual artist. New art was too raw. Who knew, until posterity's confidence had silted up around it, what was any good? They preferred their subjects cooked. Nobody would have minded if she'd studied art history.

Christine only thought of this drawing at first as doodling, passing the time while she focused her thought on particular poems, wondering what to write about them. In an art shop, ashamed of wasting money on a childish whim, she bought scraperboards. And while she bent over them, alone in the house, digging out the black wax and leaving the white lines in relief, she seemed to be gouging out some new terrain, which came out of her self and yet was unknown to her. There was something savage and exuberant in it, and high-risk. The first picture she completed showed a section cut through a turf in a graveyard, its grass wet with drops from a shower of rain, and an odd back-end view of a blackbird with its tail feathers in a fan, all very close up to the viewer's eye and cramped. A body was buried in the loamy earth, along with stones and worms: though not decomposing, rather as if it were alive – and not the whole body, but just a shoulder and neck and hair seen from behind and pressed up close against the picture frame. She knew once the picture was finished that it was horribly clumsy and faux-Victorian, and she didn't show it to anyone, hid it away under some papers in a drawer in her desk.

From the first time they went babysitting, Christine could see how Lydia was getting it wrong with Alex. She took all afternoon putting on one thing after another, trying too hard, deciding eventually on an antique blouse made of black silk chiffon embroidered with jet beads, worn over jeans, which wasn't convincing as an outfit suitable for childcare. Also she wore too much make-up, as well as her fox fur collar. Alex opened the door to them: he and Juliet were renting a little terraced cottage in Kensal Rise, with railings and a narrow strip of front garden where Juliet grew herbs in pots. He did seem to remember the girls vaguely, but not their names. When they said they were babysitting he called suspiciously for Juliet, who came out from the back kitchen, hobbled by her little boy clinging to her knees.

— Alex, you haven't forgotten! Juliet reproached him, hoisting the boy up onto her hip; she was very small and Sandy was very tall and lean and pale, so he couldn't help looking like one of those overgrown children, hanging on to babyhood too long. — We're going out to dinner at the Fairlies'. These are the girls I told you about. Say hello, Sandy.

Sandy hid his face against his mother, fingering her breast self-consciously.

— Christ, Jules, Alex said. — I don't want to go to dinner at the Fairlies'. We don't even like the Fairlies. Ring up and tell them Sandy's ill or something. And you can send these girls away.

It was obvious that he and his wife were in the middle of some bitter wrangle, much bigger than this one particular evening; Christine felt Lydia's alert attention to each sign. Alex returned inside his study and closed the door, hardly looking at them. — Don't take any notice, Juliet said smoothly. — He has to have his little sulk. You know what men are like.

Both the girls sided at once, unfairly, with Alex – Christine because of the French classes, and the *hypocrite lecteur*. Sentimentally, they took the side of art and the closed study door, against the tedium of childcare. Juliet might have been small, but there was something pugnacious and resolved about her: she was quick and light on her feet, with curling black hair caught up in a comb, dangling painted earrings in the shape of parrots, and a pale, poised little face, pretty and sharp. When she diminished Alex and cut him down to size, the girls knew how she appraised them too in her blunt way, seeing through them and their romance across her miles of married experience. She disappeared into Alex's study, leaving the girls with Sandy, who wept and pressed himself against the crack in the door as if he could squeeze through it after his mother.

The girls were transfixed and fascinated, listening to the argument – whose actual terms weren't audible – rising and falling with suppressed vehemence on the other side: much more of Juliet than Alex, his silences weighty. Eventually Juliet emerged triumphant and went to get changed upstairs – into a gypsy-dress in printed black Indian cotton, which showed off her small breasts defiantly. She tried to put Sandy to bed but he soon reappeared, haunting his babysitters, lugubriously ghostly in washed-out pyjamas: he had huge heavy eyes and skin so transparent it was almost blue. — You don't mind, do you? Juliet said blithely. — He'll take himself off to bed when he feels tired.

Alex, martyred, lifted the car keys off a hook, followed his wife out to the car without a word; Sandy cast himself against the door closed behind his parents, in a mute paroxysm. — Obviously he doesn't love her, Lydia pronounced, lighting up her first cigarette.

— Lyd, shush. Anyway, you can't possibly tell. We just don't know, about how marriage works.

— Who doesn't love who?

Sandy was suddenly attentive. Lydia laughed at him with her husky laugh; she had no idea how to behave with children. — Just some people you don't know. Friends of ours. X doesn't love Y. What do you know about love anyway? You're a little eavesdropper, aren't you?

— What's an ease-dropper?

Sandy was drawn to Lydia as if he couldn't help himself, and to begin with she exerted all her adult charm on him, flirting and teasing, asking him inappropriate questions in her deadpan voice. — Can you read and write? Why can't you? What are those pictures on your pyjamas? Yachts?

Do you own a yacht, then? Who d'you love best, your mummy or your daddy?

— My mummy, Sandy responded promptly.

Lydia pretended to be his daddy, feeling sad, rubbing her fists in her eyes and moaning. Sandy pityingly drew close, almost with tears in his own eyes: then she grabbed him and poked his tummy, playing at biting him. It was all too much. Soon he was thoroughly worked up, running round screaming with excitement. When he collapsed five minutes later in frantic sobs, Lydia grew tired of him and Christine had to take him to bed, calm him down, read him stories. Meanwhile she could hear Lydia snooping around downstairs, opening drawers and cupboards.

— It's for my survival, Lydia explained when Sandy was finally asleep. — I have to find out everything about Alex. Do you think they're sleeping together? Obviously there's only the one double bed. But do you think they're actually having sex in it? I don't think they are. I don't feel any electricity between them.

Christine didn't want to think about Alex, whom they hardly knew and were in awe of, having sex with anyone. She said she had no idea. Yet she couldn't help her own curiosity, in relation to the material thickness of these lives – Juliet, too, became glamorous by association with Alex. The girls searched in the fridge, tried the alcoholic drinks, read the postcards propped on the windowsill among the plants, even read a few letters left lying around; they felt for married secrets in the arrangements of the rooms. It was clear two forces were at odds in the tiny house, pitted against each other. On the female side there were the jars of lentils and pasta with gaily painted lids, the child's drawings stuck on the fridge, the Indian embroideries on velvet, plants everywhere. Juliet was good at growing things. Ranged against this female brightness and optimism were the books in their plain covers on the shelves in Alex's study, in English and French and other languages they didn't recognise, piled punishingly high and thick with dust. The electric typewriter, the desk with its brimming ashtray, the broken dirty venetian blind hanging at a slant against the dark outside, the swivel chair on its chrome stem: all these were so deliberately ugly, modern, an austere exhibition of the life of the mind. Black-and-white photographs propped on the shelves or pinned on the walls were all photographs of men, other writers presumably, taken in rooms very like Alex's study, also piled untidily with books and papers.

Christine flushed at something antiquarian in her own studies, her fusty lovelorn lady poets. And she felt protective on Lydia's behalf, against what was forbidding in Alex: the whole weight of a world of knowledge they didn't share, a history and prestige in other languages which shut them out, showed them up as provincial and ignorant. Lydia was betting on the power of sex, against all this monumental difference. — Are you sure that Alex's right for you? Christine wondered carefully. — I mean, even if he wasn't married and everything. I think he's quite cold. I admire him but I don't think I like him.

Lydia agreed, accepting her doom. — He's completely the wrong person. But it's love, I don't have any choice.

In spite of her lady poets, Christine didn't quite believe in that kind of love. She was always falling in love herself, with her supervisor, with a brother of one of their housemates – even with a boy who worked in the butcher's shop. And at the same time she could drily watch herself stoking her own anguish and abjection, knowing she could be free in one minute if she chose. But perhaps what Lydia felt was the authentic thing, and it was her own ironic detachment which was exceptional, shutting her out from life.

By the time Alex and Juliet returned from the dinner party – they found their babysitters watching television innocently, side by side on the sofa – Alex was in a better mood. He joked with them while Juliet searched in her purse for the money to pay them. He asked if they were still reading Baudelaire and Rimbaud. Had they given up on decadence yet? Lydia turned on all her charm and chattered eagerly, punctuating her remarks with false-sounding bursts of laughter. — Oh no, she said. — We're going to be decadent for years!

But Christine felt how Alex didn't respond to this charm as he was supposed to. Lydia's audacious frankness, her wide-eyed amused delivery, complacent like a purring cat, which had been so confounding to other men, didn't impress him. In Alex's presence, so perfected and adult, Lydia's cleverness seemed flawed and home-made, embarrassing like a precocious child's.

Soon Lydia was round at Kensal Rise almost every day. She didn't see much of Alex, though; mostly she was babysitting for Sandy or drinking coffee or wine at the kitchen table with Juliet, who poured out to her all the dissatisfactions of her marriage. Actually Lydia liked Juliet. Lydia was really very impressionable, although she appeared so disabused and knowing, and had such decided opinions. She was drawn into strong connection with women she met, studying them for clues as to how to grow up, what kind of person to be; she admired Juliet's bright little house, her tidy cupboards, her competence and toughness – and was rather afraid of her, fascinated by the idea of her intimacy with Alex. She could not imagine achieving for herself any existence so strongly flavoured, so deep.

Alex was moody and difficult, Juliet complained. He didn't know how to enjoy himself. He loved his little son but thought he could just go on with the old life he'd had before there was a child, reading all day and tapping away on his typewriter, or just leaving the house without saying anything, not coming home sometimes for hours on end. He expected Juliet to take the brunt of the childcare – which made it difficult for her to get any acting work, even though it paid much better than his poetry. In fact his poetry didn't pay at all. Juliet wasn't supposed to say a word about all the books he bought, although they were so short of money that she had to cook for weeks on end with lentils and potatoes. — He doesn't care, she said. — He hardly notices what he eats.

Lydia entered sympathetically into Juliet's difficulty in living with Alex: and yet these stories at the same time made him more desirable. She thought that if she had him she wouldn't try to tame him, tie him down. And then, who wouldn't rather buy books than lentils?

— Don't you feel bad? Christine said. — I mean, letting Juliet give all this away to you, while all the time your plan is to carry him off? Are you going to start an affair?

— But I don't even see him! The only one besotted with me is the kid. He can't get enough of me, he's always trying to put his hands up my skirt or into my bra. And he drives me up the wall with his questions. Remind me never, ever to have children.

— It would be different if it was your own.

— You think? Maybe.

The girls pored together over Alex's poems, when his book came out. Lydia read them aloud one at a time, trying to crack them like a code, find the key to what he wanted. Each poem was short enough, set apart at the centre of its creamy page, and the words weren't in themselves incomprehensible, they were the plain words of everyday speech. Superficially the poems seemed to be about real material objects – a sofa or a coal shed or a bread knife – or actual moments in the real world. And yet the girls, trained as they were, had no idea how to read them or what to take from them. They learned from the author's note that Alexandr's family had come to Britain from Czechoslovakia in 1968, when he was nine, and that his father had been a writer too, a novelist. The poems reminded Christine of the solid things in Alex's study: not charming or poignant like the poetry she was used to, but dense and heavy on the page, functional, the words fitting his thoughts as closely as tools worn smooth with handling. Their power was in the resistance they offered to any reading that was pretty or comforting.

Juliet told Lydia that publishing the collection had made

Alex miserable. He ought to have been delighted, fame at last.
— Not that anybody's reviewed it yet or anything, she said.
— Of course, that's a sore point. He says in England it's just little circles of posh poets, reviewing one another.

Lydia found out where Alex went drinking with his friends, a filthy old pub off Pentonville Road, near King's Cross. She breezed through there one night as if by accident, and got introduced to them all, and after that she began to drop in often. At first she was excited to belong to this new set of friends, the only woman among all those clever men, the shouted arguments. Alex took more notice of her, he was kind and encouraged her to talk. But his kindness was not enough, it was not what Lydia wanted, and after a while it was crushing. It reinforced her obsession: she knew there was a streak of fanaticism in her make-up, and was half frightened by the power she'd given this man over her happiness. Perhaps she'd feel better, she thought, if Christine was a part of these evenings. Christine was sane, she put things in perspective.
— Why don't you come along? she pleaded. — Please, Chris? You can tell me if there's any chance he'll ever like me – I mean, really *like* me – or if I should just start drinking myself to death right now. And anyway there's somebody else you ought to meet. Really, Zachary's the perfect one for you. I think it could work. He's a close friend of Alex's but he's so different to Alex: so easy to get along with. And terribly rich.

Just like the girls, Alex and Zachary had been friends since they were at school together. At least the girls had gone home to their families every evening. Both sets of the boys' parents had, against the grain of their progressive politics, decided to send their sons to be boarders inside the public school system – where they were, not unpredictably, thoroughly unhappy. Their parents had only wanted to keep them safe, inoculate them against exclusion: both families had histories that gave them cause to feel nervous. Zachary Samuels's grandparents had got out of the Ukraine in the early twentieth century, but so many of their relatives had not. Alex Klimec's novelist-father had never written a word, in any language, after he had to leave Bratislava so abruptly. His silence had brooded over their household.

Something in both the boys – stubbornness perhaps in Alex's case, generous self-sacrifice in Zachary's – prevented them from begging their parents, more than the statutory once or twice in the first weeks, to take them away from the ghastly place. Yet their parents should have taken in the signs of strain: the boys had come back changed from their first term, with a new brittle carapace of mockery. Probably Zachary was always too rosy and too buoyant for anyone to notice; and no doubt Alex's parents, exiled themselves, thought his pinched misery was the usual human condition. So the boys, in their small society of two – which expanded flexibly enough, in certain phases, to take in other strays – had to make up to each other, at school, for the loss of everything. Alex spoke English perfectly, that had been the first great conscious effort of his life, to pass as belonging; but he existed inside those words as if inside an alien shell, whose forms were not quite his – this made survival easier. He had to protect Zachary, who was so unguarded. When Alex first saw his friend's expectant grin, he thought of those birds and mammals on remote islands who haven't learned yet to be afraid of predators. On the other hand Zachary was liked, by the boys and the masters, and Alex wasn't; they thought he sneered at them. He could be very cutting, with his distinctive vocabulary, using with perfect fluency words the other boys hardly knew.

The great relief and release, and the beginning of their free lives, when school was over and they both got into Cambridge, didn't end the friendship – no one else would ever know what that time had been. Alex and Zachary didn't talk about school but their shared experience bound them together, closer than brothers. (And as it happened Zachary's parents sent his brother Max to the local state school, which was very good, because Zachary said that Max would be happier there – and afterwards Max always resented what he saw as Zachary's advantage.) Now Alex and Zachary were both trying to write. As well as publishing his poems, Alex was getting some university teaching and reviewing for good papers; he was making a name. Zachary was struggling with a novel, and he was making clever little light-box installations too. It was typical of his resilient good luck and his charm – and his connections, because his wealthy parents were enthusiastic patrons of the arts – that he had editors and galleries interested in his work, although he hadn't finished anything yet. Alex thought he never would finish. He didn't think Zachary had the necessary cruelty that made an artist, or the incompleteness in himself. He was too rounded and too hopeful. His work was derived from his enthusiasm for the arts, which was all upside down. But then Alex's ideas about an artist's life were based naturally on his own father, whose gifts had been so bitterly unfulfilled.

The group of friends who drank together – Alex and Zachary and Nathan Kearney and Martin Shield and others – didn't do anything so crass as discuss an artist's life or personality. If they talked about books or music or films at all it was almost always a competitive swapping of assertions: this or that was superb, or – more often – it was no good, they'd seen through it. The grounds of taste went without saying. They handled shared certainties, or poured incredulous scorn on each other's preferences, or just shut up if the other man didn't see the point, wasn't worth arguing with. Alex was often reserved in that company, he held himself apart. He was uneasy with their consensus because he felt so queasy, himself, about committing to any certainty. Everything he'd ever written he wanted to destroy when he'd finished it – or at least half wanted to. Even his poems, forged in such heat, then worked over and over with such cold scrupulousness, seemed shrunken to something disappointing as soon as he saw them exposed on the pages of a book. It was only loyalty to his past self, and also self-preservation – best not to fuss – that kept him from disowning them.

Alex's withdrawn silences, when he was with his friends, didn't do any harm to the reputation he had as the rarest, most talented among them; and then when he did talk he

was original, forceful and funny. The others took their opinions from him. The distinctive way Alex used words may
have been the last trace of his foreignness: his talk was
substantial, like his poems – he liked plain language, vocabulary drawn from daily life. But he knew so much, he'd
read everything. He read at night – his friends wondered if
he ever slept. They deferred to him and jousted for his ap-
proval, for the warming gleam of his responsiveness. Without
being aware they were doing it, they even adopted elements
of his style, wore the same kind of tight-fitting wool jumpers,
developed the same taste for drinking their coffee black.
They were afraid, too, of the hard snap of Alex's correction
sometimes, and his moods. He thought their revolutionary
fervour naïve, was scathing on the subject of the high hopes
of leftists in the West. Outside his immediate circle there
were a few who strongly disliked and resented him.

The crisis in his marriage made Alex unhappy. He had
had every intention, when he married Juliet because she
was pregnant with their son, of seeing their arrangement
through with decency. He had respect for something enduring in the institution of marriage, binding people together: the idea of a failed marriage, and fresh beginnings
over again, were clichés for the middle-aged. He'd never
been unfaithful to Juliet, although she imagined atrocities –
but he wouldn't spell out for her as she demanded where
he'd been, every hour of his day. She was always worst
when she'd been talking on the phone to her sisters, who

echoed her complaints back to her, redoubling them, eliminating any ambiguity, working her up into a fury of recrimination.

— Sandy told me you left him alone in the library, Juliet said.

He couldn't even think, for a few moments, what she was talking about.

— You left him there, and told him not to move from where he was sitting until you came back, and then you disappeared for half an hour. He was frightened.

— It was ten minutes, he said. — He was happy looking at the pictures in a book. I went upstairs into the reference section. When I came back he hadn't moved.

— My God, Juliet said. — Anything could have happened!

Alex wondered whether they'd reached a new low point, using their son as an informer in the war between them. He didn't believe that Sandy had really been frightened. When he'd tried taking him up into the reference section, Sandy had only whined to go downstairs again, disturbing the people who were working. It worried Alex that the boy wasn't more childlike and robust; Juliet encouraged him to play these games, manipulating his parents' emotions. Looking at his son, Alex could hardly recognise anything from his own childhood. — Sandy was sitting in perfect safety, he said, — in a library. Have you any idea what kinds of responsibility other children his age have to take on, around the world? Don't you actually plan to give him the freedom of his own competence?

— This isn't other children, it's our child. It isn't anywhere else in the world. He's four years old, Alex. He could have wandered out into the street, anyone could have abducted him. Why can't you see things from a normal point of view?

Inexorably they worked their way round once again to counselling: this was her sisters' solution to everything. They should have therapy, they should talk to someone. — I won't talk to anyone, Alex said. If they wanted the marriage to continue, Juliet said, then they had to make some changes in how they related to each other. He knew she told other people that he was cold, but at this moment he was making an effort to speak to her entirely without artifice or guile. — I won't change, he said. — I don't think that I can. And even if you succeeded in making me change, wouldn't you be afraid that I might hate you for it?

— I think you hate me anyway. You behave as if you hate me.

— I don't hate you.

— And why are we only talking about you, as usual? You might hate me, you might not hate me, how am I supposed to tell? Both things come out looking rather the same. Why don't you ask about me, just for once? What if I hated you?

— Then don't tell me. It's best if I don't know.

They had been in the middle of undressing for bed when this argument erupted. Now Juliet sat turned away from him on the other side of the bed with her shirt off, back bowed and her head dropped into her hands, the knobs of her vertebrae sticking up sharply on her narrow brown back, cut across by the black strap of her bra. When Juliet let her ferocity and vigilance lapse, he felt so sorry they had fallen out.

He liked her, he felt at a loss in the face of her opposition. Couldn't they just live alongside one another, leaving each other mostly alone, in peace? This bristling opposition and competition, flaring up at every hour of every day, exhausted them both. He wished they didn't always have to talk. He touched her shoulder and felt the heat of her smooth skin, on her neck under her hair. For a few moments she sat without resisting, allowed him to caress her.

— You think this is the solution for everything! she protested eventually.

— Isn't it?

But he took his hand away.

When she did finally come along to the Pentonville Road pub, Christine hardly spoke at first. She was too impressed by so many clever men talking and joking, so well-informed and witty. Their sheer physical bulk and confidence and careless loud voices were impressive in themselves, along with their liberating indifference to their appearance – the dirty old second-hand clothes, ragged jumpers with holes at the elbow, tangled unwashed hair, the spontaneity in their keen young faces. Everything else fell into place behind the men's intelligence and their ideas; beside this, Christine felt her female intelligence as fatally self-conscious. She puzzled out her ideas with genuine interest during the day, yet when she brought them out in conversation in the evening she couldn't help being aware of what she was wearing and how she might appear. Didn't that undermine her authenticity? At work on her thesis, even while her thoughts went leaping ahead under their own momentum, in the same moment she imagined her supervisor admiring her cleverness. Self-doubt gnawed at Christine: this double-think made her despondent, she couldn't find any way round it.

Lydia put in her own remarks among the men, and they all deferred to her, but Christine saw that they didn't quite take what she said seriously – not because they thought it was stupid exactly, but because her appearance blocked their attention, like a dazzle of sunlight in a reflection off glass. They were exaggeratedly solicitous and encouraging when the girls spoke, as they never were with one another. There was a danger, Christine thought, that you might end up performing for them, like a curiosity – and Lydia was inclined to show off if she had an audience. She made them laugh when she said that the only career which had ever interested her was as a *grande horizontale;* she'd like to have been the mistress of one of the great bankers or statesmen in nineteenth-century Paris. Christine looked quickly at Alex, to see if he was seduced by this idea. But it seemed to her that he was only amused and curious. Surely he guessed that Lydia was there for him. The more pointedly she flirted with the others, the more obvious it was.

Alex's looks were emphatic and un-English, slightly marked or damaged as an actor's might be, or a dancer's. He had his hair cut shorter than the others, as if he'd belonged in a different decade, and there was something light and cat-like in his movements, a tremor in his nicotine-stained fingers when he rolled a cigarette. Under the tight wool jumper his boxy narrow ribcage rose and fell with his asthmatic breathing. Christine was afraid of him, of his judgement. But she liked Zachary at once. He wasn't attractive as Alex was: he was the only one, however, who really listened to what she and Lydia said, for its own sake. He had the gift of attending to other people with his whole awareness – alert not simply to the words they spoke, but to their palpable entire selves. Moving restlessly in his seat, shifting his whole body eagerly towards her, he sat on his hands because otherwise they flew into the air, gesticulating – he had been teased for that at school, and had done his best to suppress it because Alex said he gave too much away.

— Lydia's told us about you, he said to Christine. — You're writing about your namesake, Christina Rossetti. Isn't that exciting? Won't those women writers turn out to be the most interesting thing about nineteenth-century poetry after all? The sexy secret undergrowth around all those boring lofty male intellects.

Christine was startled because what he'd said reminded her of her pictures, which she had thought of somehow as an undergrowth. — I think so, she said. — But I'm not sure my supervisor agrees.

— Oh, he doesn't matter!

— Well, he's rather important to me, as I am embarked on this wretched PhD.

She couldn't bear her own voice sounding clipped and prim in her ears, like an Oxbridge bluestocking. But Zachary was sympathetic at once. — Oh dear, is it wretched? That's what I worried, when I was toying feebly with the idea of doing one.

— I mean I'm having a wonderful time, being paid to write about the poetry I love. I'm very happy really.

— Goodness knows what I'd have written about anyway, he said — I don't seem to have turned out as any kind of expert on anything. I just liked the *idea* of the lonely endeavour. I wouldn't actually have been any good at loneliness. I fall in love with an idea: you know, the dedicated scholar, the lamplight late at night in the little carrel (don't you love that word, *carrel,* whatever it means?), the piles of books, the flash of transforming insight at two in the morning. And then I stumble into the trap of thinking I could actually be one of those scholars, instead of just imagining them. But the truth is I'm a generalist, I'm just a butterfly. My mind won't sit still on one subject. I'm not like Alex, he's the real thing.

— Alex frightens me a bit, Christine confessed.

Zachary considered this carefully. — To be honest, he frightens me a little bit too.

But he didn't start talking about Alex as she expected. Instead he asked Christine all about herself – and she didn't feel any of her usual anxiety, that whoever she was in conversation with would prefer someone more interesting. They discovered they'd grown up only half a mile apart, in Hampstead; they had their childhood terrain in common. They'd both been taken, for treats, to tea at the Louis Patisserie. Zachary seemed exaggeratedly delighted by this coincidence. Perhaps Lydia was right, Christine thought, and he was the perfect man for her. In his presence she felt at ease, and open; though she wasn't exactly drawn to him physically, not in the usual way. Yet she liked it when he touched her – which he often did, for emphasis while they were talking, and kissing her hand when they parted. Somehow he didn't remind you of sex, as some men did, at every moment. There was no hidden suggestion in their conversation – and this was mostly a relief.

Zachary was one of those men who seem only provisionally young, their youth a mere passing phase on the way to the maturity where they will be more at home. His head was too big for youth, or his features were too strongly stamped with his personality – wet red mouth, mass of frizzy black hair; no beard in those days, and a daintily cleft chin which his friends forgot in the years afterwards, when it was covered up. His vividly pink and white complexion flushed quickly with enthusiasm. There was already something bear-like in his gestures and loud deep voice and laughter, though he wasn't bulky yet, only plump. Leaning across the table, he noisily marshalled the next round; he knew all about the different beers and guzzled down pints and pints of them, pretending to discriminate between them, more voluble and insistent as he got drunker.

Christine was scraping away at another picture in her room one evening: piles of books on her desk drawn from a low angle, their chunky solidity exaggerated, the stem of her Anglepoise desk lamp snaking sinisterly behind them, one book open to show a poem magically twisting and disassembling on its page. When Lydia burst into the room excitedly, she pushed the scraperboard away under her papers and pretended to be making notes. Lydia's face was heated from the bar, her hair was sticking to her damp forehead, she reeked of cigarette smoke. Someone had told her that Alex was splitting up with Juliet, he was moving out of the house in Kensal Rise and was going to get a flat with Zachary. — It's my chance, isn't it?

— I suppose so. I'm still not sure about him.

— At least he looks at me, these days: but I can't read what he's feeling. What will I do, Chris, if I can't make him love me? I won't be able to bear it!

Christine felt a spasm of irritation. She said she expected that Lydia would be able to bear it after all. People bore worse things. — You're annoyed with me, Lydia said sadly. She sat on the side of Christine's bed, hugging her arms around her chest as if she was cold, although she was still wearing her coat and her fur collar. — I don't blame you. I've become one of those dull people droning on about their feelings. You think I'm making all this up. But it's real, it hurts so much. If I can't have Alex I'm not complete.

— You've just fixated on him because you can't have him.

— But it's not something inside my head. It's the reality of his separate existence, his body and his mind, all the details of his life and history. I need to know what he thinks before I know what to think myself. I've allowed those things to get inside me and now I can't close them off again. I've never done this with anyone before, you know that. I've always liked men but they've come after me, I've never gone in pursuit of anyone.

Lydia's expression was set and desperate. She was aware

of the tranquillity of Christine's room, which she had broken
into with her turbulent emotion: the desk was piled up with
volumes from the library, Christine had one of them open in
front of her, she had hardly lifted her head from where she
had paused with her biro still on the page. Lydia envied this
little scene of dedicated work, which seemed in that moment
unattainable to her. — Unless Alex wants me I'm not real,
she said. — I'm just a shadow.

Christine put down her biro, she made an effort. — I don't
think I've ever felt that about anyone.

— Don't hate me, Chris. It's all right for you. You're going
to be so happy with Zachary. Imagine how easy your life is
going to be. He'll adore you and look after you, and you'll
have so much money that everything will be made easy, you
won't ever have to work unless you want to. You'll be able to
buy all the beautiful clothes you want, and live in a beautiful
house.

— Don't be ridiculous, Lydia. I hardly know him.

Christine was surprised by the violence she felt, being
wrenched out of her concentration on her picture. Usually,
if she was working on her thesis, she looked forward to being interrupted at this time of the evening. She was uneasily aware of her growing preoccupation with her drawings:
as if what began as a small black inkblot at the centre of her
vision was spreading, eating up the attention she was supposed to be devoting to criticism, sapping her intellectual
rigour. She borrowed art books from home without asking
her mother, kept them under her bed and pored over them
secretly, joyously: the flame-orange hair of Degas's women,

the ferocity of his black lines, the sublime modernity of his figures cropped inside the frame, the jagged angles of their elbows, his compositions cut across with empty space. It was wrenching, humiliating, to go back from these to her own stupid efforts. And yet the noise of the nib as she scratched at the black wax felt intimate as breathing, filling up the room. She was back inside the irresponsible absorption of her childhood, when she had drawn lying on her stomach on the floor in her bedroom, inventing a whole alternative universe, an island with mountains and a city and its own history and fragments of language. She could still remember letters from her secret alphabet.

Zachary knew how Alex was humiliated by the failure of his marriage: they had thought they were so thoroughly adult, embarked on the true shape of their lives at almost thirty. It wouldn't have occurred to Zachary not to like any woman Alex chose, and he had opened his affections to take in Juliet; he enjoyed her brittle banter, she had babied him. And Sandy was the first child he'd given his heart to, as well as any number of extravagant presents; he'd spent so much time at their house, it had seemed his second home. But of course his allegiance was to Alex. He understood how his friend resented his new role as an estranged father, picking up and dropping off his child according to a fixed timetable. Manoeuvring subtly, Zachary nudged him into compliance, and Juliet was grateful. It was Zachary who built shelves at the new flat for Sandy's books and toys.

Together he and Alex took Sandy to the park to play football, and at home Zachary dug out with a knife the mud from between the studs of Sandy's football boots; by this time he had started full-time school. Later Zachary bought him his first guitar.

Painstakingly Alex began building a new relation with the boy – bought him a working miniature steam engine for Christmas, made models with him, helped him collect stamps and look up all the different countries in an atlas. He was never spontaneously very warm with Sandy, though; his strong feelings for his son were always tamped down behind the defences of that period of the end of his first marriage. Alex ought to have enjoyed himself in his new life: he could drink and smoke and entertain his friends without offending anyone, stay up talking or reading until the small hours – it was a relief not to be crowded up against Juliet's hostility at every turn, and found perpetually wanting. And yet he chafed in his freedom and wasn't quite at home in it. Zachary liked the same music and kept the same hours, his sanity was a balm, but their shared cohabitation was too frictionless. It almost reminded Alex of school, only without the antagonism of teachers. It was puerile like school.

They were domesticated in that cautious way of hetero-sexual men living together, hedging their housework about with mockery, as if it were a performance they could leave off at any moment: they painted the walls of the flat, made numberless pots of tea, washed up when the sink was full. Zachary cooked pans of curry and chili, Alex baked fish in foil in the oven with herbs and olive oil. When they smoked they found their conversations very penetrating or very funny, couldn't remember in the morning what they'd laughed at. They were carefully tactful: neither asked after the other's well-being, even when they were stoned – least of all then. Male tact was an iron law; without the tactless interventions of women, Alex thought, men would never tell each other anything. Grown men ought to live with women, he believed that. That was what his maleness was for, to be balanced against women's unlikeness, their opposition.

Lydia persuaded Alex to bring Sandy on a visit to the house she and Christine shared with other students; Alex was mildly curious, wondering how these girls lived, imagining some kind of hippie home with jam-making and patchwork. But the dirty student house, which the girls thought so romantic, shocked him to the core. It was a detached half-timbered mock-Tudor villa, tucked away behind ceaseless traffic on the Edgware Road, in a garden so wildly overgrown it was like its own little wood. Lydia took them up to her big room on the first floor; Christine was out at a meeting with her PhD supervisor. The house smelled of mothballs and decaying carpets, and even the light coming through the windows seemed brown with damp. The girls found the old rose-garlanded wallpaper – which hung off the wall in places, in wet sheets – quaintly nostalgic; it oppressed Alex with a memory from his early childhood he hadn't known he'd kept, of visiting his grandmother, his mother's mother, in a cottage in the country. No, not *cottage,* not *country:* those words were too irretrievably English. Alex had visited his grandmother in a hovel, that was more like it, amidst a terrain of relentless sodden flatness, muddy fields without hedgerows, beige-coloured in his memory.

He couldn't know that Lydia – not good with housework – had spent the morning tidying up and spraying the furniture vaguely with polish in preparation for his visit; she had even picked flowers for a vase from the garden. To her the room looked unprecedentedly ordered and elegant. And she had put out fancy cakes, with coloured icing, on a pink-and-gold painted plate: Zachary tucked into them enthusiastically. Alex never ate cake. Sandy climbed under the sheets in Lydia's bed, and she and Zachary teased him together, covering him up and asking, where's Sandy gone? Then they ripped the blankets off to expose him again, which was surely a game for babies; each time they flapped the blankets the asthmatic constriction in Alex's chest thickened. Lydia flashed glimpses of her creamy breasts from the neck of her blouse, and her belt was fastened so tightly across her velvet skirt that it must be marking the flesh of her stomach: nice English girls flaunted themselves with no fear of the consequences. He set off downstairs in search of fresh air, trying several doors: a boy eating chips doused in ketchup at the kitchen table was presumably one of the housemates, and didn't look in the least surprised at this intrusion by a stranger. Did they let just anyone in off the street, to wander around their home? He was glad he had outgrown this improvised, slumming phase of his own youth.

Pushing at another door, he found himself in a bedroom,

austerely tidy and half-dark even in the daylight, because its
French windows opened onto a conservatory overgrown with
tall weeds, watered presumably by rain coming in through
broken panes of glass. He guessed, from the sombre books
piled high on the desk, that this was Christine's room, and cast
his eye down the spines of the books, to see what she was
reading. Her passion for the musty Victorians with their virginal
frissons was a mistake. But what he also saw on her desk was
more piquant – drawings in soft pencil on thick paper: one of
an empty chair; one of a bed when someone had got out of it,
the tangled sheets as sculptural as marble; and one of clothes
on a hanger, half composing the shape of the human who would
wear them. He liked the solidity of their forms and their enigma,
their air of proposing a visual puzzle, defining a shape by its
absence. Then Christine, returned from her supervision, was
in her coat in the doorway behind him, hugging more books
and a folder to her chest.

— Don't look at those, she said agitatedly, pushing past
him and sweeping the pictures up, shoving them out of sight
into a drawer. — They're awful things. I'm only messing
around.

— They're good, Alex encouraged her. — They're interesting. You should show them to Zach, he knows about this
stuff. He knows people who buy art.

— I don't want to show them to anyone.

— I like their emptiness, the absences in them.

— That's only because I can't do people yet. I'm going to
learn how to do them. I've signed up for life-drawing classes.

— Don't put people in them. People only spoil things.

— Oh! So that's why your poems are all about furniture.

Alex laughed. He hadn't known that she had read his poems. He took this girl in properly for the first time: her stiffness and thinness, her evasive look, her dark-blooded lips in their asymmetrical smile so wary and withholding. He forgave her for preferring the kind of poetry that rhymes.

Lydia bumped into Alex accidentally on Malet Street, on her way to work in the dusk one winter evening. The foggy air was tarry with fumes, cars sloughed past on the wet road monotonously, eighteenth-century house fronts loomed against the last light. Because Lydia was always imagining Alex, it was confounding to have him suddenly substantial in front of her, hunched against the cold in his greatcoat and long scarf, blocking her path. She sounded almost accusing.

— What are you doing here?

He was on his way from teaching, with books and student work in the worn briefcase which had been his father's. Because he didn't want to go home – on these dark evenings he missed the old domesticity with his wife and child – he asked her to come for a coffee. He liked Lydia better without her playfulness, her flirting; she was flustered because their meeting had taken her by surprise. They went into a student place, found a table in the corner. Lydia had never been alone with Alex before, and almost wished they hadn't met, worrying that she hadn't washed her hair, didn't look her best. Yet this was the kind of opportunity she dreamed of in her fantasies.

Alex was full of talk left over from his teaching session. He had been given some first year undergraduate literature courses now, as well as the French language class. While he spoke about nineteenth-century French novels he allowed himself to notice Lydia's blonde hair picking up glints in the electric light, and the fineness of her jaw when she lit a cigarette; she had unbuttoned her coat and the shape of her breasts was outlined under her sweater. He thought that the white flesh of her face was bruised and dented with fatigue.

— Are you working too hard? he kindly asked.

Lydia opened her eyes wide at him. — To tell you the awful truth, Alex, I've only just got out of bed, I'm still half asleep. Don't you know that I'm horribly lazy?

He was shocked. — But it's dark already! You slept away the whole day.

— Did I miss anything? The day doesn't look that good.

— That's not the point.

Lydia was helpless to stop the confessions flooding out of her. At least she was coming clean, she thought, and Alex would know what she was really like. — Obviously I'm drifting, wasting my intelligence. I suppose I can't work in a bar forever. It's such an irony because my parents run a pub, and my one aim in life was to escape from it. You can't imagine what my life at home was, how conventional and stifling. My parents by the way support Mrs Thatcher enthusiastically. I know your father was a novelist: well, the only books my dad's ever read are books of racing form. He wins money on the horses.

— It's honestly an advantage in life, Alex said severely, — if your father isn't a novelist.

73

Lydia understood, with a leap of sympathetic imagination, how he carried this burden of his father's achievement, which blocked his own. Of course he couldn't see himself as she saw him, so perfect in his offhandedness, his handsome young sadness, squinting in the smoke from his cigarette, pale face stark against his dark coat with its collar turned up. — I could change, Alex, she said, — if you helped me. What do you think I ought to do? Perhaps I could become quite noble and self-sacrificing if you told me to do something. I would really try.

— You ought to read more, he said.

She was disappointed, she'd hoped for some impossible mission against the grain of her nature: charity work or travel to some rugged, miserable place. — Is that all? That's not enough.

He lent her a book, which he took out from his briefcase: Foucault's *Madness and Civilization*. — I don't know whether this is a good thing, he said. — But you ought to know what's going on.

Lydia took it without enthusiasm. — I won't understand it. I'm not as clever as you think.

When Alex asked after Christine, Lydia said she was fine, she was working hard. Chris was really the clever one, Lydia explained. — She's the real thing. Why, do you like her? Yes, I'm not surprised that you like her. She has her own ideas, she's not like me, she doesn't just follow what everyone else thinks.

———

Christine and Zachary Samuels did go out together for a while. They really got on well. They spent hours in the National Gallery and the Tate, showing each other all their favourites, discussing them absorbedly. They enjoyed the same films and books, shared the same politics, spoke uninhibitedly. When they slept together it was very purely pleasurable: Zachary was so physically at ease and generous, enjoyed their lovemaking so frankly, undid something knotted and watchful in Christine. Yet when she remembered their happy companionship afterwards, she never quite thought of calling them lovers, even to herself. The word had too much excess in it, couldn't convey how economically and smoothly they had been conjoined. There was supposed to be some violence in sexual love, which swept you away in its adventure; when she was with Zachary she had hardly felt the jolt to her own sensibility.

One afternoon they met for tea at the Louis, to commemorate the occasions they'd missed meeting there in childhood. She had given him her drawings and a couple of small paintings to look at, things she'd done in her life classes, where she was learning to give her human subjects the same exaggerated presence she'd given to books and clothes in the old scraperboards. She contracted the human forms for density and pushed them forward to fill the picture frame. Zachary talked through the pieces one by one and said he loved them, they were so exciting. She had never spoken to anyone before about her art. He said she should take it very seriously. She should give up the PhD, put everything into it.

Christine was fearful, joyous. — But won't I fail?

— You won't fail.

She bowed her head, staring down at the brown tea circling in the flowery cup, and felt tears of happiness spring in her eyes. His confidence had the momentousness for her of an annunciation. He said it was a good thing she hadn't been to art school, her kind of work wasn't fashionable, they'd have set themselves against it and tried to change her. But she must have the conviction of her style. Afterwards, when they came out of the cafe into a thin rain, neither of them had an umbrella. — I could take you home, she suddenly suggested, although the idea hadn't occurred to her until that moment: their relationship wasn't at the point of needing to meet parents. — I mean, to my real home. The house where I grew up.

— I'd love that, Zachary said.

Christine still kept a key in her purse to her old front door, broad unpretentious entrance to a plain, well-proportioned eighteenth-century house. She was proud of herself, bringing home a real man – almost thirty – who would make clever conversation, and know the sort of people her family knew. The boys she'd brought home before had been too impossible. Christine's mother Barbara was small and soft and pretty, full of subtle discriminations, exacting over her clothes, aiming for a French look with a tincture of earthy, arty colours; Christine took after her tall, thin father, an expert in health systems who worked for the UN. She and her father would decide from time to time that Barbara was frivolous, while her two sturdy brothers took their mother's side.

It turned out that the Drinkwaters did indeed have friends in common with the Samuels, they moved on the fringes of one another's circles. Zachary was immediately, expansively, at home in the terracotta-painted drawing room on the first floor, full of interesting *objets*. He threw his coat and scarf onto a chair and sprawled on the comfortable sofa, willingly drinking more tea although they'd had second helpings at the Louis. Barbara asked how they knew each other and Zachary said it was through Lydia. — Oh, we adore Lydia, Barbara said. — We've known her forever. So funny when she was eleven, in her frilly party dress. A solid little pudding in those days. A force of nature! Now she and I confabulate over silly subjects like make-up and hairstyles — I can't talk about them to Christine, she's too intelligent.

— Mum, you make intelligence sound insufferable.

— But it's true, darling! You're not interested in make-up.

Zachary had promised not to mention Christine's pictures. — Your daughter's a genius, he said. — She's so talented.

— Isn't she wonderful? Though rather terrifying. She's awfully hard on her poor old mother, who can't keep up.

— Well she's very nice to me, he defended her stoutly. — And doesn't terrify me in the least. Lydia's the terrifying one.

Christine was surprised. — Really? Lydia? You've never said that to me before.

— Haven't I?

He looked at her with some trouble in his pink bright face. — She rather squelches me. As far as she's concerned, I think I'm a piece of the furniture, for tripping over. I'm turned into a jelly by a girl like that.

— She's very attractive, Barbara said with interest. — Is that what you mean?

— Oh yes, she's marvellous. Sumptuous. You know, like ... He was frankly nonplussed. — Like an actress. Like a goddess in a painting.

Christine stared. — Is that what you think of her?

— One of the goddesses who punish mortal men if they get too close. She makes me think I'm going to be turned into a deer and eaten by my own hounds or something. But in a good way.

Barbara sat smiling, from her daughter to Zachary and back again.

Then she asked how Christine's research was going and Christine reported briefly that her supervisor said she was on track – she bored herself, if she ever talked to her mother about her academic work. She didn't mention that she was contemplating giving all that up: she hugged to herself her knowledge of what Zachary had said about her pictures. Barbara wondered if Zachary was keen on the Victorians too, and he said he was mad about them, they were the next big thing. Barbara sighed, she said she preferred the eighteenth century.

— Good taste's all over, Zachary said. — Now we all want feelings.

— Oh dear, I'm so much better on good taste.

She and Zachary were teasing already, they were getting on. Christine was thinking judgementally that her mother didn't actually *know* anything about the eighteenth century, just liked her idea of it. At first they were sitting in the dusk. Then while Zachary and Barbara were talking, Christine got up and went around switching on the lamps, prowling in the shadowy margins of the room, picking things up from the shelves and putting them down. From childhood, she had got into the habit of letting her mind drift while her mother spoke, not following her words, only letting their tone wrap round her, familiar and reassuring as a blanket. Zachary fitted in so perfectly, she needn't make any efforts on his behalf. There was some latest new novelist he had read, who was the son of her mother's friends. Barbara made a conspiratorial face of distaste. — But wasn't his book *boring?* Such a shame, what a nice chap.

Zachary was delighted. It was boring of course, she was quite right. And then they discussed some marvellous French film that they'd both seen. Christine had seen it too but she didn't say anything. Barbara eventually invited them both to stay to supper – Zachary was suffused with regret, he'd made other arrangements. Downstairs in the hall he and Christine kissed affectionately. She waved goodbye to him from the front door, then climbed the stairs again slowly, hesitating on the landing before she stepped into the drawing room, where her mother hadn't moved yet to draw the curtains. The lamplight seemed weak, pouring into the night beyond, which was restless with rain. Barbara put down her book. — I like your new friend, darling, she said. — Such a nice chap. Very sweet.

— What's that supposed to mean? You're holding something back.

— I'm not holding anything back. I thought he was lovely. But he's just a friend?

Christine knew her telltale face was hot. — Yes of course, just a friend.

— Because he's not right for you: I mean, if there had been anything more to it. I can see how it wouldn't have worked out.

It wasn't unheard of for Christine to be explosive in that room. She had been known in her childhood for her tantrums – jagged marks on an Italian antique chest had never quite been polished out, where she'd scored them savagely in revenge for something, using a penknife belonging to one of her brothers. She had always been lovingly understood, lavishly forgiven — It's because he's Jewish, isn't it? she cried. — I can't believe this of you. What would Daddy say? I'm so ashamed.

— Good gracious! Don't be so silly, her mother calmly said. — Of course it isn't that. How idiotic. That's not what the problem is. Have you fallen for him? I wouldn't be surprised, he's very nice. He likes you. I think he *likes* you, Chris, tremendously. But the problem is Lydia, isn't it?

When she got home later that night – though her mother had pressed her to stay over, in her old bedroom – Lydia was still up, just as Christine had hoped she wouldn't be, sitting reading in the kitchen. She had the three-bar electric fire plugged in and blazing away, careless of the expense. It was only when Christine came in from Hampstead that she noticed how their rented house smelled stale with damp and gas and vegetables past their best. Lydia was undressed for bed, in a vintage satin nightdress splashed with a pattern of peach-coloured roses, wrinkled against her smooth skin because she never ironed anything. In her drenched dark coat, flushing with the sudden heat, hair lank with wet, Christine felt painfully that she was not beautiful. Lydia's hair, naturally the colour of streaked wild honey, was pinned up on her head in a floppy bow and her bare feet, tucked under her on the chair, showed rosy heels.

— This floor's sticky, Lydia remarked in surprised distaste, as if it hadn't occurred to her that someone ought to wash it. Alex's Foucault was open on the table in front of her, along with a Mars bar on a plate, sliced into thin slivers – she kept this in the fridge, and allowed herself one slice per night. She lived on eked-out morsels of cakes and treats and was an awful cook, too easily bored to follow a recipe, inventing dishes out of unlikely combinations – grilled banana with tuna or cold pasta salad with tinned peaches and sweetcorn – then throwing away her disasters almost in triumph, as if she'd cheated her own appetite. She said that she was struggling with the book, whose passionate polemic was too remote to make sense to her: like an explosion far off among the stars. And eyeing the Mars bar she confessed that she'd had her slice already, but wanted another one. — I want it now, but if I eat it then in a minute I'll wish I hadn't. So, is it going well? Isn't Zachary just the nicest? Didn't I make a good plan for you?

Christine lifted eyes heavy with her doom. — Haven't you noticed, Lydia? Zachary doesn't really want me.

— You're made for each other!

— Well no, actually. He wants you, it's obvious. He just can't help himself - talking about you, for instance, at every opportunity.

— What are you saying?

— I was just pretending not to know.

Zachary was besotted with Lydia, Christine explained, but he didn't think he had a chance, he saw that all her attention was for Alex. And anyway he believed she was a goddess, and was so sweetly modest he'd never hope that goddesses might condescend to him. He didn't think he was much good with women, not in that way: although he was quite wrong, he could make any woman very happy. Lydia's face for once was quite slack and empty with surprise as she took in what her friend was telling her. Then gradually her expression filled up with new knowledge – which was not even slyly jubilant, only disturbed and heavy. — But are you quite sure? she insisted.

— Aren't you sure too, now you think about it?

Slowly, one by one, Lydia picked up all the rest of the slices of Mars bar in her chipped, blue-painted nails, and ate them. Christine wouldn't sit down with her at the table or even take her coat off. — You can have the whole thing now, if you want it, Lyd, she said. — I mean, the money and the beautiful houses and the life of leisure and everything you were selling so hard to me. You might as well, because I don't think Alex is interested.

She saw how carefully Lydia was listening.

Alex came with Juliet to Lydia and Zachary's wedding and they both drank too much champagne. Apparently they were back together but it wasn't working out, and Alex's best-man speech was so sardonic no one knew whether to laugh. Sandy was obnoxious, running out of control, pretending to knock into the guests' wine glasses accidentally. Christine had asked Lydia before the wedding how she felt now about Alex. Lydia was sublimely assured, impatient as if Christine were dragging up ancient history. — Oh no, all that's completely over. It was just a silly game. You were right at the time, you're always right. I set my heart on what I couldn't have, although I knew it was bad for me. Just *because* I knew it was bad for me.

The wedding was registry office, with a reception afterwards in the Samuels parents' Hampstead garden – on an autumn day of showery fitful sunshine, fine rain floating in the gleams like dust motes, clouds liquid with light, thick cobwebs in the hedge glittering with raindrops. Zachary's parents had turned out to be wonderfully worldly, with a house full of modern art. There had been some private consternation, because of the wife he had chosen; generously and for their son's sake, on the day this was tidied out of sight. They had taken on Zachary's passion for Lydia, along with her languid delivery and odd ironies and white wedding trouser suit and non-Jewishness, without betraying the least flicker of anything but warm welcome and interest. It was Lydia's family who hung back, suspicious of what their daughter was getting into. Tibs and Pam would only thaw into their party mood, Lydia gloomily predicted, at just that point in the evening when all the other guests were taking leave and everybody wanted to go to bed. Zachary insisted his parents would love that, drawing up chairs for a cosy chat, getting out the cognac and cigars. — It won't be cosy, Lydia said. — My mother will still be on her high horse for some reason she's forgotten: for fear, really. And she takes Babycham in her cognac.

— Trust me, Zachary said. — Everything will work out.

Christine was avoiding Alex, though he seemed to be trying to talk to her; the more champagne she drank, the more numb and dull and solitary she felt. He cornered her eventually at the buffet when, very late for dessert, she stood indecisively before the wrecked white damask cloth and the ravaged remains of the chocolate gateau and fruit salad, not fancying anything. She'd never seen Alex in a suit before: it looked cheap and too tight on him, the shiny grey material creased at the elbows and across the shoulders. His jacket was unbuttoned and he'd spilled something on his shirt. — You're thin, he said, doling out syllabub into her dish, sticking it full of finger biscuits. – You need feeding up.

— I don't even know if I like this, she protested, pushing the dish back at him.

— You need to feed yourself so you can make more drawings. I hear that Zachary's keen on your drawings?

— I don't want to talk about them.

— He's going to ask that friend of his, isn't he? If she'll show them in her restaurant, where they put exhibitions on the walls. Quite a big deal, he says.

Anxiously Christine said she didn't have enough to show, she couldn't just make them to order. Anyway, Zachary and Lydia were moving to New York, so there was no point in starting anything. — I could take care of you, Alex said.

— You, take care of me? Oh dear.

— What's so amusing?

— You've had too much to drink, Alex. What about that speech of yours? It's supposed to be funny, you know. You're not supposed to make it sound as if the wedding's all a disastrous mistake.

— It is a mistake. He's chosen the wrong woman. She's pretty, but I thought that he'd want someone with more depth.

— You hardly know Lydia, Christine said indignantly.
— You don't know what her depths are.

Juliet was heading through the crowd towards them, purposeful but unsteady on her high heels. Relieved, presuming she was coming to take Alex home, Christine stepped back to be out of her way; then in an ugly transformation, Juliet was suddenly hissing into her face with pent-up vindictiveness. — Don't think I didn't know what you were up to, she said. — You little cow. Worming your way into my home and all the time making those soft eyes at my husband, imagining you could fool around behind my back.

— Christ, Juliet, Alex said. — You're humiliating yourself.

— I think you've got the wrong end of the stick, said Christine, astonished – though not without some twinge of unease, thinking of that night they'd rummaged through Juliet's cupboards and read her letters. Then Juliet lunged and slapped her very hard, knocking her head sideways. Scuffling with his wife, Alex grabbed at her flailing wrists and swore at her. Wedding guests began to look over at them. Juliet kicked at her husband's shins with her heels and tried to kick Christine, who jumped back out of range. Someone who knew Juliet took her by the arm, persuaded her to sit down inside the house. — That's not the end of it, she shouted across her shoulder. Christine put her hand to her face; tears sprang into her eyes for the shock and stinging pain, and for how virtuous she was, and how wronged. — I can't believe she just did that, Alex said, appalled. — She was drunk, I can't believe her stupidity. Did she hurt you? I'm so sorry. Did she leave marks? Let me see.

He touched her face gently with his fingers, tilting it up towards him, scrutinising it tenderly and close up, frowning; she proffered herself for his attention acceptingly. Then he put his cool palm on the hot marks on her cheek.

For such a long time, when Alex declared his feelings for her, Christine couldn't allow herself to believe in them. She was in no hurry to introduce him to her parents.

— Why have you chosen me? Why would you choose someone like me?

She was reluctant to be overwhelmed, afraid of his completeness, the force of his manner, his knowledge and inexorable critical judgement. He said things which bewildered or upset her: that England was run by grown-up clever public-school boys in thrall to their nanny, as if life was a sport. — I can't forgive their furtive, stunted sexuality. And how they're so serenely oblivious.

— But I'm English.

— You're different.

— My brothers are English and they're not like that.

Yet she felt the glow too, the golden good fortune of being chosen. At first she liked him best when he was with other people, and she could steal looks at him shyly and obliquely, as if she didn't know him. When she tried to tease him and deflect him, which was what she did with her brothers, he wouldn't let her, he was too serious. Christine agonised over whether Lydia would feel betrayed. — It doesn't matter what Lydia thinks, he said. — She's too young, she sleeps until four in the afternoon. She's silly, she's still a child.

Christine stared at him. — Then that's what I am too, she said. — We're the same. You don't know me.

— You don't know yourself, he said.

When he made love to her eventually – she was still afraid of him, but didn't like to seem a prude – his nicotine-stained scalding fingers, stripping away layer upon layer in the dark, seemed to expose her as if to a stranger; she wanted to keep up her guard at first, didn't want him to know if she was carried away. She found herself thinking of his old study in Kensal Rise, with its heavy typewriter and broken blind, its shelves full of books in unknown languages.

THREE

THEY DECIDED TO BRING ZACHARY'S body to lie in the Garret's Lane gallery which had been his life work. This was Grace's idea. — It's always been a sacred place, she said. The art gallery was a conversion of an eighteenth-century chapel, and had won prizes for the architect: the airy purity of the original interior had been preserved, the maze-like display spaces were composed of a sequence of white folding walls, which could be arranged in different combinations. Zachary had died in the light-filled office with its walls of pink brick, modernist furniture and arched window looking out onto an acacia tree in the courtyard garden. In the week before the funeral, artists associated with the gallery came and went, bringing in pieces on loan for the unique occasion: some of the big names who'd begun with Zachary or been with him from the beginning – Jane Ogden, Hari Rostami, Martin Shield – along with others more modestly successful whose work he'd championed, and those young artists out from art school who'd won the coveted Garret's Lane Trust apprentice-ships, and had studios in the outbuildings. The Trust was

Zachary's characteristic invention. He'd decided that some of his old friends in art were making too much money and needed to be relieved of the burden of it. As well as the apprenticeships, the Trust helped to fund the gallery's work in taking art into local schools and bringing schoolchildren into the gallery, and the art projects with refugees and victims of torture. Two of the current apprentices had come through from the refugee group.

It was Grace's idea to bring her father's body home to the gallery but it was effective, judicious Hannah – compact and heavy-bosomed, dyed red hair swinging in her eyes – who made the arrangements, cajoling and forceful on her phone, always seeing the shortest way through any problem. They closed the gallery to the public though they kept the cafe-bookshop open. The team that had worked with Zachary and Hannah came in at all hours, they hardly seemed to take a break, helping to store away the exhibition which had been in progress, hanging and re-hanging according to what turned up, solving the problem of display for those fragile pieces which might be in danger in a crowd. Zachary had always had one of Christine's paintings in his office, opposite the desk where he worked – one of the series of self-portraits she'd done when she was pregnant with Isobel. This was carried downstairs for the occasion, to hang among the others.

Lydia and Grace moved back into their home adjacent to the gallery; Alex and Christine and Isobel came to keep them company, at least for these first nights. Alex and

Christine took the big front bedroom because Lydia said she wasn't ready to sleep in there, not yet. Isobel put a mattress on the floor beside the bed where Grace slept naked on her front, with her arm hanging down, hand curled as if she was half-holding something. Isobel slipped her own fingers inside her friend's, found nothing there. She didn't know if Grace could feel her, in her sleep; perhaps her hand tightened on Isobel's – but that might have only been a spasm of the thrumming, manic, overheated engine Isobel could feel driving Grace along, never letting up its effort onwards into this grief. At least she had let go the idea of the death mask. Now instead she was obsessing about photographing her father in his coffin. She'd made up her mind that the picture itself must represent the emotional difficulty of its taking, and she was working with a family friend, a photographer who used the wet-plate collodion process. He would prepare the glass plates for her and make a temporary darkroom in the gallery, because they must be processed immediately. Grace spent hours researching, calling Isobel over to her laptop to admire the mournful old photographs with their depth of light and hair-fine detail, mossy darkness eating away at their edges.

Christine stripped the bed where Zachary and Lydia had last slept, then put the linen in the washing machine. She opened the window wide, snapping the clean sheets in the air as she spread them, raising dust, trying to exorcise the significance of the scene. Sitting down on Zachary's side of the bed she picked up his things one by one, glad to be alone with them: the book with its marker a third of the way through, the stale glass of water, its sides furred with bubbles, the Fitbit he had neglected to wear – he couldn't resist a gadget. Morocco-leather slippers, backs trodden sloppily down, lay where they'd fallen when he last kicked them off, holding the shape of his feet, darkened with his sweat; picking them up tenderly, she arranged them side by side. He had liked to prowl around at home in his slippers, heavy-footed and at ease, unbuttoned, domesticated, leaving a trail behind him of half-drunk cups of strong black coffee. All these objects ought to compose him – they promised solidity and permanence, she was incredulous that he could have slipped away between them. Opening his book to the place his marker kept for him, she stared at the page – were these the last words Zachary had read? It was about criminal justice in Baltimore: Christine remembered him full of outrage, declaiming statistics about young black men in the US prison system. But the book was dusty, his bookmark was only a third of the way through, he didn't finish things. She couldn't find any message from him in the words.

Lydia's hair was dishevelled, she hadn't put on any make-up for days, her long face was blotched and naked. The room where she was sleeping seemed rank with her distress, like a den with an animal ranging around in it; the duvet was kicked into a heap on the bed and the bottom sheet was pulled out wildly from its moorings, snaking in a thick rope across the bare mattress.

— Oh, you're reading, said Christine in surprise, picking

up a paperback book, a Scandi thriller, from where it lay face down on a pillow, its spine cracked.

— Is that awful? Lydia said. — I mean, I should be reading Tolstoy or Keats or something.

— You need to lose yourself, that's natural.

— I know Alex thinks I'm a coward. But really I've never pretended to be anything else – have I?

— Nobody thinks you're a coward.

— How am I supposed to get through the hours, Chris? Everyone's dreaming up beautiful and dignified things to do for Zachary; the funeral will be a work of art in itself. But I'm really quite ordinary without him, I haven't got any talent for anything. I'm not like you.

— I don't feel very talented right now. I feel useless.

Lydia marvelled at herself. — I'm the useless one. I never even did my own housework or learned to cook – and I had a nanny when Grace was little. Now I don't know how I'm going to fill my days! I can't go on with what we did before. What would I do in all those exciting places, meeting those wonderful people, on my own, without Zach's unstoppable enthusiasm? His enthusiasm always seemed so risky to me, as if he was setting himself up for disappointment – though he never was disappointed. The world went on supplying him with beautiful people making their beautiful gestures: good things came into being, to fulfil his expectations. They won't come into being for me, that's for sure.

— Something will come into being for you. I know that as surely as I know anything.

— I can't be here. I can't stay in these rooms.

— You don't have to be here. You can come back and stay with us, for as long as you like.

The heavy coffin was carried in as if some singular and controversial work were arriving for exhibition. Quite a crowd was gathered in the gallery: family and friends and helpers hung back around the edges of the space. It was Isobel who bravely went up first to look at Zachary, when the undertakers had gone: she did it for Grace. She had had this magnanimous ideal of duty since she was a little girl, befriending all the doomed, lonely children in her class. — Oh, it's not too bad, she reported with relief. — It's sort of like him but not like him.

— I'm so glad to see his face again, Grace said when she went over to look. — It makes me feel better.

The two girls stood holding onto each other, Grace weeping into Isobel's shoulder, Isobel stroking her shorn head. Hannah carried flowers down from the office, vases full with tall white foxgloves and delphiniums and hollyhocks, fat peonies. But the sight of Zachary's body was a horror to Christine, the darkness in the nostrils, his closed face. He looked like a stuffed doll, with his stubby-fingered hand laid in rhetorical gesture across his heart, wedding ring on ostentatious display. Lydia had given the undertakers one of the lightweight wool suits he'd had made in Hong Kong – a clownish tobacco-brown check.

They heard Lydia's steps then, resonant in high heels, on the staircase which linked the living quarters with the gallery, through the office on the mezzanine. When she appeared in the office doorway above them it was clear that she had dressed up for the occasion – in a vermilion satin dress fitting her figure tightly, with a patterned scarf wrapped around her hair like a turban. Stepping down with assurance in her teetering high shoes, in the silence that had fallen with her arrival, she was as striking as a visiting queen, or a tropical bird alighting in the room. Her smile was faintly defiant – she had smiled like that, Christine thought, when she was scolded once at school for forgetting her homework. Their geography teacher had hated Lydia, spitting with loathing, shaking her violently by the shoulders so that her plaits flew: *Lydia – Smith – you – nasty – little – piece – of – work.* Now Lydia looked into the coffin, gripping its wooden side tightly. Then she said a few words, thanking people for their help, for rallying around the family. Her small, dry voice was lonely in the absence of Zachary's loud informality, his booming, commanding bass.

Grace embarked on taking her photograph. The cranky ancient camera was specially adapted to hold a glass plate. Its broken imperfection, Gilby the photographer said, made for the beauty of the end result; glue peeling off between the layers of the lens meant that when the light struck, it diffused to beautiful effect. Because they couldn't zoom, and the camera needed to be held steady for thirty seconds' exposure, they had to set up a platform of sorts – two planks balanced across between two sets of steps – where Grace could crouch under her black cloth, looking down on where her father lay. A whiff of ether floated from the storage cupboard which was their temporary darkroom, and the syrupy collodion mixture dripped from the camera onto the floor. Lydia wouldn't watch what was going on. Grace kept her hand clamped across the lens, pulled it away, counted to thirty, covered the aperture again. They went through the whole process with two separate plates, in case anything went wrong with the first one. No one could look at the pictures yet. They had to be varnished, the backs of the plates had to be painted over and the whole thing sealed inside a protective frame.

Alex sat up all night with Zachary. They set up steel spotlights at either end of the coffin and switched off all the other lights; briefly the chapel burned with the sunset, and the high pink walls seemed transparent as shells. Spotlit in gold, the coffin seemed unreal as a tableau, or a kitsch artwork. Christine went upstairs early with Lydia, to see her into bed; Grace was determined to stay, and sat in a plastic chair pulled up close beside her father, hugging her jack-knifed long legs in her arms, her chin on her knees, staring bleakly. Then she fell awkwardly asleep, and Alex signed to Isobel to take her up to her own room. Roused, Grace opened her eyes wide on her friend in incomprehension, wondering where she was, like a child who'd fallen asleep at an adult party: she submitted to being led away. Hannah in her stocking-feet took round the teapot and the whisky bottle among those mourners left; then her wife Jenny took her home to rest.

Alex must have fallen asleep because when he woke up his mouth was full of bile, as if he'd drunk something disgusting. When he looked at Zachary's dead face he thought that it was doughy and flaccid. Had he really grown so fat? Alex hadn't noticed it when he was still alive. As a boy at school Zachary had been so keenly hopeful, with his fresh pink cheeks and irrepressible laughter, bubbling up even as it got him into trouble and he was ducking to avoid blows, sobbing and laughing at the same time, snotty and blubbing and giggling because the punishment was ridiculous too. And now he was extinguished, easily as putting out a candle.

Zachary's send-off in the gallery was beautiful, everybody said so. The undertakers came in the morning to close the coffin. There wasn't enough room for everyone, people were standing outside in the bookshop and cafe, lapsing into the tradition of so many other convivial occasions in this same space, in much the same company, with the same wine and flowers and interesting things to look at on the walls. The artworks were their own strong statements: an angry Jane Ogden glowered over the gathering, debris erupting through a crust of filthy paint. Children threaded tactfully through the adults' solemnity; patches of sunshine bloomed and withdrew on the floor tiles like tentative reassurances. Then a squall of rain blew against the windows and latecomers hurried in apologetically, shaking their umbrellas. So many friends brought flowers, which they heaped up on top of the coffin. A huge wreath spelled out *Goodbye,* in acid yellow against vivid red: no one knew who'd sent it. Another gallery with a grudge, Hannah suggested.

Friends and family stood up at the lectern one after another. Gina Brennan played a sarabande from a Bach suite on her cello, Alex read a poem, Nathan Kearney read extracts from a satirical mag he and Zachary had edited when they were undergraduates. Kids from the Art Club played steel pans, then Tomo Okamoto danced as a warrior re-enacting the scene of his own death, in full Noh costume and mask. Hannah in her tight black dress, with her slash of brilliant lipstick, couldn't finish reading out what she'd written, Jenny had to do it for her; Martin Shield made everyone laugh. Christine sat with her mother and Isobel and Sandy, struggling against weeping, pressing her knees together in her blue dress, gripping her screwed-up wet tissue in her fist. She envied her mother's poised, dry face, so carefully made-up, with its sad little smile of regret lifted towards the lectern or the dancing – when you were eighty you were more used to funerals. Scowling into her lap, she tried to hold off every real thought of Zachary, rehearsing trivialities. She would need new keys cut if Lydia was going to stay with them. Had she remembered to arrange for the cat sitter to come in today? Fixing her gaze on a painting hung on a side wall, she was furious with its daubed hieroglyphs, its stupid posturing. Dislike was a relief, it dried her eyes. Some of the art Zachary had liked was awful.

Sandy had come alone, because he was between girlfriends. He was pale – but then Sandy was always pale, as if he didn't often see daylight. Unexpectedly he'd turned up in a suit, which was sweet, and of course he looked gorgeous in it, with his dishevelled beauty. And he played something on the guitar too, with that simplicity he only ever had when he performed: a little instrumental he'd written years ago for

Zachary, who'd first encouraged him to play. It was very touching. Max had told Hannah that he didn't want to say anything, but at the last moment he stood up abruptly to recite the prayer for Kaddish, stumbling and forgetting half of it, then ripped his cotton jacket down noisily, from the lapels. Lydia and Grace exchanged quick glances, sitting straight-backed side by side at the centre of the front row of chairs. It was so like Max, they both thought, who hadn't been inside a synagogue since his bar mitzvah, to confound them all today with a dramatic gesture. Was it his best jacket, or had he worn an old one specially? Seen together from the front, Grace and Lydia were so unlike that no one could have guessed they were mother and daughter: one small and self-possessed and fair, one tall and dark, athletic and careless as a boy. From behind, though, a likeness was visible in their tensed shoulders. Both were rigidly attentive to the tributes playing out in front of them, holding their heads stiffly as if they expected further blows.

— Poor old Max, last one left, whispered Lydia's mother Pam. Pam had had any number of operations and complained of pains everywhere, but was still handsome; she had her hair done with bronze highlights and wore good hats. — Lucky Zach's parents didn't live to know they'd lost him, she added with sententiousness. — I wonder if you ever appreciated, Lydia, what a lovely man you had.

Lydia smiled constrainedly, patted her mother's hand. — You know me, she said. — Famously unappreciative.

— How can you joke at such a time? You heartless creature.

— Heartless? Now who might I get that from?

Tibs and Pam had worn set faces through the Japanese dancing, but at least understood the requirement for poetry at funerals. Dapper faded Tibs sat beside Grace and held her hand in his, out of his depth but kind. When Grace was little she had bloomed amid the hectic sociability of their pub-life, she'd been a great hit with their regulars, dancing for them uninhibitedly to the Spice Girls, gyrating her hips and pouting, sticking out her bottom. — It's unsettling, Ma, Zachary had mildly protested to Pam, laughing and loving it.

Everything overran, despite Hannah's best efforts: the hearse arrived and the undertakers had to wait, discreetly and sympathetically consulting their watches. Then Max and Alex and Sandy and a couple of Zachary's cousins carried out the coffin, strained and tense with the difficulty of it; family and a few close friends followed the hearse to the crematorium, where there was a brief last ceremony. Christine was grateful for this displacement onto alien territory, with its exhausted neutral sanctimony, limp from use. Pink silky curtains, jerking along their rail, reminded her of a cinema. She could abstract herself at last, be absent, think about nothing.

Afterwards Grace had hardly any recollection of the day.

— But I wanted to keep it all up here, she cried in dismay to Isobel in her bedroom, putting her hands to her temples. — Now I wish I'd videoed it. I should have.

— You'll have your photographs, Isobel reassured her. — Anyway, it will come back to you. For now, your poor mind is overloaded. It needs rest.

— I do remember Sandy's instrumental. Wasn't he great?

— He was great.

— Do you think he'll take me more seriously, now that I'm grieving? Not that I'm looking for a sympathy fuck or anything. Though perhaps I am. I wouldn't mind.

— Lie down now. Stop thinking.

They were to spend one last night in the chapel rooms before Lydia came to stay with Christine and Alex, and Grace went to Isobel's. Grace didn't know if she'd go back to Glasgow for her fourth year. She couldn't imagine what would happen next, couldn't imagine her life resuming where it had left off. All the women went to bed in the late afternoon and slept deeply, then woke to a honey-coloured evening light, emptiness in the rooms, syrupy birdsong. They were at a loss now that the funeral was over, which had been an end point in their imagination. Its burden was lifted and they were weightless; Hannah's team had tidied the gallery, closed it for a week. Alex was out, who knew where? He sometimes walked for miles around the city streets. Christine cut some ham and put it out on the kitchen table with pickles and tomato salad, she boiled new potatoes and put butter on them, picked parsley in the yard where Zachary had grown herbs in all the pots. Lydia had held up wonderfully, everyone said, she had smiled graciously and talked to all the friends who came. She swallowed one of the pills the doctor had prescribed.

When they'd eaten Lydia turned on the television and found the soap opera they all watched because Juliet was in it. Christine rarely saw Juliet in person these days, now there was no need for contact over Sandy; she couldn't come to the funeral because she was away filming somewhere in Europe. Christine and Lydia kept up with her religiously on the telly though, taking a huge interest in her character, a harassed middle-aged doctor in a country practice. Lydia said she was beginning to forget which bits were the real Juliet and which belonged to the part she played. What about the dodgy accent? Wasn't that fake? But perhaps if you were a bad enough actor even your own voice sounded as if you were putting it on. She was still slight and energetic, but it was difficult to recognise the gypsy looks of the young Juliet behind the doctor with her stony features and pragmatic short haircut, her repertoire of exasperated expressions, through fraught to grimly resentful. Apparently she had a following of younger fans, because of Sandy.

The living area was arranged over two levels. In the dusky light later, looking for the telephone – she ought to call her mother, and Alex's mother too, who didn't come to funerals because of her feet – Christine climbed the steps into the mezzanine, which was lined with bookshelves. One volume caught her eye, pulled out slightly from the shelf or pushed back incompletely, gleaming white in the dimness, claiming her, familiar. More than familiar: it was the collection of Alex's poems, published long ago, before they were together. The edges of its pages were yellowed and the book had lost its freshness; the cover, whose plainness had been austerely striking at the time, seemed of its period now, its curly purple lettering dated. She felt towards Alex's book a complex reflex of protective tenderness mixed with faint derision. Because she had just been watching her on the television, she remembered that there were poems about Juliet in this book – not exactly love poems, although some of them were sexual. Hesitating, Christine almost pulled it out to look inside it, as she hadn't done for years; then she pushed it back into its place instead. All that was over with, she felt impatiently. She got on better with Alex these days because so much was smoothed off between them, the surfaces of their lives sliding fairly effortlessly together. Anyway, there wasn't enough light for reading, and she was reluctant to turn on any lamps. The dimness was restful.

Who could have taken his book down from the shelf? Alex himself would never look at it. Could Zachary have been reading Alex's poems in the days before he died? Perhaps that would touch Alex if he was aware of it. But Christine knew she wouldn't try to tell him: he'd only be exasperated by what he'd see as her clumsy efforts to comfort him, and by her even mentioning those poems. She pushed the book back into its place, where it was inconspicuous among so many others. She and Alex hadn't spoken now for years about his writing, or his having given it up. Once or twice long ago, when they were first together, she'd urged him to set aside time for more poetry, thinking this would make him happier. He'd turned on her in irritation: what could she possibly understand about his writing, or not writing?

Christine didn't tell Alex that she'd invited Lydia to live with them for as long as she liked. But he was uncomplaining when after the funeral she closed up her own home with obvious relief and came to set up camp again in their spare room. This time Lydia unpacked her bags, putting her clothes away in the drawers which Christine had emptied for her, or hanging them in the space she'd made in the wardrobe. Her sumptuous, interesting dresses and skirts and jackets made Christine's clothes look dowdy and worn-out. Lydia tried to give her things, told her to help herself to anything she liked, and Christine was tempted by the heavy, silky fabrics, the fine sewing and good designs. Her mother loved Lydia's clothes, she was always hinting to Christine that she ought to wear something more colourful and striking. — To show off your wonderful figure darling, she said.

Christine reproached her mother, they didn't have the Samuels' kind of money. But it wasn't only the money, she'd have made a fool of herself if she tried to carry off Lydia's style. Now Lydia set out her brushes and mirror and all the apparatus of her make-up and skin care on top of the chest of drawers: pots and tubes of cream, lipsticks and eyeshadows spilling from bags that were pretty curiosities in themselves, embroidered and patterned zip-bags, or pouches with tasselled silk drawstrings. She draped the mirror and the chair backs with her jewellery and scarves, and the room began to smell of her perfume. Soon all the surfaces and the floor space were cluttered. Lydia had always been untidy, and was used to having cleaners.

In the mornings she didn't get up until long after Alex had left for school. When Christine took coffee into her room she would be lying reading her thrillers under the duvet, with the tabby cat sprawled across her legs or curled up beside her. Christine would have been up and dressed by this time for hours already, busy with housework, tidying or washing dishes, filling the washing machine or hanging the washing out, popping out for milk from the corner shop, cakes from the Algerian bakery, mint and mangoes from the chaotic greengrocer where customers haggled over the price of a yam or a handful of chilies. In the evenings she cooked elaborate meals, trying out new recipes. She knew that she was using Lydia's presence in their house to justify these wasted, absorbed, peculiar days when she never once let herself think about entering her locked studio. She still carried its key around with her, hidden in the back pocket of her handbag. Alex was annoyed that he couldn't get at certain books in the studio, but stubbornly she avoided his questioning about the lost key.

The gallery had opened its doors again, Hannah was working with Jane Ogden on the assumption that her exhibition was still going ahead. But perhaps she ought to be looking around for another job? Lydia fended Alex off when he asked what her plans were, she put her hands over her ears, asking him not to torment her. She was so sorry, she knew she was behaving badly, but she wasn't ready to talk yet about what happened next. He said he would help her any time she liked, to sort out Zachary's things, but she couldn't bear to think about that either, and eventually he did it with Grace and Isobel. Grace came in with a black bag full of Zachary's suits and shirts and ties, emptied them in a heap on the floor in Christine's sitting room, suggested that they should cut them up and make a quilt out of them, with Zachary's name sewn into it to commemorate him. At first Christine hated watching Grace attack the precious clothes with her sharp scissors. But the sewing gave them all something to do. Christine was good with that kind of dainty work, she had made patchwork when she was a girl; Lydia didn't have the patience, she gave up quickly. The quilt grew under Grace's direction, a spiral in brilliant orange and scarlet burgeoning from its centre, against a more sombre background cut from the dark suits.

One afternoon Grace brought round her photographs of Zachary, packaged up in brown paper, and handed them to her mother with a stricken face. — Actually I haven't looked at them. I can't unwrap them. Gilby was so nice about helping me, I'm ashamed to tell him that I haven't seen them yet. He says they're beautiful, but I've lost my nerve. I had my nerve, but now I've lost it.

Lydia pushed the parcel away in horror. — Grace, I can't. I told you, darling, I don't want to see them. You don't have to look at them either. We could just put them away somewhere and forget about them.

Grace cried bitterly that this was just so typical of her mother. She offered the photographs to Christine, who only shook her head and bent lower over her sewing. Alex came home from school to find them all in tears. He was as calmly tactful with Grace as if she had been a child upset in his classroom, taking her into his study and sitting with his arm around her while with trepidation she unwrapped the parcel so carefully padded with bubble wrap, lifted out the frames. In the interval since the images had been made, it was as if

Zachary had finally taken leave from the face they saw. They didn't know him any longer, his living personality had withdrawn from behind the darkened, shapely lids which were closed with such stern finality. Grace wrapped the photographs up and gave them to Alex to hide, said she didn't want to look at them again for a long time. — He frightens me, she said. — He isn't funny any more, is he?

Alex watched his wife from over the top of his book as she undressed in their bedroom. The straight brows which met above the bridge of her nose were still dark, and her veiled, quick, oblique glance was the same as when she was young, but her light-brown hair, cut in its short bob, was full of grey. You could hardly tell, apart from the little slack round belly, that Christine had ever given birth to Isobel: she was still girlish, but an ageing girl. Her un-made-up worn face and thin naked body made him think of the austerity and angularity of farmers' wives in photographs of the Dust Bowl, with their sculptural raw cheekbones and hip bones – although those women were probably twenty years younger than Chris, aged by work and poverty. In repose and in animation his wife could seem two different characters. Alone with him, absorbed in her thoughts – her long dark mouth, with its deep recess under the lower lip, closed as if on a reservation or hesitation, holding something back – she was appealing, unfathomable. But in company with other people she talked too eagerly and waved her hands about with that gracelessness of educated Englishwomen of her class and her generation. She had been fighting him ever since Zachary died, Alex thought, flinching if he touched her on the breast or her waist, turning her face from his kisses. Now, she put on her boyish pyjamas and tied the cord decisively. — Don't watch me, Alex, she protested. — It makes me uncomfortable.

— How long is Lydia staying here? he asked sternly. — Because I'm not sure that it's working out. She needs to start up some kind of a life again.

— But what life?

— Be resolved, take responsibility.

— Those are such cold, hard words though. You're only using them as a punishment against her. Can you imagine her managing all alone in Garret's Lane? What would she do all day?

— Well, what's she doing here?

— She's waiting. She's not ready yet. We can't abandon her.

— But she's stopping you from working.

Christine shied away from any discussion of her work. — Oh no, it isn't Lydia. She'd prefer it if I was working: I think she even feels the need to entertain me. Look, she's painted my nails.

Alex only glanced at her crimson fingernails, frowning. Everywhere she touched, Lydia left her mark. He was full of pity for her but avoided being alone with her in a room – she was too potently present, with her blue-white skin and mask of beauty, in her eternal place in the corner of his sofa. Her play-acting made him think of some ancient dreadful tragic art. She was adrift without Zachary, lost in chaos, and Alex thought he must protect himself from chaos. When Christine put down her book and fell asleep at his side, with her back turned and her knees drawn up to her chest like a child, snoring lightly, he imagined that in their spare room Lydia too was lying awake, and that she was aware of his wakefulness reciprocally, panic and confusion alive in both of them, a muffled violence inside the darkness of their bodies lying still.

Grace threw herself into partying, she drank too much and confided in strangers, telling them all her sorrows, spilling over with noisy grief, bringing men home with her to the spare bed in Isobel's flat.

— I have to live life to the full, she said. — That's what Dad did.

Isobel found this difficult. She couldn't sleep and her work was suffering, because she was always listening out to make sure Grace came home – or trying not to listen, when Grace did. When she had to go through her sitting room in the mornings, visiting the bathroom, she tried not to look at the sleeping forms on her sofa bed. She didn't want to share this problem with Lydia or her own mother, who were already dazed with sadness and hardly thinking straight. She didn't trust either of them, anyway, to be sympathetic to Grace. Instead she confided in her grandmother Margita: called Czech Granny to distinguish her from the English one. Margita had bloated ankles and Alex's beautiful eyes; thick pink foundation was creased into her wrinkles, her dry stiffly lacquered hair was her own but looked like a cheap wig, and the heaps of her half-smoked cigarettes in an ashtray were stained with lipstick. Her eyes were so clear that they were almost glassy; it was a surprise when she had to put on spectacles for her crosswords – she did the *Telegraph* cryptic every day, although her English was thickly accented still, false in her mouth like her too-white false teeth. Margita's vases of silk flowers on crocheted doilies, and her greasy bottles of alcohol on their painted tin tray, labelled in an unknown language, had always stood for Isobel as signs of foreignness and otherness.

— Poor little Grace, Margita said. — Let her get it out of her system.

— Some of these men are awful, Granny. I can't be sure they are, of course, as I don't meet them. But I hear them, they sound awful. I think there've been three different ones, or maybe one of them was there twice. But you know, I only have a tiny flat.

Her grandmother shrugged. — As long as she doesn't get pregnant, or infectious diseases. It takes her mind off.

— But is it *right*?

— Who cares? She's crazy because she loved her dad. Mine was a bastard, I was dancing when I heard he died, maybe it's the better way.

In her attitudes Margita was surprisingly free of prejudice and up to date. She watched television for hours on end, but despised the credulity of anyone taken in by it. Once, in another life in Bratislava, she had been a teacher of literature, but all she ever did with her dead husband's books these days was dust them, and not very frequently. Isobel always imagined that her grandmother's life under Communism – which might as well have been a mythic era in Isobel's perspective, for she was born the year it more or less ended – had purged her of every superstition and sentimentality. She was fairly lonely: had never made friends among the English, and liked the dwindled, doomed community of exiles even less. Her husband had taken up so much space in her attention: with his ambition first, then with his disappointment and his affairs, then his absence.

Margita had learned to do her shopping on a computer – which, like the vases, was displayed on a crocheted doily on the sideboard – so that she hardly left her flat except on Sundays, when she was borne off to Alex and Christine's for lunch. She sat at their table stiffly in her too-tight white patent shoes with kitten heels; hurt, but only half-heartedly, because they didn't invite her to live with them, although this wasn't really what she wanted. Aware of her superior intelligence in competition with English Granny, she knew that she lacked Barbara's emollient social lightness and deprecating charm. Margita complained that Alex never talked to her on the telephone. He only wished she was dead and out of the way, it was always Christine who called.

One hand clutched Isobel's, its wedding ring bedded deep in loose flesh, while the other scrabbled in the cigarette carton with its photographs of cancerous lungs. — And what about you, hey, Izabelka darling? How's your love life?

— Granny, it's non-existent. What am I to do? Nobody wants me! Am I so horrible?

— You're too nice, Margita soothed her. — Be patient. These selfish boys, they don't deserve you. Something good is waiting, just you see.

— At least Grace just goes out there and takes what she can get!

They settled down to browsing the men on Tinder on Isobel's phone. Not that Isobel ever actually went as far as Tinder – she drew the line, she said, at anything worse than Guardian Soulmates. — What about this one? Margita encouraged her. — He's more mature. Lawyer maybe: sporty, nice car.

But Isobel couldn't warm to his carnivorous smile.

One night when Alex couldn't sleep and went downstairs, he found Lydia in her nightdress in the sitting room, on the sofa with her feet tucked under her. He shut the door quietly behind him, so that they wouldn't wake Christine. — You aren't even reading, he said sympathetically, sitting down beside her, close but not touching. — What are you doing? Aren't you cold?

The blinds were pulled down at the windows, but the street lamp outside gave them light to see each other. — I'm just being, I'm not doing anything.

— Can I get you a drink? Or a cup of tea?

— Sit there for a bit, Alex, she said. — That might help.

Don't go away. Talk to me about something abstract and very clever.

— Now you've put me on the spot.

— It doesn't matter, you don't have to talk to me. Just keep me company.

Alex poured himself vodka and then when he sat down again Lydia took the glass from him and drank from it, they shared it, both of them feeling its heat spread inside them. She was unsettled by sitting at such close quarters with him, in the T-shirt and stretch cotton shorts he wore to bed, his physique in these disconcertingly youthful: she was used to him in the jacket and tie he wore for school. She was beginning to see Alex again with the old intensity – that dangerous sprung tension in his posture, the keen lines of his face. Her awareness of him was a taut wire. He told her he was reading a comparative study of educational systems around the world, showing how each system was formed by the culture and ideology of that country, and also shaped and influenced by it. — But I'm boring you, he said. — You're not interested in this.

— You always think I'm not interested. I was listening carefully.

— All the richness of the book is in the detail, which I can't do justice to.

A few hours ago they had all sat watching a film, a thriller, on television in this room – with Christine's mother, Barbara, too, who'd come for supper. Their chairs were still pulled around the screen, there were dregs in the wine glasses and coffee cups left out on a low table; Christine sewed pieces of

Zachary's quilt while she watched. Afterwards they'd enjoyed picking the film to pieces; all evening their collective domesticity had seemed friendly and inevitable, almost ordinary. But now in the thin middle of the night it appeared to Lydia too strange and strained to last. — I should go home, Alex, she said. — I don't know what I'm doing here. I know it's difficult for you two.

In that moment she was guileless and helpless, with her hands clasped between her knees, naked shoulders hunched. — We need to stick together, he said.

— Are you sure? I'm not sure.

She was shivering in her skimpy nightdress. Christine had left her cardigan on the arm of a chair and before he went upstairs again he picked it up, dropped it across Lydia's bare shoulders.

Isobel begged Sandy to take Grace out somewhere, just to calm her down. He invited her to eat with him in an expensive, fashionable place, relieved to have the distance of a tabletop between them, pouring her wine parsimoniously so that she didn't get carried away. Alone with Sandy, however, Grace lost all her bravado; she sat meekly in her cheeky T-shirt, ordering whatever he recommended, intimidated as if she hadn't been used to eating in nice restaurants since she was a baby. She blushed when she dropped her fork on the floor with a clatter, and questioned him eagerly about the band, regressing to the little worshipping cousin who'd trotted round everywhere after Sandy like a devoted dog whenever their two families holidayed together. Sandy had used to torture Grace, calling her Mop-head, tying her hands behind her back with her own skipping rope, requiring her to stand unflinching while he fired potato pellets at her. He had taken her out once in an inflatable boat into the middle of a pond, and then swum back and left her alone without a paddle, gripping the sides of the boat and not calling out for help for such a long time – she couldn't swim, and Sandy had known it. That had got him into awful trouble.

Grace could remember waiting for him in the close, humming, buzzing afternoon, under a lid of cloud – water boatmen scudding across the surface tension between fat lily pads, unseen fish mouthing their spreading rings, and after a while a shower of rain pocking the water all around her with a prickling sound, secretive and teasing as if it rose from the depths of the pond rather than falling from above. Of course Sandy was nicer now. Grace had every reason to be grateful to the saving veneer of adult decency: there was a wince of contrition in his new consideration for her. He even unwound a little in the balm of her uncritical attention, with no one else listening – dropped news of a forthcoming US tour into the conversation with unguarded self-importance. In the restaurant he brought off the performance required of him by his public, sophisticated celebrity combined with rebel youth. He spoke with extreme courtesy to the staff, signed an autograph without fuss, and didn't finish anything he'd ordered; staring around him restlessly he shifted on his seat, crossing and uncrossing his long legs. Grace ate up all the food he didn't want. — You know me, I'm so greedy, she said, with chocolate on her cheek, which he leaned over wordlessly to wipe off with his napkin, dipped in his water glass.

Only at the very last minute, outside the restaurant, when he was about to put her into a cab back to Isobel's – sliding out two virgin twenty-pound notes from his wallet while they made their farewells, pleating them in his fingers, ready to slip them inconspicuously to the cabbie – did she fling her arms around his neck and kiss him, tasting for one heady moment, mingled with coffee and amaretto, his clean young skin and salty hair. — Take me home with you, why don't you, Sandy? Please, just for this once? You know I'd never ask anything more of you, afterwards. Don't you think I'm pretty? Aren't I pretty enough for you? Just for one night?

Sandy extricated himself, ducking under her arm and leaning into the cab window, handing over the money, giving the driver Isobel's address. — Grace, you're very pretty. You know how fond I am of you. You're a wonderful girl. But I respect you too much to ever take advantage of you.

— Oh please, don't respect me, she cried too loudly in the street. — Please take advantage.

His respect, however, was inexorable.

Christine sometimes went guiltily back to bed in the afternoons, before Alex came in from school, to read or doze. Coming downstairs once when she woke after a nap, treading quietly because she thought Lydia too might be asleep, she saw through the open doorway that her friend was reading on the sofa in the sitting room. Something prevented her from stepping forward across that threshold, offering to make tea, breaking the spell of Lydia's solitude. Her concentration on her book was so intense, almost severe; frowning, straight-backed, wearing her reading glasses, sitting forward from the sofa cushions, her face uncharacteristically slack and plain because she believed herself unobserved. Lydia was reading Alex's poems. Her hair, fastened in a clip at the nape of her neck, glinted with bronze in the sunlight from the window, and she wound and unwound one loose strand around her finger.

A breeze fanned the newspaper on the table, the smells of a city summer were wafted through the open window: tar and car exhaust, the bitter-green of the flowering privet hedge. Police horses went past in the broad street, their hooves clip-clopping conversationally alongside the voices of the women who rode them; the stables were nearby. Christine saw in the hard light how the flesh was beginning to be puffy under Lydia's eyes and drag down her cheeks. Yet this late ripeness was attractive in itself, she could see that too, softening Lydia's haughty beauty, filling it out with character and experience. Lydia must be so afraid, now she was left alone, of wasting this late flare of her power on no one, on emptiness. In a few years they would be old women: sixty! There wasn't much time.

Christine stepped back from the door, then sat down on the stairs in the dim light, to think where it was cool. Lydia appeared to be studying Alex, setting herself the problem of what he was. Long ago, when Isobel was a baby, Christine had fought Alex for her life, so that he would acknowledge that in the domain of the mind they were equals, separate as equals. She couldn't remember now why this had mattered so much, or where her appetite had come from for those long late-night sessions, prising away layer upon layer of resistance and falsity, confession matched with counter-confession. The lovemaking that usually ended things had sometimes amazed and reconciled them, sometimes seemed the continuation of their fight by other means. When Isobel woke them in the early morning their eyes had been sore with lack of sleep, they'd gone about in a daze of exposure.

She had been so keenly interested, then, in what Alex thought. But after a while things weren't so difficult after all, and she never really knew how much that had to do with all those sessions of interrogation. Anyway, she didn't think any longer about the truth in that same way: as a core underneath a series of obfuscations and disguises. In the long run, weren't the disguises just as interesting, weren't they real too? She and Alex were so unlike, really: associated through some accident in their youth – the accident of his choosing her, because of what he thought she was. Since that beginning, they had both changed their skins so often. Marriage simply meant that you hung on to each other through the succession of metamorphoses. Or failed to.

Lydia must have sensed Christine's presence in the doorway, or felt its alteration in the light, at just the instant she withdrew it. After a pause Christine heard her stand up from the sofa and walk over to the door; she stood at the foot of the stairs, staring up, her eyes taking time to adjust to the different light. Alex's book was still in her hand dropped by her side, finger holding it open at a certain page – she made no attempt to conceal what she'd been reading. Why should she?

— Chris, what are you doing there?

— Just thinking, Christine said. — I was thinking about the four of us.

— What about us?

— You know, all our history together, the way we were.

— Oh, I see.

Lydia sounded disappointed, as if she'd waited for something else.

— Is it drawing to a close, do you think? Our bourgeois sensibility. All our sadness and our subtlety, our complicated arrangements. Our privilege of subtlety and irony is at an end. What's in that Polish poem Alex quotes? Something about how the barbarians don't object to irony. They just grind it up and use it as their salt.

— So it's all up for us, the lilies of the field.

— You're a lily. I've never been a lily.

Lydia climbed the stairs and sat down beside Christine with the book in her lap. — Who wants to be a fucking lily? Although I must say, look how nice I was once, in your picture. What fun we had in those days.

One of Christine's acrylics, a painting of Lydia from years ago, hung on the opposite wall. Lydia was holding a fan, with a scarf of black lace over her hair, like a Maja; she was painted in dense brushstrokes with a lot of black, the room behind in an exaggerated childlike perspective, decorated with symbols which were deliberately obvious – a goldfinch, cherries.

Christine had been thinking of her work then as set designs for plays that were never performed or even written. It was from around the time when she won the Whitechapel Prize, and everyone had been so surprised – painting was still unfashionable, and they hadn't thought anyway it would go to a woman – that it hadn't given the boost to her career it should have done. — Can I have it when you're tired of it? Lydia said. — It means a lot to me, it's beautiful. It's my past.

— You can have it now. It's yours.

— Why aren't you painting, Chris? Is it because I'm here?

— You think everything's about you. It isn't about you, Lydia.

— About Zachary then. I think it's about him.

Lydia felt Christine stiffen against her in repudiation. She said she didn't want to talk about her work – she was taking a break, that was all. Why was everyone making such a fuss? Her face closed stubbornly.

— Talk to me about Zachary, Lydia said. — I need to think about him. He was so transparent in his life and now in his death he's an enigma, I can't get through to him. Tell me things you know about him, that I don't know.

— I can't, Lydia. I can't bear to. Not just now, I'm sorry.

Grace wanted to get back to her friends in Glasgow. — It's bad for me down here, she said to Isobel. — I'm just dwelling on Dad. I'm longing to do something with my hands, without my mind in it.

— I'll miss you so much, I'll be so solitary. Don't stay away too long.

— I want to get back to my chisels, and vent all my pent-up feelings on some stones. Not that they're very pent up, you're thinking, Iz. Anyway, I've got to do something with the rest of my life.

The four women sat up late one night, finishing their quilt – even Lydia joined in, stitching with a frowning effort dispro-portionate to the tiny progress she made. When they held the quilt up finally, they were moved by what they'd brought into being between them. They hadn't appliquéd Zachary's whole name in the end, only woven a huge Z into their spiral design, cut out of a bright red flannel that had once been his waistcoat. Christine said she would sew on the backing fabric, with cotton wadding, on her machine.

— And who's going to have it then? Grace challenged. — To sleep under.

Christine had imagined hanging it up somewhere. — It would look gorgeous against a white wall.

— No, we have to use it, Grace was adamant. — Not just look at it. We have to touch it every day and love it and spill things on it. It has to be part of life. Mum should have it, shouldn't she? She can sleep underneath Dad's name, to cheer herself up.

— We should drink to the completion of the quilt, ex-claimed Christine. — Where's that bottle of the Czech brandy Zach liked? The kind Vaclav Havel drank when he met up with Polish dissidents in the Harz mountains.

— Not the Harz mountains, Mum, Isobel said. — They're in Germany.

— Isn't she just like her father? Christine appealed to the others. — With the two of them, it's like being trapped for life inside a general knowledge quiz. Can you imagine just how *corrected* I perpetually feel?

— The funniest thing happened to me, by the way, Isobel said, smiling round at them all. — I meant to tell you. I had a date for once – someone at work had fixed it up for me, friend of a friend.

Isobel was so wholesomely attractive, Christine thought with a rush of love, in her neat blue cotton skirt and print shirt, with sturdy bare brown legs and sensible brogues. Her appearance made you imagine preparatory rituals, bathing and tending and ironing; a distinctive tight fold under her green eyes was edged in dark lashes as densely and precisely as if in pencil. — When was this? she said anxiously. — I do like to know, darling, just in case.

— At the weekend, Mum, don't be silly: it was fine, Sunday lunchtime. But you just won't believe my bad luck, it's so typical. He was really quite nice, we drove out to a pub on the river in Henley, and we were both thirsty. He bought two pints of beer, we were standing up together, we chinked glasses. Maybe I was nervous, but really, we didn't chink that hard. And my glass just broke! Around the middle, so that the bottom fell out neatly onto my feet and both of us were simply deluged in a whole pint of beer, from the waist down. I mean, I hardly knew him! It wasn't exactly an auspicious beginning.

— It was a baptism, Iz, Lydia pronounced. — I think he's the one.

— He was very nice about it, Isobel said. — But I haven't heard from him since.

Alex took Grace back to Glasgow. He cleaned up the kitchen in the shared house above the shop and filled it with bread and cheese and pasta and fruit, unpacked the fruit cake which Christine had made for her. Two of her housemates were in residence and he didn't know whether it was Grace's bereavement which made them creep around so meekly, bursting with their repressed shy sympathy, or his inhibiting presence and forbidding age. He stayed overnight, in a sleeping bag on a dank sofa whose springs had collapsed, and the next day he escorted her to the Art School. In a chilly damp studio looming with unborn or half-born forms amid sodden sandbags, filthy with stone dust, he watched Grace in goggles and dust mask cut vindictively into the lump of half-carved limestone she'd left behind her in another life. He had a feeling she was only obliterating every trace of her old intentions, returning her artwork to pre-existence. He offered to stay another night, make sure she was OK, but she didn't want him. He wasn't any use to her, he was the wrong person, he wasn't Zachary. He telephoned Christine to let her know he was setting out for home.

— Alex is en route, Christine announced to Lydia, yawning and then rousing herself, wifely. She ought to cook something, get some milk in, tidy up. Lydia said vaguely then, only half meaning it, that she should go back to Garret's Lane. Alex had had enough of her, she should leave them alone, couldn't really spend the rest of her life battening on to her friends' domestic arrangements. The two women had lapsed, in Alex's absence, into slow hours of reading and desultory talk, not quite intimate, amidst a debris of dirty coffee cups and wine glasses, plates of crumbs.

— Don't go!

Christine protested, but in that same moment was aware that there might be something stale in their conversation, if it continued any longer. They were falling back on old patterns inherited from their past, and might be wearing out their shared present. Now it was as if Alex's impending arrival tolled a bell; blinking, they looked around them, surprised by the time. He gave a form to their formlessness, punctuated it with necessity. Lydia insisted, her idea taking hold.
— Seriously, I'm in the mood. Alex will be exhausted after all that driving. He won't want me in the way. I'll call Grace up and talk to her for company.

— In the way of what? Don't be silly. But just for one night perhaps. Your home is always here, if you want it. Don't be afraid or sad, will you, in that place on your own?

— I will be sad, Lydia said. — But I'd better get used to it.

She called a cab and packed a bag, the two women embraced quickly at the door. They said affectionate things, but under the surface of their parting Christine was aware of haste, as if each of them suddenly, urgently, needed to be free of the other's company. When Lydia had gone she felt full of energy, throwing the windows up high, looking out onto the wide sleepy street, the semi-detached brick villas with their white-painted fretwork porches, some smartened up and some with flaking paintwork and torn curtains, steeped in the yellow light of the summer evening. The plane trees cast their blue shadows; parakeets sliced across the stillness, shrieking with derision. She stacked glasses and plates in the dishwasher, and dusted and vacuumed the front room, changed the sheets on their bed upstairs, put clean towels and fresh scented soap in the bathroom. It would be late by the time Alex got home, he wouldn't want a heavy meal. So she went out to the Co-op to buy eggs and peppers for a frittata, which would be just as nice cold; when that was cooked, and sprinkled with sea salt and lemon on a plate in the kitchen, she showered and washed her hair, changed into her navy dress, sprayed on perfume, poured herself a glass of wine, then sat down with her book under a single lamp switched on in the front room, to wait.

Her perception was a skin stretched taut, prickling with response to each change in the light outside as it ran through the drama of its sunset performance at the end of the street, in a mass of gilded pink cloud. When eventually the copper beech was only a silhouette cut out against the blue of the last light, Christine pulled down the blinds, put on all the lamps, turned her awareness inwards. From half past ten she began to think she heard Alex's car draw up outside: each time, she braced herself. The more a homecoming was anticipated, the more disconcerting the actuality was prone to be, she knew that: the arriving one walked into a shape prepared for him, not actually his own. Just because she was relieved to be free of Lydia and looking forward to seeing Alex, the reality of him would be an affront: he wouldn't fit into her preparations or even notice them, would arrive burdened with purposes of his own, breaking into the tension of her waiting. Men didn't care anyway about clean sheets or scented soap. It would be better, really, if she watched telly and forgot she was waiting.

But in the summer night the spell of her expectation was too strong. She lost herself inside short passages of her novel, then couldn't proceed because they affected her too much – she dropped the book and looked about her restlessly, filled up her glass again. It was only once midnight had come and gone that panic lifted up in Christine's chest like a great bird, between one moment of its not occurring to her to worry, and the next when she was certain something must have happened. He'd said he might be home by ten o'clock, hadn't he? No doubt the traffic was bad. And he wouldn't have called to let her know because Alex never used his phone while he was driving – also, he despised that whole infantile obsession with calling, needing to be in touch at every moment. Yet her imagination, working outside her control, began to conjure disasters that were more awful for being indefinite. The poised perfection of her scene was spoiled, a mockery: and yet she couldn't possibly go to bed, sleeplessness there would be worse. Anyway he would surely arrive any minute, and there wouldn't have been anything to be afraid of after all. When he did arrive she would never forgive him, she thought, for putting her through this.

In interludes of respite she forced her awareness down into her novel, then awoke from its dream in palpitations of dread. She hadn't eaten anything since cake at lunchtime, she'd waited to have something with Alex, so the white wine she'd been drinking had given her a headache. There was nothing to think about except the worst. For a long time she wouldn't let herself call his phone, then she tried it, and found it was switched off. Her helpless fear was a paralysis, hollowing her out, and yet was probably absurd: she kept hearing a car whose drone seemed familiar, which then droned past. Or a car would park in the street outside, a car door slam, her heart would lift in a paroxysm of relief – but Alex didn't come. She thought of calling Grace, to make sure he'd left when he said he would. But wouldn't that be unforgivable, burdening the poor burdened girl with her stupid worry? There was no point in frightening Isobel either. This madness of anxiety was her own to bear; and at any moment Alex would turn up, it would have all been for nothing. She remembered Mary Shelley going from house to house, the night Shelley went missing on the lake. *Ha visto Shelley?*

By two o'clock she couldn't help herself, she rang Lydia. She told herself Lydia often stayed awake late, reading – and indeed, she picked up the phone almost at once, spoke into it warily. Christine knew there was a handset on the bedside table at Garret's Lane. She poured out her distress, so glad to talk to someone. — Lyd, I'm so really, really sorry to call at this time of night. I know it's completely selfish of me, but I'm so stuck, I don't know what to do, I don't know who else to call. I don't want to bother the children. It's Alex. He's not back yet, I don't know where he is, he said he'd be back by ten and he isn't here, and his phone's turned off. I've got myself worked up into a state, imagining every kind of disaster. D'you think he's had an accident?

Lydia's voice was hesitant, but not as if she'd been woken from sleep. — Oh Chris, she said. — Don't worry, he's all right.

— I know it's stupid, he'll be fine. But I am worrying.

— Don't worry though, really. Alex is here.

She could hardly take in what she heard, at first. — What d'you mean he's there? What's he doing there? Why hasn't he rung me?

— I don't know what to say. I don't know how to tell you.

It was as if dark forms crowded suddenly into the room around Christine, recognition was so violent; one stark and ghastly white face showed in the mirror – she didn't know her own self for a moment. Lydia ploughed on, as if bemused by wonders. — Everything's so strange, Chris. I'm so sorry.

Alex had reached the outskirts of London at about eleven, and although he was exhausted from driving he hadn't wanted to go straight home. He'd got into the habit of calling in at Garret's Lane, telling himself he was just checking that the premises were secure, everything was OK. The place was a solace to him, it soothed his restlessness to be in there, browsing among Zachary's books or just sitting. If he went home, he'd only be breaking in on Christine's days-long conversation with Lydia. The air would be thick with their confidences;

he knew just how they'd turn to look at him as he entered, faces replete with interpretation as if they knew him.

He kept the Garret's Lane keys on his key ring. When he pulled up in the gallery's cobbled parking space – beside Zach's old plum-coloured Jaguar which Lydia didn't want because she hated driving – his body was chilly from air conditioning, numb from his long journey; it was a relief breathing in the warm night outside the car, meaty and beery and tainted with traffic fumes. Taking the stone steps two at a time he turned his key in the lock, anticipating the peace of the empty rooms, where a faint veil of dust would have had time to settle on the designer furniture between the cleaner's visits. The nothingness in him needed silence and stillness. Yet even before he pushed open the door he was aware of an assault of music, incomprehensible and outraging: Beethoven, Fischer-Dieskau singing 'An die ferne Geliebte', one of Zachary's perennials, played on the sound system at top volume. Zachary had used to sing along to it in his enormous, tuneless voice, so delighted with himself and so stirred, his eyes and his heart full, big beard wagging, waving his arms around, conducting encouragingly towards his imaginary accompanist, missing every note.

Alex was almost vengeful; it didn't occur to him to deduce logically that it must have been Lydia who put the music on and had every right to, in her own home. He didn't deduce anything, only came striding aggrievedly, bewildered, from the hall through the sitting room and study into the kitchen, flinging the open doors noisily back against the walls. Then he set out up the stairs, in pursuit of his explanation. The music couldn't be playing by itself. And Lydia in her bathrobe at her dressing table in the bedroom, warm from her shower, didn't deduce anything logically either: only heard the front door slammed shut, and then the doors of the downstairs rooms banging open, someone advancing heavily upstairs. She seemed to be hunted down. When Alex stood in her bedroom doorway she was as shocked as he was, sitting staring in her bathrobe with her hairdryer turned off, raised in one hand, her other hand over her heart. Her iPod – or more likely Zachary's, because he was always spending money on new devices to play his music – was in its socket on a chest of drawers, puny bland origin of so much magnificent tender drama. *Auf dem Hügel sitz ich spähend/In das blaue Nebelland.* Alex took a step inside the room and when Lydia stood up an antique ebony hand mirror fell out of her lap and cracked on the wood floor.

— Christ, Alex, she said: quavering, tearful. — I didn't know who you were.

At first he took her into his arms because he was sorry for frightening her. They were only reassuring each other, at first; each meant to restore the other's equanimity. Then their reassuring altered into something else, Alex's blind-sided up against the surprise – which was not a surprise after all, more like something long guessed at, anticipated – of Lydia's warm nakedness under her unfastened robe, and then her quickened breathing, her eager trembling offer of herself, pressing herself against him, pulling him in deeper, confounding him and swallowing him up. Alex hardly took the trouble to make any bargain with his fate: that whatever was happening might be sealed inside its moment, without consequences. It was as if he wasn't himself, the bargaining man he knew, but a different man who was capable of this. And afterwards – when they lay still, beached and naked in the chaos of white linen on the bed, the enormity of their act having crashed over them and left behind its significance, like a wave withdrawing – Christine telephoned, and Lydia spoke to her, and it was too late.

FOUR

GRACE WAS THREE YEARS OLD when Zachary and Lydia came back from New York to live in London, in the mid-nineties. Of course the two couples had visited each other in the years between, they had holidayed together, Isobel had already found her role as Grace's protector and interpreter. Grace had been a difficult baby: she cried, she wouldn't breastfeed, she didn't sleep, she was a fussy eater. When Isobel stayed in the Manhattan apartment, she and Zachary together had devoted long hours to encouraging the fiercely scowling little girl to walk and talk and be happy. Isobel taught her to fit the pieces of her puzzle into the right holes, the square into the square hole, the triangle into the triangle. — Why couldn't I have had a sweet one like yours? Lydia complained to Christine. She employed a succession of nannies, none of whom were satisfactory. Privately, self-righteously, Christine disapproved. Surely it was the nannies who made Grace difficult?

Zachary's parents had died, his mother first and then his father, within the space of a few months. He had needed to come to London often when they were ill – he loved them dearly and grieved for them hugely – and then afterwards to arrange the family affairs with Max. The family affairs were on a large scale, there was a lot of money. Zachary sat up late one night with Alex and Christine, drinking vodka and discussing what he ought to do with his inheritance. Their ideas got wilder and wilder – buy a Picasso, buy an orchestra, set up a foundation to promote renewable energy. — But you don't know anything about renewable energy, Alex reasonably pointed out. Christine thought he ought to spend it on a crumbling palazzo in Italy where they could all live together like aristocrats, growing grapes and keeping goats, making their own wine and cheese. Zachary loved the Italian idea. Or perhaps he should just change it all into cash and throw it into the wind off Tower Bridge.

— Buy a premises in the East End, Alex suggested. — Come back to live in London. Start an art gallery.

— What does Lydia think? Christine asked. — What does she want?

Between Zachary and Christine there was quite a tradition of analysing Lydia. He loved to talk about his wife, combing his fingers excitedly through the lustrous black beard which he had newly grown, idiosyncratic in those days before all the young men in art had beards. It suited him and added point to his soft face; even Lydia was resigned to it.

— You'd think she was materialistic, he said musingly. — I mean, she is materialistic. She's awfully lazy, and she loves nice things. But I think that the idea of real money bores her.

I mean, the kind that you have to do something with. It's too much like hard work. She'd like to go on just the way we are, really, with me working at the Gagosian, the nice parties, the shopping.

— She's quite an ascetic sort of materialist, you're saying.

— D'you know, she is, Zachary agreed. — I really don't think she's interested in the power that money brings. Or any kind of power. She's actually quite unworldly, though she doesn't look it. The world's only unworldly materialist.

— And are you interested, Zach, in the power that money brings?

— Aha! I'm terrified of it. But it's exciting, isn't it?

Alex wouldn't discuss being part of any commune in Italy, not even playfully. At this point he was working part-time as a postman as well as tutoring in English as a foreign language; he and Christine were living in a tiny cramped place in Streatham, behind Brixton prison, and between them they hardly made enough to cover their rent and bills and food. Christine had a job helping in a school office three days a week; it wasn't the same school as Isobel's, and at the end of those afternoons there was always an awful hiatus, worst in the rain, when she had to dash like mad on her bike to be in time to pick Isobel up. On the other two days Christine painted – or drew, or scratched – in her box-room studio at the end of the landing. Zachary had to sleep among her paints when he stayed, and said he felt the beneficence of her art sifting down upon him in the dark, doing him good. When Zachary tried to give them money to help out, Alex walked out of the house in a cold rage without saying a word, and Christine with Zachary's arm around her sobbed into his broad accommodating chest, his soft good shirt.

— Why couldn't he just have refused your generous, loving offer in kind words, like any normal person? He's so horrible, Zach!

— Or accepted it.

— No, of course we do refuse it: although thank you, you're lovely, you're so kind.

This was another tradition: that she accused Alex of intransigence and intolerance, of having impossible lofty standards, and Zachary – perplexed and upset on her behalf – managed to comfort her without giving away his friend. — I was tactless and he's fine-tuned, he said, furious with himself. — I'm an oaf, I should think before I speak.

Christine sat up and mopped at her eyes with a tissue, blew her nose. — Why does everyone have to tiptoe round Alex's moods? I'm never, ever supposed to criticise him in any way. I have to tread so carefully, taking care not to say the wrong thing, because it's too tedious, frankly, if we get into another fight, and then he's sulking and doesn't speak to me for days, so that eventually I have to make the effort and coax him round, and he doesn't even *know* that he's been coaxed. I want to make everything nice, Zach, I want us to have a happy home. Why shouldn't it be happy? Isn't it better to live pleasantly? You and Lydia aren't like this!

Zachary considered carefully. — Alex must feel as though we're always all watching him. That must be awful. Waiting to see him do what he ought to do. Wondering why he's expending all that brilliance of his on things that are too small for him. He must know we're all asking why he isn't writing.

Christine felt negligent then, wondering if she cared that Alex wasn't writing. She didn't think about it much. People did seem to like his poems. Although they hadn't been much reviewed at first, in the years since they were published they'd acquired a certain cult following. Anyway, he had seemed stubbornly perverse to her, taking on seasonal work at the post office on top of his language classes, getting up in the freezing flat at an hour when it was still dark, when it wasn't even conceivably morning. Why didn't he try to find a job he liked? There was something self-dramatising in his sacrifices, though stoically he never uttered one word of complaint.

It was always a relief, pouring out her hoarded grievances for Zachary to hear. And yet when Christine had finished she was half ashamed, because they weren't the whole truth – although Alex really was impossible and she really was afraid of him sometimes, of his cold look cast at her, shutting her out of his favour. In their early days – when his favour had fallen on her uninvited, like Jove's shower of gold, and before she'd had Isobel – she'd felt that she could leave him easily if they quarrelled or she changed her mind. She was free! Love was his idea, not hers. Then as time passed Alex's force had melted something resisting in her, so that she had taken on a new shape, fitting against his. But it wasn't always his fault when things were difficult. Under the surface of their relationship she often fought against him: against his authority, which he took for granted. He was bewildered sometimes, she thought, by the twists and turns of her dissatisfaction, and how she manoeuvred to put herself in the right. Women used their pleasantness sometimes as a weapon, a subtle knife.

Zachary began to give her a small amount of money secretly, and she paid one of the other mothers to pick up Isobel from school on her painting days, so that she could go on working for two precious extra hours, while Alex taught. Zach said he was investing in her career. There was even a relish, a hot triumph, in keeping secrets from her husband. She knew that Alex didn't really attend to her opinions, or weigh them against his own. He liked to talk with men, or to have women listen to him; in company he was surprised if the women made too much noise, too insistently – he retreated then into his privacy, his irony. Christine beat against his indifference, in her mind. He wasn't indifferent to her moods or her feelings, only her ideas. If he loved her, it was for what she was unconsciously. He didn't mind her having opinions, but that wasn't the same thing as his really taking notice of them – as he might do, for instance, if he thoroughly attended to a book which changed his mind. She desired this real, mind-changing attention from him, for her thoughts, for her work. Was it out of petulance or egoism merely? Otherwise her husband didn't really know her. Didn't she love him for the content of his thoughts? Didn't she take so much of her truth from him?

It had been obvious all along that Zachary must open his own art gallery. And then almost as soon as he went looking for a premises he found a red-brick chapel, built by the Huguenots in a modest back street of terraced eighteenth-century cottages in Clerkenwell. The chapel's main entrance and its row of arched side-windows fronted directly onto the street: the windows still had their original thick flawed greenish glass. In its proportions the place was domestic, friendly – the interior with its floor tiles worn by human passage into a shallow relief landscape, its dreamy underwater light, its gracefully curving upper gallery supported on iron pillars. After the Huguenots the chapel had been Wesleyan and the Wesleys themselves had preached there, then it was a school for a while, and then a chapel again – Bethesda, into the 1970s. An arched gateway wide enough for a wagon, fitted at some point with corrugated iron doors now rusted fantastically, gave access to a cobbled courtyard overgrown with buddleia and nettles and filled up high with junk – old chapel pews ripped out when the chapel was used as storage for a builders' merchant, heaps of rotted drugget, plastic sacks of hardened cement, abandoned steel scaffolding poles and bolts, an ancient Gurney stove, hymn books rotted down to pulp.

The place fitted every part of Zachary's idea and even surpassed it because he could make a home for his family as well, in the adjoining parish rooms which had been added on in the nineteenth century and came as part of the purchase. And the sensation of dropping down into this pocket of stillness and neglect – sometimes no one passed in the little cul-de-sac for half an hour at a time – was somehow significantly related to the roaring traffic and filthy air just around the corner on the main road. The chapel wouldn't have appealed half as much, Zachary explained, if it hadn't been less than a minute's walk from the clamour of car body repair shops and kebab shops, printworks, fabric wholesalers, a funeral director's with sculpted ebony horses' heads on folds of sky-blue satin in the window, a dingy pub with yellow bottle-glass in mock-Tudor windows where a star cut out from fluorescent card, hand-lettered in felt pen, announced Topless Waitress's.

Lydia flew over with Grace from New York to take a look. — This is a crazy place, she said. — I think you're crazy. We can't live in a church! We will be haunted. Think how these people would have hated us.

— They don't hate us now, Zachary said. — They're dead, they've transcended mortal prejudice. If they're watching us they'll understand our idea, they'll like it. We'll plant a tree in the middle of the courtyard.

Looking into the courtyard, Lydia was appalled by the accretions of so many generations of rotted filth, piled up to the level of the windows: this chaos seemed unalterable to her, like something fixed and cruel. She couldn't have faced it herself, but she trusted Zachary. Contracts were exchanged, he was given the keys, and they invited Christine and Alex – who else? – to drink champagne with them that same afternoon in the chapel, consecrating its new life in art. Zachary kissed the keys ceremoniously in the street outside – where still, perhaps disconcertingly, no one passed. Would anyone ever visit the gallery? The keys themselves, anyhow, were things of beauty, with their austerely slender iron stems and the ellipse of their bow-ends, drawn fine as italic calligraphy. It seemed a miracle that after almost three hundred years you could put the same key in the same lock and turn it, and the mechanism would respond to its cue: they had brought WD40 but didn't need it. The door swinging back on its hinges allowed them inside, where they had visited before, of course, but only under the inhibiting scrutiny of the estate agent. The musty, dusty, empty, softly echoing high space belonged to them now – they could do what they liked with it. Pale October light filtered through cobwebs as thick as cloth in the windows.

— What money can buy, Alex marvelled, looking round him: if it was a criticism then Zachary, in any case, would never apologise, not even to Alex, for what he insisted on thinking of as his great good luck. It was good luck for all of them, for everyone, for art, wasn't it? And the chapel was saved from dereliction. The little girls went running off, up and down the stairs to the gallery, giving out screams of freedom, dizzied by the emptiness, their hard shoes pounding on the bare boards, Isobel hanging onto Grace's hand responsibly, Grace protesting, trying to tug her hand away and run by herself. Sandy, who stayed with Alex and Christine at weekends, traipsed after the girls, bored as usual, with his hands in his pockets; he was thirteen and his peaky face, faintly freckled, with a fine uneasy jawline, had just begun to be good-looking. He gelled his pale hair and wore it flopped in a thick wave across his forehead, or falling forward into his eyes; his gaze melted away reluctantly from any encounter, especially with his father. And Alex responded to his son's withdrawal coolly, although Christine urged him to try harder. He accepted as if it were inevitable that Sandy had finished with him and they must go their separate ways.

They found whole rooms whose existence they had forgotten since they were last shown round: cubbyholes and sculleries and pantries and outhouses; a back kitchen with a brass tap hanging on its pipe away from a wall tiled in ocean green, over a stone sink; the stone steps of a curving stair worn by the passage of many feet; a porcelain toilet in its own throne room, the Thunderer, with an overhead cistern and a chain to pull. In an office a great desk of warped mahogany held record books and accounts from Bethesda chapel days. Breathless from running, Isobel pleaded with Zachary, seizing his hands. — Never, never change this place Zacky, will you? Always leave it like this. Me and Grace love it how it is.

Isobel was stocky and earnest, with a shy sense of decorum and a woman's developed features, too expressive for her soft face. — Izzy's right, Zachary said, hunkering down to her level. — It's perfect like this. Shall we just keep things this way forever, and come picnicking here every weekend?

— It has to change, my darling, Christine said, quick to feel her daughter's deep attachments and disenchantments. — Zachary's going to make it into a gallery with paintings and sculptures and installations: that will be lovely too.

Isobel reassured herself. — It will just be lovely in a new way.

There were still a few pews piled up against the chapel walls; they pulled them together and Zachary set out his feast of bread and foie gras, Italian cheeses and *mostarda di frutta* pickle, with baklava and pears and brownies – they used paper plates, and had to share one plastic knife. Everyone wore their coats; the electricity wasn't switched on yet so they didn't have any heating, and a stony cold rose up through the brick-red floor tiles crusted with cement dust. The women kept on their gloves because their hands were freezing. Zachary lit candles when the light began to fade, and the children invented some game of advancing into the dark then running screaming back into the safety of the illuminated circle. After a while even Sandy couldn't resist joining in, inventing things to make the game more seriously terrifying, darkness covering the sacrifice of his grown-up aplomb.

The adults huddled closer for warmth among the candle shadows blooming and elongating on the chapel walls, Christine and Alex on one pew and Lydia and Zachary on another pew facing them, all their knees pressed together across the gap; the restless candlelight seemed like an ema-nation of their young inner lives, urgent and expectant and sensuous. Christine's animation – her awkward thinness, her quick attention and talk, the plait of her light brown hair wound round her head and slipping loose – offset Lydia's self-possession. There was a sheen of new sophisti-cation on Lydia, from New York; she had shed her sulky, punky look and was groomed and sleek, looked the world in the eye with a new candour. But Christine felt with relief that this candour was only another subtle layer of Lydia's performance. She was not translated wholly into the worldly woman whose part she played.

The four of them were happy to be back together again.

The champagne went to their heads, and Zachary had bought dope from Alex's dealer; Christine was the only one who didn't smoke, it made her sick. Arguing over Tarkovsky's *Nostalghia,* which they had seen the night before as part of a retrospective at the BFI, they hardly took the trouble to hide their smoking from the children, who knew about funny cigarettes. Christine said she only really liked the bit at the beginning of the film, when they stop the car in the mist and walk to see the painting in the little church; the woman says it's so beautiful, and following her the man says he's had enough of beauty. — But then it gets silly, she said. — It's just an idea of life, one man's idea. At every point after that I could see they were actors, acting, and I could imagine the director, directing them.

— Christine's very literal-minded, Alex said. — She likes the art of everyday.

— That's so unfair, she said, — because I love all kinds of art, I've loved other Tarkovsky. But isn't it a cliché, because the man is pursuing meaning and art and truth, and the woman only wants love and happiness? It's somewhat more likely to have been the other way round, in real life: the middle-aged writer pursuing the attractive young woman, and her fending him off.

— That's such an uninteresting way of thinking about the film, Alex protested.

— I believed it implicitly anyway, Lydia said. — There are men like that.

Zachary asked if Christine hadn't loved the famous single shot of the writer carrying a lit candle the whole length of the empty pool, and Christine conceded wholeheartedly, with sudden emotion, that yes, that was so meaningful and moving, it had made up for everything. And then the children came screaming out of the darkness, flinging recklessly into the circle of grown-ups, hiccuping with fear and laughter, taking refuge between Christine's knees and Zachary's, the adults kissing them and hanging onto them, holding them safe, the children breathing in the fumes of drink and marijuana. They flung away again, into the terrors hidden in the dark. Sometimes Zachary went charging after them, growling like a bear, to their extreme delight although they shrieked with fear. He had put on weight, he had the authority of a substantial man these days, with his booming voice and laughter, his air of knowing where to find all the good things worth having. But he kept a quick concern in his expression from boyhood: the blinking watchful eyes following everyone with his enquiry into their well-being. Were they all right? Did they have everything they wanted? They told him to stop fussing, relax, they were fine. Lydia complained that Zachary was always the enabler, concealing himself behind his attentions to others. — I don't know what I want for myself, he conceded happily. — I've got everything.

Alex was the moody prince with his pent-up angst. He was still slight at the waist and hips, still had his thick hair with its bronze gleam cut in the old style, fringe hanging into his eyes. The hazel cat's eyes and curving mouth – too often closed in disappointment – were sensual and feminine despite himself. He'd have liked to give nothing away. And yet he was also vain, he was human, he was like everyone else:

Christine knew how, although he avoided mirrors, if he caught sight inadvertently of his own reflection he straightened his shoulders and stood taller, renewed by these glimpses of his good looks, his power. When they went out in company other women looked at Alex surreptitiously or hungrily, and Christine was gratified that such a man had chosen her. But how long would the women admire him if he persisted in refusing to take on any substantial role in the world, or any status? Reading so much and knowing so much, but with nothing to show for it.

They stayed in the chapel until long past the little girls' bedtime; Grace was wild with fatigue. They were all disinhibited in the new, strange place, and because of the drink and the smoking. Lydia spoke about the therapist she'd been seeing in New York. Or rather, the two therapists: she couldn't make up her mind which one had the right insights to unlock her problem. With one of them it was all about her mother. — The other one's a man, she said, — and he's much harder on me, but I trust his judgement more. Though he says that's part of my problem, always seeking out the people who will judge against me, so that I can't break out of a fatal cycle in which I self-sabotage, punishing myself for being myself.

— But what is your problem exactly? Alex said severely.

She gazed at him, eyes glittering in the candlelight. — Well, I'm not very good at being happy.

— You are good at it! Christine cried out in protest.

— I don't feel entitled to happiness, Lydia said. — For instance how I was at school, always thinking the other girls

146

were the real thing and I was only passing myself off, I was a sham.

— No you didn't, Lyd! That's not what you thought! We despised school!

— Lydia is more melancholy than you'd ever guess, put in Zachary, as if it was another of her marvels.

She held herself upright and steady, submitting to their scrutiny; if she wasn't happy then it was to her credit that she didn't mope, always appeared unruffled and serene. — You should work, Alex said. — You should fill up the hours of your day with discipline.

— Because of Zach's money though, she patiently explained, — I don't have to. When I worked in bars and waitressing I wasn't doing it to fill up my time. Or are you suggesting I should join a committee, supporting the arts or doing good or something? But I think that I'd hate doing good. My idea is that Zachary does the good, on my behalf.

— Isn't it Lydia's genius, Christine said, — just to live, like an aristocrat in another era? To be herself, while the rest of us are running round like idiots, because we've inherited a punishing puritanism.

Alex said therapy was a parade of suffering, everyone poking their fingers into their own wounds in a competition to see who'd suffered most. — It's magical thinking. Believing that every random thing happening is an element in an encoded secret story, and that if only you can crack the code, you can be set free.

— But can't I be set free? Lydia said plaintively, self-mockingly.

— Freedom isn't about liking yourself, Alex said. — That's just an indulgence, a distraction from freedom in the real world.

— Politics is Alex's trump card, Christine said. — He uses his real world to squash everyone else's argument. Why is your real world always the realest, Alex?

She could see he was spoiling something which had seemed to Lydia to matter and be hopeful, in New York. To distract them from quarrelling Zachary tried to carry a candle ceremoniously the length of the draughty chapel, like the writer in the film. After he'd done it they all had to have a go: Alex went too fast, his candle blew out and he had to begin again twice. Lydia did it the first time, her stately pace in her high heels was just right.

In bed at home later that night, Alex suggested unexpectedly to Christine that they should forget about taking care and make another baby, and she agreed, she was carefree, the shape of her own history felt loose and open, anything was possible. And in fact she did get pregnant again around that time, but lost the baby at ten weeks, and although she grieved for it, and was bereft and humbled for a while, she was also half-relieved. She'd have loved the baby utterly if it had come, of course – she loved Isobel more than anything in the world. But it hadn't been a baby, only a cluster of cells. Babies took up so much time, so much of your life energy, and she was working well at the moment. She was thinking a lot about Paula Rego and influenced by her had started on a new series, pictures of men and women embracing imaginary birds as harbingers and emblems. These were small, cramped inside the picture frame: a cock robin, a phoenix, a pelican piercing its own breast to feed its young, a jaunty folkloric crow. She was working in acrylics for the first time. Anyone could make a baby. Only a few could make a painting.

When tens of thousands of refugees from East Germany had begun pouring into Czechoslovakia in November 1989, Alex had brought his mother round to their flat so they could watch together the events unfolding on the television. For a few nights Margita slept in their spare bed. Zachary had telephoned from New York; Alex had stayed home from his classes in the language school and walked from room to room with the radio pressed to his ear in case he missed anything. Christine sat breastfeeding Isobel, watching the abandoned Trabants blocking the Prague streets, the tent city growing in the courtyard of the West German Embassy, the police trying to stop the men and women climbing over the embassy walls. There were mass demonstrations, the crowds jangled their key rings, Alex thought you could pick out on the television the StB men moving amongst them, taking photographs. In Bratislava they broadcast dissident music via television signals from Vienna. Alex and Margita and Christine couldn't turn their eyes away from the police in their white helmets breaking up demonstrations, using tear gas, pulling the peaceful demonstrators down by the hair, kicking at them and beating them with their truncheons.

Then Havel in his leather coat was addressing the crowds in Prague, and the crowds were waltzing in slow motion and waving sparklers. Havel was embracing Dubček, recalled from his desk job working for the Forestry Service – somehow he had not been hanged or shot. A bust of Stalin was paraded with *Nic Netrva Vecne* written on a paper strung around his neck; the cameras loved that, Nothing Lasts Forever. Margita turned to look at Christine on the sofa, tears running down her face, making runnels in the pink powder. She said she'd thought it would last another hundred years, or four hundred. She was still handsome at sixty, with her fierce stare and thick shock of hair, home-dyed, streaked blonde; her hand was pressed to her heavy bosom in its close-fitting jazz-print dress as if she were holding in something fighting to get out, and she pulled her cardigan tight across her chest, squeezing its buttons in her fist, in tense concentration on the TV screen. She and Alex spoke together in their own language, which Christine hadn't often heard him use. The family had always tried to speak in English, it had been the first rule Margita and Tomas adopted on arriving in the new country, to save their son. *Stesk* was homesickness, Margita explained to Christine, it was for sentimentalists, she'd refused to feel it on principle. But on a day like this …

Alex's spoken Czech was rusty and he felt ill at ease, trying to express himself in it. He had experienced the same pain of exile as his parents but now was unable to share wholly in the joy of liberation: he was exultant but felt shut out at the same time, cheated. There was no part for him to play in their revolution – you had to be there, you had to belong. 'My eyes are dry,' he quoted from some poet. 'I need them for looking with.' And at first Margita was adamant, she didn't want to go back to Czechoslovakia even for a visit, there was nothing for her there, her life was in London now. Her sister and her cousins were narrow-minded country Catholics; they'd hated Tomas first because he was a Communist, then because he was a dissident. And the regime hadn't made things easy, she said, for the relatives of émigrés. Also, they would think she was sniffing after a share of the value of the farm in Galanta, which they were trying to get back into ownership under the restitution. Margita didn't want anything, she hadn't brought anything out with her and wanted nothing back. In 1968 she and Tomas had left their rented flat without packing suitcases or telling anyone, and had posted the keys to a dear friend, long dead, who had rescued a few of their books and possessions. Though it turned out now that he'd also been informing on them to the authorities. Ah well, that's what life was like, back in the old days.

When the fuss had died down, after two or three years, Margita changed her mind. She could afford to pay for a trip home out of her inheritance from her uncle Vas, who had owned a delicatessen and took care of Tomas and Margita when they first came to London – Margita had worked behind the shop counter, while Vas paid for Alex's schooling. She began to think that going back to the old country would put a stop to her bad dreams. But she would only go if Alex would accompany her. One cousin nicer than the rest had an apartment in Bratislava – by this time capital of its own republic. She could stay with her cousin and pay for Alex to stay in a hotel. They stopped off in Prague first, sharing a room in a guest house: Alex had no memory of the city, though he'd lived there for a couple of years as a small child. The baroque houses were restored and painted in candy colours, there were restaurants and gift shops on every corner; he had felt no connection to it. Margita bubbled over with delight at using her own language, chattering uncharacteristically to women in the shops and cafes; she waxed lyrical, remembering the little backstreet theatres and cabarets of the sixties, occasions when she'd skied in hilly lanes in the suburbs. You could smell the pine forests in the heart of the city, she insisted. There was something feverish and inauthentic, her son thought, in this rush of romantic enthusiasm. The cafe customers looked as if they'd heard it all before.

In Bratislava he had begun to remember things, standing with his mother outside their old apartment on the second floor of an austere nineteenth-century tenement – inevitably now repainted candy pink – and then outside the school he'd attended, and in a little park where once he had played on the swings. For a few uncanny minutes it was as if two epochs of their lives were superimposed and coexistent, the present transparent and the past showing through behind it. Then the superior solidity of the here and now was bound to prevail over fragile memory; a different generation of children, born into a different politics, came pouring out through the school gate, jostling and calling. Margita's shy cousin was a radiographer and read poetry, her tiny apartment hadn't been updated yet to the new more affluent reality, was still lit by forty-watt bulbs, decorated with sample squares of carpet nailed to the walls, faux-bronze reliefs of Bohemian castles. The family were invited up from the country one Sunday to meet the visitors, and arrived full of curiosity and welcome, bringing dishes of prepared food and their own wine from the farm, in yellow plastic bottles. They toasted the home-comers gravely, courteously. But after the first warm rush of reminiscence they didn't have much to say to one another. Alex could just about follow their conversation in Slovak, but he knew his speech sounded alien and formal to them. He and Margita wanted to know more about tumultuous events and political change, but it was clear that the questions they asked seemed banal and outdated to their relatives. Any passion about the country seemed exhausted too, even the idea of the new Slovakia.

All that was over with. And how could they be interested in what Margita and Tomas's lives in London had been? — I realise that while we were away, we no longer existed for them, Margita said. She grew more subdued and in fact, Alex realised to his surprise, she began to seem rather distinctively, awkwardly English – smaller than her whole self, private and diffident – in contrast to the formal country manners of her relatives, and their broad humour. She mentioned his father's work insistently, as she never did at home; the others responded with vague embarrassment. Certainly they hadn't read Tomas's books – they probably didn't read any books, let alone the clever, difficult kind of novel that his father wrote. Margita and Alex visited Tomas's older brother, who edited history texts for schools and had been busy recently, revising them. He was smaller and neater than Tomas had ever been, his silvery hair floated with static. His skull was polished as ivory, he was worn very fine: like his ironies, so mild they hardly registered in his tone or facial expression. In place of a 'diligent and modest Lenin', he told them, children now learned about the 'ruthless and cunning Stalin'. Once revolutionary movements had been 'thriving', now it was independence movements.

Alex had a suspicion that, as far as he could understand their conversations, his mother told everyone about his own job as if he were lecturing at a university, not teaching English part-time in a language school. She must be ashamed that her son didn't have more to show for all the opportunities he'd enjoyed. When they were alone together he asked her if she were disappointed in him, but she brushed him off with her quick irritation. What was he talking about? He'd got the wrong idea completely. What did she care about whether he was some kind of big success, admired by everyone? That was his own business. Hadn't she had enough disappointment with his father?

Every morning, coming out from his small hotel in a side street, heading for the apartment where his mother waited for him to join her for breakfast, Alex had crossed a bridge over a river which pooled in muddy, stony shallows, then made his way along a street planted with lime trees. A new road was under construction, whose concrete viaduct would carry it over the top of the street he walked in, which seemed to belong already to an old world in retreat. Passing a neighbourhood bar which was no more than a small cubbyhole off the street, he fell into a pattern of stepping inside for a coffee and a shot of plum brandy, and to smoke a cigarette. For those moments each morning he felt some slender thread of connection with the place.

Was it possible, he wondered in his intervals of solitude, that without knowing he was doing it, he'd held off from choosing his life until he could come back here? He had been waiting to rejoin these places and people he'd left behind as a child; naturally, now he'd rejoined them it turned out they meant nothing to him. So now that the waiting was over, could he do something at last? He felt his own strength, not at all abated, locked up in potential, only he didn't know what it was for. Not for putting things into words; he felt a violent revulsion from that. Late one evening, making his way to the hotel, he saw that his bar was still open; as he stepped inside the bartender recognised him, put his hand ready on the brandy bottle. A young woman, blonde, wearing a leather skirt and a white ribbed jumper tight over her breasts, was standing alone at the bar drinking coffee, her light mac folded over her arm because the night was warm. The bartender didn't seem to know her. Perhaps she was a prostitute; Alex wasn't confident that he could read the signs, in a strange country. Anyhow, he liked her pale skin and defined, small features, faintly cruel and impersonal – he thought of a Venus in a Cranach painting. She asked him for a cigarette and when he lit it for her she tilted her head and dropped her glance in a certain way – at once flirtatious and withheld – which made him nostalgic, as if it were a gesture from an old film. The bartender was cashing up, the bar was closing.

He had walked companionably with the woman as far as the bridge, where they heard the river hurrying below them. In the darkness Alex pulled her into his arms and began to kiss her, tentatively at first and then more urgently. She yielded passively to his kisses, he tasted alcohol in her mouth. The two of them had hardly exchanged ten words. Stroking her neck and her hair, and then her breasts, he was murmuring, trying to persuade her to come back with him, to his hotel. Since his marriage to Christine he hadn't been seriously tempted, until this moment, to make love to any other woman. The girl managed to wriggle out of his grasp, laughing. — I don't know you.

— Or we could find somewhere to get another drink?

Smiling, she wasn't offended. But she wouldn't stay. — No, no. *Někdy jindy.* Another time perhaps.

Lydia said she was lost in wonderment, watching her offhanded parents transform into doting grandparents. Apparently they had been heartbroken when their only grandchild was born so far away in America. — How was I supposed to know? Lydia exclaimed. — As far as I was concerned, they were bored to death by babies. Mum made it clear to me how she'd resented all the mess I made. I even thought they'd be relieved, only having to be grandparents long distance. Turns out they had reservoirs of familial devotion which they'd decided in their wisdom not to waste on me. They were saving it all for Gracie.

Now they had Grace back in Britain, Pam and Tibs couldn't get enough of her. She stayed for days at a time in their new pub out at Epping, ruling over it like a little princess; Pam bought her smocked Victorian-style dresses and white lace tights, black patent leather shoes with straps across the instep, a furry-dog hot water bottle cover. They adored how thoroughly she was unlike her guarded mother or grandmother: Grace was incapable of calculating to please anyone, or of holding anything back. She looked like a little African, Pam said proudly; no diamanté barrettes or Alice bands could tame the fierce black fuzz of her mop of hair. Out of hours, she was allowed to have the same thing played over and over on the jukebox; on her birthday her grandparents invited her friends from nursery to a party in their upstairs function room, whose violently patterned wallpaper and prints of hunting scenes usually presided over meetings of the local Rotary Club.

This new pub was Tibs's grandest venture yet: 1930s half-timbered, painted black and white, with eight guest rooms which were often full, standing back from a wide road that had been a trunk road until it was superseded by the M25. Pam's only grumble was getting up early to do the breakfasts – they had someone in to do lunches and dinners; though even when things were going well she always had her aura of trouble stoically endured. She was more firmly upholstered and gilded than ever, in response to their move upmarket; Tibs was still racy in his slim-cut suits and narrow ties, with his shifting glance and chronic restlessness. Even serving behind the bar, he always seemed on his way out somewhere else, though they didn't know where he went. Fifty yards down the road, a shabby sixties shopping precinct – video rentals, hairdressers, Chinese takeaway, newsagents – had fallen on hard times; opposite the pub, on the other side of the road, the forest mysteriously began, its grey beech trunks receding in stately order across the washed-out tan of fallen leaves. At night the Earl of Essex glowed with coloured lights, strung along under the eaves. — It's a roadhouse! Zachary exclaimed. — A jewel from a more spacious age of motoring.

Tibs was itching to modernise the place, Zachary begged him not to do it. Alex and Christine brought Isobel to the birthday party, then sat drinking out of hours with Lydia in the empty bar downstairs, while Zachary threw himself with the grandparents into party games, only coming down to report delightedly that all the layers in Pass the Parcel were wrapped in pages from the *Sun*, including the breasts, and that Tibs was a sinister Pied Piper with his doting gang of four-year-olds. In the bar a red carpet, patterned with scrolled gold leaves, exhaling stale smoke and beer, rolled everywhere like a tide; mirror glass behind the bars replicated over and over, like infinite riches, the glitter of bottles and labels and coloured liquors, the cut lemons and maraschino cherries, the packets of peanuts on their card. The space was cavernous, segregated into cosy nooks and corners behind sections of banister, shallow flights of unexpected stairs. No fire was ever lit in the stone fireplace under its gleaming pink copper hood, but the air was hot and dry from central heating, sealed imperviously against whatever weather was outside. Children in their herd-ecstasy thundered in the room above, and a leftover Christmas decoration in gold paper, drawing-pinned to a beam, swayed in response.

— It's hard to believe in progress, in here, Lydia said. — If I try to imagine eternity, I think it might feel like an English pub on a Saturday afternoon. Time's actually standing still, isn't it? It's like a ghastly syrup and we're all preserved in it.

No, not standing still, ticking away inexorably towards the doom of opening. I swear those same novelty teapots have stood on that same windowsill since the world began.

She was prodding in her drink with a plastic cocktail stirrer, trying to spear the cherry; looking surprisingly at home behind the bar, she had concocted Manhattans for the three of them. There was some irony in the fact that Pam and Tibs's daughter – whom they'd shucked off, she claimed, so coolly – seemed made for pub life. Weren't her sumptuous looks perfect for a barmaid – and her preferences for late hours and for company, and her dry remarks? She had her mother's gift, Zachary said, of reeling the men in and throwing them back at the same time.

— Zacky, you're such a flatterer, said Pam complacently. She extended the same fond indulgence to Zachary as to Grace: these two were the exceptions to all her iron rules.

— To me it's exotic, Alex said. — I never visited anywhere like this in my childhood. My parents wouldn't have known such a place existed.

— Nor mine, said Christine enthusiastically. — That's why I love it.

— I'm too unsophisticated to love it, Lydia said. — I hate it. It makes me want to die. Except that I might wake up in an afterlife which looked just exactly the same. How would we even know that we were dead?

— Alex doesn't believe in progress anyway, said Christine.

— Oh Alex, don't you? Believe me, it was progress when I got to stop living in a place that smelled of other people's beer and cigarettes.

He was only faintly amused, opening up Tibs's newspaper

from yesterday which he'd found folded under the bar counter. Alex preferred to get his news from the enemy. He believed you risked banality if you only read to confirm your
prejudices – though there wasn't much news of any sort in
Tibs's paper.

— Don't you think Alex's pessimism is so mid-century?
Christine said. — So Central European. He can't adapt. But
I say, let's shake off all the horrible old burdens! Why must
we always be expecting the worst?

— Because the worst mostly happens? he suggested, not
looking up.

— Not always, though. It doesn't always. Things sometimes
change for the better, you know: anaesthetics for instance. Or
antibiotics, or flush toilets. The end of the Cold War! You've
got to have something to believe in, Alex!

— Why?

She displayed him triumphantly to Lydia. — You see?

— Something's always lost though. Even in the end of the
Cold War.

— Nothing good was lost! Really, was it?

He thought about it. — Something crabbed and cobwebby
and disenchanted. I hated that crabbed thing in my father.
Yet it was also very ambitious, very purely intellectual. We
may come to think that those dissident Central European
cultures were the last to keep a classical ideal alive, an ideal
of disenchantment.

Christine was watching him closely, and she spoke with
sudden sympathy. — Oh, yes, I can see that, I can see what
you mean.

— But most people wanted Adidas trainers more than they wanted classical ideals, Lydia said.

The women were filled with an infectious lightness, which partly came from the excitement of the gallery project. Zachary had told Christine he wanted her pictures in his first show, she was exuberant; Lydia was dizzy with choosing designs and furniture for their new home. She and Zachary were renting an apartment by the river while the chapel premises were transformed. Both women felt some balance of power in their lives had been restored in relation to their men, after the initial blow of becoming mothers to young babies, which had knocked them back; now their children filled them out rather than depleting them. Christine was aware too of a new strength in her relation to Alex, a private agnosticism like a resource of insight which she'd been collecting together slowly and invisibly. Perhaps this questioning of impervious male knowledge had always come to women at a certain age, in their prime, as they grew out of the illusions of girlhood. Or was it a new thing coming about in history, because of cultural change?

— By the way I've a plan for next year, Alex announced casually.

— What kind of a plan?

— Oh, just *something to believe in,* as you put it.

He'd thought he might do a year's course, train as a schoolteacher. They were incredulous: that wouldn't suit him, he'd never stick at it. — You haven't got the patience for school teaching, Alex. You don't know what it's like, having to spend all day cooped up with children. And even if you got onto the PGCE, you'd hate being a student again, people telling you how to keep discipline in the classroom and all that stupid stuff. You'll never actually get round to applying.

— I've had the interview already, as it happens. They offered me a place, I've accepted it. There's funding, and I could keep up some evening work at the language school.

Christine looked at Lydia. — This is just like when he passed his driving test. He didn't even tell me he was having lessons, until he'd passed! Why's he so *secretive?*

Parents arriving to pick up their children came rattling at the pub's locked doors eventually; Pam and Tibs, descending into the lounge, kept on their party hats, sporting them with stiff dignity. Pam's paper crown even helped her maintain a regal kind of order — the naughtier children glanced nervously in her direction, hurrying to play the video games Tibs had promised, which were ranged like robot-sentinels against the walls downstairs, flashing their coloured lights. The children in their ignorance were satisfied without putting any money in, pushing levers and pressing buttons. Grace's white satin party dress was stained with orange squash, her cheeks were shiny with sugar and flushed with power, she was intoxicated from so much attention; hurtling towards Lydia she clasped her about the knees, rubbing a sticky face against her skirts, shrieking *My Mummy!* Lydia sat down abruptly on the padded banquette, awkward for once, seduced and flattered by Grace's peremptory claim. Amazing that such a child, so wild and full of force, could possibly belong to her – or she to it! Pam came holding Isobel by the hand, saying she had been such a help with the little ones; *so sensible and mature.* And stolid, conscious Isobel blushed with pleasure, although Christine knew Pam meant she wasn't spirited like Grace.

— Lydia's parents don't like me, Christine said to Alex later, when they were at home and Isobel was asleep, mumbling anxiously in her dreams. — They never did. Or at least, Pam doesn't. Tibs doesn't even notice me.

— It's class, said Alex. — You're not their type. They think that you think you're superior. Perhaps they think you took Lydia away from them.

She considered this idea for an instant, conscience-stricken. — But they couldn't seriously think I took her anywhere! It's always Lydia who takes me. And if it's class, then how come they like you? Pam likes you, anyhow. But you're an intellectual, you're more superior than I ever was. I try so hard with them!

— They feel you trying. And I doubt whether Pam has any thoughts about me either way. I don't think we've ever exchanged more than a few platitudes.

— It isn't words, Alex. She watches you, I see it; women watch you. Pam thinks you're wasted on me, she's always thought that. She admires you from a safe distance – relieved at the same time that Lydia's got Zachary, who makes everything easy.

There was a private view and party for the opening of the Garret's Lane gallery, and all the right people found their way to the little cul-de-sac; the write-ups for the opening exhibition were good, the critics were encouraging, there were nice photographs of the conversion as well in an architectural magazine. It was a good beginning. Zachary by this time had taken on inspired, shrewd, calculating Hannah as his manager, and there had been an awful morning six months before the opening when Hannah came to talk to Christine in confidence. — I love your pictures, she had said. — I love them. But they're not the right thing for Zach's opening. They're not big enough. He needs to aim at something big, right from the beginning. You're not a big enough name, not yet. And he shouldn't begin anyway with a mixed exhibition: it's too timid, not enough of a statement. I've talked to Hari Rostami, he could be interested in putting together a new show for us. He's what the gallery needs, as a launch pad – you know, the name, the noise! Later, when Garret's Lane is big, Zachary can do what he likes. He can put you on properly, and you'll be big then *because* he's put you on.

In her hurt Christine cast around vindictively: she thought that Hannah was head-girlish, leaning forward so eagerly to placate her, the glossy wings of her red hair swinging. Her dark fitted suit, no doubt intended as *film noir*-ish, was more like a school uniform, and her figure was top-heavy with incongruous bosom. Christine felt pinned to the spot, faking smiling carelessness, as if she were being lectured for not pulling her weight on the hockey team. — You'll never forgive me for saying this, Hannah apologised. — I hate myself for saying it. But it's my business to have Zach's interests and the interests of the gallery at heart. Of course I've said it all to Zachary already, he knows what I think, but he's adamant, he's faithful to you because you're his friend – and because he believes in your work. He thinks I'm wrong, and even if he didn't think I was wrong I don't think that he'd change his mind because he promised, and he couldn't bear to let you down. You know him, you know what he's like. And of course if you decide to take no notice of me, which I'd completely and utterly understand, then you'll just hate me for it, and I'll understand that too, and I'll also back your work to the hilt. I'll do everything in my power to prove myself wrong.

It was a wound, and Christine, sick with the humiliation, crawled to bed all alone in the middle of the day while Alex was out at college and Isobel was at school, curled up around her own disgust at the pain of it, the shame. — We could always hang some of your things in the cafe, Hannah had said, and that had been the worst moment. But then Christine went to Zachary and confessed that she didn't think she'd have enough work ready for the show, and was quite sure that she didn't want to be in the cafe either. He was so disappointed, but he asked her what she thought of Hari Rostami instead of a mixed exhibition, and she said that sounded just perfect, although in her heart she believed that Rostami's installations were just empty, clever things: empty and ugly. By the time of the opening night she was all right. She never told anyone what had gone on between her and Hannah, the two of them never spoke about it, and she did hate Hannah for a while afterwards, until eventually she forgot to. And later, as the years passed, Christine was part of several mixed exhibitions in the gallery space, and had two solo shows there.

Naturally she knew people, at least some, at the opening night party. Once it was actually happening she felt light-hearted, relieved that it wasn't her work exposed on the walls – costing her peace of mind, crushing her with its importance. She could go on clasping its secrets to herself, her treasure which did not have to be weighed yet or found wanting. Hannah had been right, this wouldn't have been a suitable occasion for showing off anyone's subtle art. So she didn't have to be an artist at the party, and Zachary had given her the money to buy something nice to wear. The folded notes when she took them had been warm from his trouser pocket, and the gift had made her feel as if everything that had ever been between them – including even Hannah's secret visit, which perhaps he really didn't know about, or only half-knew – was understood without needing explanation. Christine had bought a full-length vintage blue silk-crêpe dress whose bodice was sewn with silver beads, and had pinned up her hair and made up her face carefully; she was aware of snagging a few appraising glances. The heavy silk swung satisfyingly as she circulated; she was thin, she'd lost weight since she had Isobel. And the dress was very naked around her throat and arms, plunging bare to her waist at the back. She had her grandmother's silver chain around her neck and nothing on underneath except her knickers.

She didn't stand out, the place was full of women dressed

up gorgeously. Lydia, in a white lace dress by Helmut Lang, seemed almost to have attained the aplomb of a consort, becoming a still point around which all the circles moved – while Zachary went everywhere in the crowd, greeting and blessing. Even when they were students, at parties in basement flats with warm white wine in plastic cups, Lydia had had a way of settling herself on a mattress on the floor as if it were a throne where she received petitioners, dispensing favours or cutting them off. Christine was as disdainful in her judgements as Lydia and yet didn't know how to convey that she too was clever, superior, easily bored. She knew she seemed too eagerly apologetic, too quick to blame herself for any faltering of interest; she probably ought to be less amenable, if she wanted to be taken seriously. Weren't great artists always difficult? At least the lovely spaces of the new gallery were so crowded that quite literally you couldn't be left standing alone. Pushing past so many interesting strangers, she scrambled out onto little islets of acquaintance and then regretted it, felt stranded and looked round surreptitiously for rescue.

From time to time the press of bodies parting afforded her a moment's glimpse of Alex. She expected him to be prowling, disaffected and moody. He hated parties, and she'd made him wear a suit which she'd found for him in an Oxfam shop – dark wool, fitting him perfectly. But he wasn't moody, he was talking to people, making himself charming, looking as if he was amused and in his element. The teaching course was good for him, she thought. He was taken outside himself, learning to perform for others. Christine saw how he was touching with particularity the women he was talking to, fingertips on the inside of an elbow or palm on a bare shoulder – perhaps she ought to be afraid of this, but was just curious. He was striking in his new suit, which had played its trick of conferring authority. She thought she'd have been attracted to this clubbable, suave, urgent Alex, if he'd been a stranger. And would he have liked her, in her blue dress?

Then she was distracted because Hari spoke to her and surprised her by being friendly, making a point of saying nice things about her work, so that she was buoyantly afloat at the heart of the occasion for ten minutes. When Hari turned away she didn't mind sinking under its surface again, slipping between the turned animated backs, sipping at her drink for something to do, getting drunker, pretending to give Hari's installations her sustained attention. The crowds were beginning to thin out because the party had started early; its high-pitched excitement wound down amiably. Long before it was even midnight Hannah was chasing the last stubborn pleasure-seekers out of the gallery. — But we can't go to bed! protested Zachary. — I'm not ready for bed, not for hours and hours! I'm just getting into my party mood.

A few old friends retreated into Lydia and Zach's new place next door. They'd moved in a few weeks ago. Isobel was asleep upstairs with Grace; they had paid a babysitter for the duration of the party, a nice teenager – Alex walked her home, she only lived around the corner. They weren't any of them habituated yet to the new rooms – glass and steel fitted cleverly inside the lovely old forms, blond parquet floors restored, a new spiral stair, features made of the great chapel desk and the stone sink in the kitchen, huge as a cattle trough, with its brass tap. It was like staying in some-body else's house which you coveted madly, Christine said: you found yourself playing at being the somebody else. They were all showing off, in the unfamiliar spaces – and they were suddenly shivering too, exhausted from socialising. Christine, going up to check on the children, swayed from the door jamb dizzily: the little girls were flung in sweetly unconscious disorder in their sleep, Grace on her tummy with her arms up in surrender, Isobel curled around herself protectively. When Alex got back from dropping off the sitter he lit a fire in the new wood-burner, crouching on his heels in front of its window in his smart suit, jacket undone and tie loose, hands hanging between his knees, watching the flames take hold. — You're like primitive man, Alex, the fire-maker, Jane Ogden admired. He flashed his palms at her, filthy with ash and charcoal, mock-threatening, then went to wash. The women eased out of their shoes, groan-ing. Zachary came in dangling a choice of bottles at them – which? More champagne or Armagnac or both?

He threw his bag of weed at Nathan Kearney, for rolling up. Coffee, coffee, they all insisted. But Zachary poured them out spirits with their coffee, something very sweet made of rose petals and flavoured with bergamot, the kind of thing that Alex would never usually have touched, but he drank it too because they were all under the spell of the occasion. All of them were drunk already, anyway: on the glamour of their success, Zachary's success, as well as on the champagne. — Hari said such good things about you! Zachary put his arm around Christine, stretching his feet in their crimson socks out towards the stove; she arranged her own bare feet – nice enough, with their high arches and aristocratic long second toe – alongside his. Her toenails were elegantly painted for once, in a crimson that happened to match his socks. They were all sprawled across cushions on the thick Turkish rugs in front of the stove, holding out their hands to its warmth which melted and unknotted them invidiously and deliciously. Lydia, sitting upright with her back to the sofa, was the only one still alert, turning her head in her deliberate way towards whoever was speaking. The gossip went on desultorily. But one by one, once the coffee was finished, people were bound to make their farewells – even Jane Ogden, even Nathan – until only the four of them were left.

Zachary poured more of the rose-petal spirit, then sat down with his arm around Christine again; Alex put another log in the stove. They all slid down to stretch out full length on the cushions, and had given up on talking in complete sentences – they may have been exaggerating their drunkenness, clearing a way through to what happened next. Lying in the space between the two women, Alex began kissing Christine on the neck, under her hair. After a while he turned to Lydia and kissed her too, as if it were only fair; he was stroking Christine at the same time, his hand was moving on her lazily. Both the women made sleepily responsive noises, to convey they were only half conscious of what was happening. Then Christine turned over on her side towards Zachary. Smiling, she kissed him full on the mouth, tasting the liquor and the dope and all the piquant familiarity and strangeness of him – when they'd made love together such a long time ago, he hadn't had a beard. Alex's hand was gliding over the top of her dress and then sliding underneath it, exploring; sometimes his hands were on her and sometimes they were on Lydia, sometimes he was touching them both at once. Christine turned around to give her attention to Alex again and Zachary came cuddling up behind so that she felt his beard against her bare back, his purposeful kisses moving down her spine, on the bare skin between her shoulder blades. Lydia with her arm flung out found Christine's hand. Zachary was pushing the straps of Christine's dress from her shoulders and Alex was exploring with one hand under the lacy white fabric of Lydia's bodice. He seemed intent on Lydia but with his other hand he was searching intently too, fumbling down between Christine's knees, pushing apart the thick folds of the material of her dress, finding his way up.

Later that night, when they were alone in the new spare room, Christine interrogated Alex incredulously. — Would you? Would you really have done it?

They were half-undressed in the lamplight, still excited; she was kneeling over him where he lay on his back on the bed with his suit jacket and shoes off, shirt unbuttoned halfway. The blue dress was pushed up around her thighs. — Would you have gone through with it? Are you disappointed?

His hazel eyes were gleaming, pupils dilated. — Would you?

Christine was amazed by what they'd done. — What came over us? We must have been mad! But really, how could we have arranged things, if they'd gone on any further? I mean, what …?

— And are *you* disappointed?

She was laughing but put her hand over his mouth to stop him, said she couldn't think about it, they mustn't think. Or at least they mustn't speak their thoughts aloud. Her hair was falling down from where it had been pinned, her make-up was smudged under her eyes, her face was blurry and dissolute with tiredness and drink, she was thoroughly desirable in that moment of their married love.

The opportunity for their debauchery in a foursome never came around again. It must have depended on being so innocently unplanned. They hadn't got much further along than the preliminaries, in any case, and were all still quite decently in their clothes, when Zachary had caught sight of little Isobel in her nightie standing like a sentinel angel at the bottom of the spiral staircase, looking at them with frightened and fierce eyes. Alex reassured Christine afterwards that there hadn't been anything for Isobel to see: at any rate she wouldn't remember seeing it in the morning. Righteously Isobel had announced that Grace was crying.
— She's been crying for hours and hours. How come you didn't hear her calling? She wants her mummy. Lydia, she wants you.

FIVE

AFTER CHRISTINE HAD TELEPHONED AND Lydia had spoken to her, Alex got up out of the bed, Zachary's bed, and began putting on his clothes without looking at Lydia. She sat naked against the pillows with the white sheet across her breasts, watching him, drinking in his reality fearfully. Her eyes were unguarded for once, naked as her body – she had taken off her make-up before her shower. Lydia knew that in speaking to Christine she might have lost him. She waited for him to say something, to break the silence. What now? She couldn't even make conversation or ask about her own daughter, how Grace's spirits were when Alex left her in Glasgow. That domestic way was closed to Lydia for the moment, the prohibition heavy as a hand across her mouth. She and Alex had entered a forbidden terrain where their paths were blocked in all directions. And now, by speaking to Christine, Lydia had cut them off from saving themselves, from stepping back again into what they were before. She'd made it impossible – though not premeditatedly, she hadn't had any plan when she picked up the phone – for Alex to step back.

Lydia knew he was scalded by what she had said to Christine. Not because he was a coward or had calculated on deceiving anyone, but because there was something ingenuous in how she'd delivered her news – so baldly, like a teenager who intervenes out of her depth, precipitating adult consequences beyond what she can understand. Recalled to himself, Alex had been appalled by finding he was embroiled with Lydia, the Lydia he knew, with her exasperating passivity and fatalism like a child's. His arm sticky with sweat had been around her neck the whole time she was talking to Christine, strands of her honey-coloured hair alien against his chest. He had been helpless not to overhear Chris's utterly unsuspecting innocence: she was so slow to understand at first, and then so wounded and bewildered. Casting around to make sense, she hadn't even accused them or been outraged – not yet. How could Alex and Lydia not dread each other after that? When Christine cut off the call he'd pulled away from Lydia in cold horror.

Yet Lydia persisted in clinging to those truths of the body she'd found out when she was a teenager. Their act couldn't be undone because it wasn't nothing: their awareness of it was present in the room all around them like a shadow-play, overmastering their reasoning. There was no redemption in the world, only in this: teenagers knew. Alex had lost himself, and if Lydia let him go now he would hate her. He pissed in the bathroom then ran the tap full force and washed his face, dried it in her towel; without looking at her or speaking, he left the room and she heard him go downstairs. She waited without moving, listening out for the sound of the front door closing with finality behind him, shutting her out. But it didn't come. Eventually she got out of bed and put on her gown, glancing at her reflection in the wall-mirror, running her fingers through her hair – dishevelled because she hadn't finished drying it when Alex turned up. She didn't look too bad.

She found him on the sofa downstairs in front of the cold stove, sitting with his head bowed, fingers tensed against his temples, frowning at the floor in a despair that might have appeared theatrical at a different moment. Bringing the whisky bottle and one glass, she crouched between his knees on the rug, poured for both of them and drank first and deeply, then handed the glass to him. Her elbows on his knees, her face turned up to his, she claimed him for herself – whatever was between them wasn't over. Alex touched her hair with re-signed kindness. In the pressure of his hand, cupping the back of her skull as his eyes with their irony sought out something in her face – did he find it? her own irony? – Lydia felt all the reproaches he held back and explanations he gave up. He yielded to her and she was almost frightened, because the relation of her passion had always been to Alex's resis-tance, his difficulty. He said that he had to go to Christine, talk to her.

— She won't want to see you, not yet. She won't let you in.
— I have to try.

She took his hand and put it inside her gown, on her warm breast. — But you'll come back to me? Don't just drop me, Alex, will you – not after this? I don't know what I'd do.

He drove through the fitful imperfect darkness of the night streets, furtive with their intermittent traffic, red-eyed with lights; then alongside the shrouded Heath. What had happened? This new reality seemed like a trick of the darkness: momentous but so accidental. He had almost not gone to Garret's Lane. And he had no idea what came next: much gnashing of teeth and wailing, no doubt. They had broken, he and Lydia, something that had been a monument containing everyone's sorrow – how could they not be punished? He was in his fifties and for all he knew, the shape of all their lives was shaken loose now; his awareness burned with the hurt he had done to his wife. Yet an intimation surfaced, like a post standing up out of a tide for him to steer by: that he was strong enough for whatever it was, this twist of his fate. He had always known what lay behind this opening, more or less decently closed in his married life so far: the ocean depths of sex. This possibility had existed in him always, he was like his father.

When he'd found a parking space in their street he tried to open the front door to the flat with his key, but Christine had pushed the bolt across. He rang the bell and seemed to sense her listening very close to him, on the other side of the door – he was sure he heard her breathing. He called her name in a low voice but didn't knock, in case he woke their neighbours downstairs in the divided house – Chris would hate that. From the car he tried phoning but her mobile was turned off; she let the landline ring and didn't answer it. A light was on in their first-floor sitting room, the blinds were drawn down: he thought he saw her shadow passing behind them and then the light went out, definitive as an eye closing, repudiating sight and being seen. When he drove away he didn't go back to Garret's Lane at once but chose a different route through the centre, parked somewhere by the Thames where he wasn't supposed to, and got out of the car. He stood for twenty minutes watching the broad river slipping past on its own urgent business from bridge to bridge, its brown water oily as mud in the oblique half-light. But he wasn't imagining throwing himself in. Something cruel and cold had come to the surface in his life, appalling and exhilarating. He could smell the river's mineral breath, hear a rhythmic slow knocking from one of the static pontoons moored in the current.

Replacing the phone in its socket after she'd spoken to Lydia, Christine sat poised on the edge of the sofa with her knees pressed together, waiting to see how she would feel. Her knees were trembling so that perhaps she couldn't have stood even if she'd wanted to. Of course, she was devastated. But she floated above that in her mind, observing it wryly. This humiliated her: it was as if she'd been stripped bare in public. And now everyone would have to condemn them and be horrified by what they'd done – Alex and Lydia, Lydia and Alex! Their pairing seemed suddenly so inevitable, it had been bound to happen. And Christine was bored in advance with all the sympathy she would enlist, and the outrage – she was furious with distaste at their incurring it, those two, and at the stupid necessity for emotion and action and reaction they had unloosed. What an unattractively dreary role she, Christine, would have to play – the wronged wife!

— I knew, I knew, she said, needing to reassure herself.

Hadn't she known and not known – what had she ever

thought Lydia would do, now that she didn't have Zachary? And why had Christine called her and no one else, when Alex was missing? At least, anyway, Alex wasn't smashed up in an accident, she was let off that hook. No horrifying maiming, no hospital visiting: she could get on with things. But what things? Now, how would she live, if Alex left – or if she threw him out? Recognition after recognition tumbled down, giving way under her, leaving their gaping vacancies; when she thought of the word *husband* she was most stricken, although in all the time she and Alex had been married she'd never used it quite sincerely. Now perhaps she would be no one's wife. Christine stood up confidently enough then and went all around the flat, up to the top bedroom and into the kitchen, seeing it differently, in a surge of possessive passion. Whatever else happens, she thought, this place is mine. They don't get this. And she was almost pleased, picking up objects in the rooms and putting them down again, straightening pictures, admiring the rich accumulation of interesting things as if she'd just come into some inheritance. It would be so convenient, to have all this to herself.

Everything she saw that was Lydia's she snatched up, stuffing it into a black bin bag: her scarf, magazines, bits of her wet washing on the clothes horse, letters from the bank and her solicitors, lighter, shoes. Lydia had taken a few of her things home, but left most of them. How untidy she was, how she spread herself everywhere! In the spare room Christine began dragging Lydia's clothes off the hangers, shoving them into the bag, dropping bottles from the dressing table and bathroom in on top. In her vindictive cold soul she repudiated the other two, felt herself retracting away from them. It was a kind of freedom. But could she manage solitude? Wasn't she a coward? All the years with Alex might have been only the staving off of solitude. For a moment she imagined explaining this to Lydia, who understood things.

Confronted with the door to her studio, she remembered that its key was in her handbag. No, not in her handbag, she'd moved the key recently to a blue coffee pot where they kept receipts, on a kitchen shelf. She could fetch it easily: wasn't her art her resource in this crisis, now she was left alone? Art was supposed to come out of what was ripped open. Also she would need money, she'd need to start earning again. But she was too afraid of what lay behind the door, she veered away and felt nausea at the idea of it, in case it was a failure, a rotten dead nullity – in case she never sold another thing. The time hadn't come for testing her work, not yet. Too much was at stake. She might sink altogether, if it turned out she was no good any longer.

When she heard the car draw up in the street outside she hurried to push the bolt across the front door to the flat, then watched from the sitting room, through the crack of sight down the side of the blind, as Alex approached the house. How strange that he was entirely familiar even though everything else was changed: in his quick abstracted walk, head down, hands clenched into fists – in the past, with a cigarette half concealed, poking between the knuckles. She used to think, he walks as if his path is marked out for him on the pavement, taking him somewhere, only no one else sees the marks: when she'd drawn him, she'd tried to draw this. From her viewpoint above, when the security light came on, she watched as he used his key in the outer door, saw the vulnerable spot where his faded tow-coloured hair was thinning. If only Lydia hadn't spoken, and she hadn't had to know! This stupid spasm of sex could have been buried decently, under the surface of the rest of their lives; they could have gone on growing old together, the three of them left. Then Christine thought of dropping something on Alex's head, to kill him. She returned to sit in her usual place on the sofa, arms hugged around her ribs, listening out for his step on the stair – so that she wasn't really on the other side of their front door when Alex was so sure he sensed her closeness. He gave up calling her name and went downstairs again and tried to phone her from the car; the peremptory loud ringing was like an invasion into her self-possession, excruciating. Yet until the last moment she expected herself to let him in, pick up the phone, have explanations out with him. She switched off the lights and stood waiting in the dark.

When he had driven away at last she felt sleepy, and thought she could lie down on the bed to rest: in all her clothes be-cause she'd never taken them off. But the moment she put her head on the pillow – with her knees up and her hands clasped calmly between them, closing her eyes – a great grey panic, crowded with very specific images and ideas, seized her and smothered her. She had to sit up again quickly to recover. Her heart leaped in her chest so painfully that she was sure she must be having a heart attack – which would solve every-thing, she thought melodramatically.

In a reckless moment Isobel had texted the man she'd drenched in beer on their first date. He'd done his generous best to rescue that afternoon from its sticky beginning, making a joke of it; clearly though, once he'd delivered her home, he hadn't wanted to take a chance on her again. She hadn't heard a word from him. If she'd had any sense, Isobel thought, then she'd have felt the same: been relieved that she worked for the Department of Communities and Local Government and Blaise for the Foreign Office, so that their paths would probably never cross. Isobel was in a project on youth homelessness; he said he spent a lot of time counting Afghani Taliban and marking their positions on a map. Yet she felt regret for some affinity between them which hadn't had time to show itself – probably existed only in her hoping for it. She felt as if they'd known each other as children, although they hadn't; she had liked something stolid and gauche in him, and how he had been as scrupulous not to open doors for her, or help her off with her coat or pay for her, as a man like him in another generation would have been scrupulous to do those things. Blaise was shorter than she was, pudgy around the waist, with woolly gingery hair and clever eyes like chips of blue glass, set rather far back in his head; he'd seemed awkward in his jeans and she guessed that he'd always look better in his suit, tie loosened and shirt only half tucked into his trousers. He was one of those thirty-year-old men rushing headlong into middle age, with their boyishness still alive in their faces.

He had replied to her text almost at once. She'd expected a painful interval of waiting while he composed the right gently regretful let-down; imagined him wincing over it in front of one of his maps stuck with Taliban-pins, in a dingy office with an eighteenth-century fireplace.

— Do you fancy throwing a coffee over me? he wrote.

At her desk, Isobel laughed in relief, and they arranged to meet the next day. She dressed up for the occasion in a cotton summer top and striped skirt, white patent leather belt, sandals; by the time she left the office it was bright enough for sunglasses, and she'd thought happily that she looked like a girl in a film hurrying to meet her lover. Then she'd sat alone in the cafe for forty minutes, digesting her disappointment, feeling overdressed as a doll. How could he? When he texted her later she wouldn't even look to see what he said straight away, she was so hurt and offended. She didn't want to read that something had come up, or that he'd forgotten, or been unavoidably detained in a meeting.

— Where were you? he wrote.

With hasty fingers she replied with the same question. Of course, there were two Prêt à Mangers in Trafalgar Square. And so their unlucky pattern was set. Both of them really, in the rest of their lives, they swore it, were very competent people. But when Blaise invited her round to his place, to cook for her, and they both intended – without either of them hinting it or even suggesting it by a significant look – for it to be the first occasion they slept together, she got some sickness bug. Blaise had to wipe the hair from her forehead as she hung vomiting over his toilet – and he'd prepared such a lovely meal, buying everything fresh from the farmers' market. He might have given up then, Isobel thought. And perhaps she had seemed almost insanely persistent; she hoped that he didn't begin to dread her. Aspects of his character which she might not have liked – his deliberateness, a certain unassailable privacy, some self-satisfaction – gained power over her because she was afraid she'd lose him. Blaise was self-sufficient like a much older single man: already he'd started collecting things and knowing about them, wine and antique books and clocks. He said he was conservative with a small c, voted Lib Dem and read the *Economist* and the *Financial Times*. — I suppose you're a *Guardian* reader? he enquired sympathetically. She tried to tell him about Alex. — My father's very brilliant. He's special.

— Oh, what does he do?

When she said he was a primary school teacher she saw Blaise stop believing in the brilliance. — But he's an inspired teacher, she explained. — And he could have been a poet or just about anything, except that he carries this burden about with him from his Czech legacy, because they had to leave when he was a boy and his father never recovered.

Isobel realised that Alex would never think Blaise was good enough for her. She would never be able to explain to him about that nugget of Blaise's wholeness and goodness she was attracted to, seeking it out inexorably as a Geiger counter under all the layers of his stuffiness. Blaise's education was Eton and Balliol; his mother was a barrister, his father farmed and hunted. Isobel wanted to ask him, if you had children, would you have to have all that for them too? And although they hadn't actually even kissed yet, except for hello and goodbye, she lay awake worrying about her principles, whether if they had children together her commitment to state education would give way in the face of Blaise's intransigence, if he were intransigent. When she'd recovered from her sickness bug she asked him round to her place, and as they poured their third glass of wine her mother rang. Isobel turned her phone over, but then while Blaise was in the bathroom listened to her messages, just in case. — Something happened last night, Christine said in a heavy voice, irritatingly portentous. — I'd like to talk about it. But it's all right, don't worry. Could you come round?

— Would you like me to go with you? Blaise asked when she told him.

— Oh no, hell, Isobel said unhappily. — Perhaps I'll just ignore it.

— You could do that.

She hesitated. — We've had this awful thing recently, that's the trouble. We're all so sad, Mum's sad. Someone very close to us died, the last person you'd ever think would die: so full of force. He just dropped dead one day in the middle of talking in his office. He was my dad's best friend, my best friend's father, Mum's best friend's husband.

— It sounds like one of those puzzles, Blaise said ineptly. — You know: 'who is my father's brother's mother's husband's grandson', that kind of thing.

Isobel didn't know whether she ought to break up their evening early, to go to her mother; she stood agonising in her flowered dress, hugging her bare arms tightly in a chill from the open window; their plates were still on the table, smeared with the remains of Thai noodles. She wasn't a good cook:

Blaise's meal, which she hadn't been able to eat, had been much more impressive. This story of their family misfortune, she thought, must seem like a final clinching stroke of the bad news she brought. — Actually you remind me of him a little bit, she ploughed on. — I mean, you're not really alike at all: he was Jewish and arty and extrovert. And much older, of course. But I suppose he was sane and solid, and you are.

Blaise found he didn't even mind being sane and solid. He saw Isobel's responsible anxiety for her mother, and also her frank disappointment, cheated of what she wanted: which, surprisingly, was him. Her eyes were strange as he looked into them in decent concern, with their short dense black lashes and concentrated gaze, a taut crease under the lower lids. When he remembered that her father was Czech her rather thick calves and ankles seemed romantic, and the downy hair on her arms. He understood for the first time then how she was desirable and exceptional, not at all ordinary. He never told anyone afterwards that to begin with he'd thought Isobel was ordinary. For everyday, she wore her disguise as a nice girl.

Lydia brought Alex coffee in bed like a handmaiden – she who was more accustomed to being the princess. She knelt in her silk nightdress on the bed beside him, watching him drink. — I've always loved you, Alex, she said, in that intensely serious voice it was impossible to distinguish from her mock-serious one. — You do know that? From the moment I first set eyes on you in the French class. I've never wavered.

— These are fairy stories, he said, not unkindly. — No one believes in them any more. You should have lived in the nineteenth century for all that: true love, the one and only. It helped when everyone died young. If this had happened twenty years ago you'd be disenchanted by now, I can assure you.

She shook her head. — I won't be disenchanted, ever. Don't misunderstand me though: you'll never know how nice I was to Zachary. You never believed I was good enough for him: but I was. And I swear he never had any inkling of what I felt about you. I knew how lucky I was to be married to him. I made him happy. He saved me when my heart was broken because I knew I couldn't have you.

Alex marvelled at her. — You're wilful. You invented a romantic story and you've stuck to it in your wilful heart. It's an act of will.

Lydia thought about that. — But how else does anyone live?

When Alex first returned inside his own home, he felt how everything was changed by what he'd done. He wanted to say to Christine that nothing need be different between them just because he'd slept with Lydia, but he didn't actually feel that this was true. Even the rooms as he moved around in them felt different. Christine had let him in eventually, after he'd come back to the house for the third or fourth time and tried to use his key in the door to the flat: she'd had the locks changed, she told him. Waiting outside on the landing Alex could hear her on the other side of the door, fumbling with the bolt and a new mortice lock like some elderly pensioner afraid of callers. — That's crazy, he said, trying to speak loud enough for her to hear him, and at the same time keep his voice steady and somehow open. He must be whatever Christine wanted, make himself instrumental to her needs in some way not yet defined – it was up to her to define it.

She looked so altered, when eventually she opened the door: he saw her almost as if he didn't know her – stooping and thin, with bent shoulders. Walking ahead of him into the sitting room, she was careful like someone who has been ill for a long time. — You didn't need to change the locks, he went on gently. — I could have given you my keys.

— I didn't want you coming in and out without my knowledge.

— Chris, what did you think I would try to do?

— Something's over. I'm getting used to the idea. I've packed your stuff into suitcases, you can take all the CDs, or most of them. The books are more complicated.

— So you want me to move out?

— Isn't that what you want? Aren't you going to move in with her?

— I don't know. What do you want me to do?

For a long time Christine wouldn't look at him directly. They went back and forth over the same ground. She'd waited up for him so anxiously that night, she'd been so worried. Had Lydia called him, while he was driving from Glasgow, invited him to come to Garret's Lane? No, of course not. He'd gone in there to check the place as usual, never expecting to find her. And Lydia couldn't have expected him. — I suppose she was frightened, Christine imagined, — when she heard you come in. You comforted her.

— Something like that, he said.

How could they come back from this to what they'd been before, the three of them? He said he didn't know. — And when you arrived, where was she exactly – downstairs or up in the bedroom? What did she say, when she saw you? What was she wearing? Was it because she was so attractive that you made love to her, or was it more like affection for an old friend?

— I can't tell you those things.

— But tell me, she urged him feverishly. — And I'll tell you things too. There are things I've never told you.

Alex couldn't expose to her his relation with Lydia: that was his only way to keep faith with it, to try and balance keeping faith with both of them. Christine said that in that case she didn't want her name in his mouth, even, when he spoke to Lydia. — You're not to talk to her about me. Don't tell her how I am, or one word that I've said or anything I've done.

And as if this was perfectly reasonable he agreed to it, and tried to keep his promise. Lydia's face was shocked, as if she'd been slapped, when he explained why he couldn't tell her how Christine was taking things. In the awful days that followed he had the odd sensation sometimes that his vital function was as a live wire connecting the two women in their extreme estrangement. He went over to be with Christine as often as was bearable, as often as she allowed – told himself she mustn't feel abandoned. Once Isobel was in the flat when he turned up, but she wouldn't speak to him or look at him, wouldn't stay while he was there. Her face was blotched and red from crying; she flung her arms around her mother, threw on her coat and went out, slamming the door. He had wronged all his daughter's hopes, her belief in him. Christine was gratified and dry-eyed, when Isobel had gone. — They're more puritanical than us, she said, — this generation of our children. She can't open her mind to it.

When Alex made himself coffee in the kitchen, he noticed that Christine was keeping things in different places already, the teaspoons in a pottery jug, cafétière beside the stove. At first she didn't want coffee, then she changed her mind; her hands were shaking when she took the cup from him. He wanted to tell himself this was a lot of fuss to make over nothing, yet he knew it wasn't nothing, this change was absolute. No, he said, he hadn't moved into Garret's Lane, though he was seeing Lydia. Lisa the Class Five teacher had a spare room in her flat in Gospel Oak, he was sleeping there for the moment. No, he wasn't sleeping with Lisa. Christine wept and said that she'd lost everyone. — First Zachary, and now both of you.

— I'm sorry. I'm so sorry.

— But do you wish it hadn't happened?

He searched in his heart and told her the truth. Strangely, that was one of the moments when they drew closest. They comforted each other. Pressing Christine closely to him, he was back inside the lifelong familiarity of the smell of her skin

and her hair, her warmth, her whole character – its wholesome-
ness and clumsiness, her honesty and her guarded, prickly
private self. For a few days then he moved back in, sleeping in
the spare room, but that was worse. That was when they quarrelled most violently, said the most awful things. He was dismayed with guilt. Christine demanded again to know what
Alex wanted and he said he didn't know, he didn't know what
was possible.

Isobel met Sandy in a bleakly cavernous pub where he thought
no one would recognise him; he arrived in dark glasses, with
his collar turned up. For hours they drank shots together,
working up their indignation against their father and Lydia,
Isobel melting into tears. All her life she'd been making efforts
of sympathetic imagination – but she couldn't surely, in all
fairness, be required to sympathise with this. — I dreamed
once when I was little, she said, — that Dad was touching
Lydia, inside her dress. And I never liked Lydia because of
it – though I told myself it wasn't fair, to dislike somebody
because of your own dream.

Sandy didn't want to think about his father's sex life, but
held forth on the defects in his character, his arrogance. He
said Alex was a hypocrite, he was so selfish. Sandy's usual
wary, wandering attention was transformed into tense bel-
ligerence; squeamish, he wouldn't repeat what Juliet had remarked when she heard. The barmaid meanwhile stared over
at him, and was muffled but excitable on her phone.

Grace took it more easily than anyone else in the two

families. When they rang her in Glasgow at the end of the evening, out of solidarity and fairly drunk, she said she didn't really care that much. — To be honest, if it helps them to feel better then good luck to them. It's life, isn't it? I mean, at least they're still alive. I'm only sorry if it's made Christine unhappy.

— But wouldn't Zachary have cared? Doesn't it dishonour his memory?

Grace sighed. — Iz, are you serious? What does that mean?

The next morning Isobel was nauseous from the drink. — I can't bear to tell you what's happened with my parents, she said to Blaise. They had actually sent each other this time, to make sure, the map coordinates for a Caffè Nero in the Haymarket. — I'll never be able to convince you that up until now, my life's been so straightforward. Almost too straightforward. I wish you'd known me in the past, just so that you'd believe me, how boring I used to be.

Blaise only smiled fondly; he had brought her as a present a leather-bound Victorian anthology of poetry – inevitably she lost it almost at once on the Tube. She asked if nothing awful ever happened to him. — I was in a helicopter last year in Pakistan, he offered helpfully. — And my ear protectors blew off in a backdraught. I was too embarrassed to say anything, you know, civil servant among all those military types. But I couldn't hear properly afterwards for months.

Isobel laughed, touched his hand across the table. They still hadn't had their chance to sleep together, or do much more than exchange friendly kisses in greeting, like old chums – she was afraid that their moment would pass without them. She had gone to her mother's alone, eventually, that evening of the Thai noodles when she was summoned, and found her on her knees in the kitchen, weeping and scrubbing the floor. Apparently Christine had spent all that day without speaking to anyone, spring-cleaning the house from top to bottom, pulling all Alex's clothes out of the drawers and wardrobes. Isobel had persuaded her to undress and get into a hot bath, then couldn't forget the sight of the pale knobs of her mother's bent spine in the bathroom steam; she'd hugged her knees while she told Isobel what had happened, her nakedness vulnerable as a child's or an old woman's.

One afternoon, Christine was at her mother's house with Isobel. The sash windows overlooking the garden were pushed up high, a slanting dusty light slicked Barbara's antiques in honey colour, faded tasteful curtains scuffed in the breeze along the floor. Christine couldn't help bringing all their conversation round to a discussion of her situation with Alex; patiently, feeling the strain, her mother and her daughter heard her out, went over and over the same ground with her. They wondered if Alex had told Margita yet. — She thinks her son's so marvellous of course, said Barbara.

— She has no illusions, she's convinced all men are like that, Christine said. — After Tomas.

Isobel put her hands over her ears. — Don't tell me about him too!

— Do you really not know about Tomas?

— No, I do know. I just don't want to hear it all again, not now.

In Isobel's idea of her paternal grandfather, dead before she was born, his unreadable bleak books and his adulteries had the same affronting texture: chunks of Central European gristle you were supposed to swallow and couldn't. She knew, because her father had told her, that Tomas had also cut out storybook characters from paper and made animal shadows on the wall with his hands, but these accomplishments seemed improbable, folkloric.

Alex rang Christine's mobile and asked if he could see her.

— Isobel is here too, Christine said warily into her phone.

— Does she object to me coming?

Isobel shrugged when Christine asked. — I can't stop him. Tell him I won't ever forgive him, though.

— Poor Alex, he hates having your bad opinion, Christine said after he'd rung off. — But of course you'll forgive him eventually. Anyway, there's nothing to forgive. I never owned your father, I don't possess him.

— How could he abandon everything he had, Mum? Isn't it grotesque, at his age?

— It's Lydia I can't forgive, said Barbara. — When I think of her scheming to get Alex. She always wanted him, she was always jealous of Christine.

— Mum, don't be absurd, Christine said. — You've never thought any of those things. You've always loved Lydia.

— But I never trusted her. You are too trusting.

— She was lonely without Zachary. She's no good on her own.

Isobel demanded to know what Lydia actually did all day; Christine speculated disingenuously. — Well, I suppose she lives for Alex, now.

The three women looked at one another: for a moment it was funny. — I didn't think anyone did that any more, Barbara said, almost wistfully. — Aren't men ridiculous?

Isobel, softening, said she couldn't imagine how bad Lydia must be feeling. Christine could imagine it. She knew Lydia better than Alex ever would or could, she thought; Lydia would always be performing for him. — She tells herself it was fated, it was bound to happen. And also that passion is always selfish and amoral, but can't be resisted, only submitted to. She thinks what a selfish person she is, but thinks it luxuriantly.

— Lets herself off the hook, you mean.

— Twists on the hook, not trying to escape.

Christine seemed calm enough, but Isobel had found pages and pages of her mother's writing that morning, stuffed into a wastepaper basket, scrawled in black ink on lined file paper in her spiky italic hand, the same letter begun again, over and over. *Dear Alex, I feel so Dear Alex, I can't get over ... I feel crushed. Alex, I know that I haven't been ... I'm so angry Dear Alex, How could you, what did you think I'd ...* Words were scored into the page and underlined five or six times. *Dear Lydia, I feel so, I can't ... although Why did you have to ...* Isobel hadn't been able to stop herself reading what she could see, but she wouldn't pick the letters up out of the basket, she was afraid of them. She was more used to her mother's writing on shopping lists or birthday cards, or in contained, funny little postcard messages from holidays abroad. It was excruciating for her to see this turmoil exposed, garrulous and banally confessional as a teenager's: like a mature person falling down in the street, all their accumulated self-possession turned to heaviness.

As he entered the room where the women waited, Alex's face was keen with consciousness of their condemnation; uneasily he defied it. Barbara sat smiling ruefully on the sofa, hostess-like out of long habit; Isobel had her back turned, looking out of the window. He most of all wants Isobel to look round, Christine thought. — Oh Alex, Barbara said, putting up the parchment-skin of her cheek for his kiss. — What have you done?

He took both his mother-in-law's hands in his, kissed them too, then sank into the armchair opposite her, sighing: as if of all things he'd only called in for their usual prickly, wary chat. For a moment Christine didn't recognise the clothes he was wearing, and thought in her craziness that Lydia was buying him things already. Then she realised it wasn't his clothes that were different: he came flaunting his satisfaction at them, he was vivid and sleek with sex. How horrible! Whatever had been loosening and fading in him was drawn tighter now and brightened; whereas Christine hadn't washed her hair in days, it was lank and she was wearing an old top like a rag. Barbara kept telling her this was no way to win her husband's interest back. She had said she didn't want to win it back but now she felt obliterated because he didn't approach or touch her. — This is such a mess, Alex, said Barbara severely. — What are you going to do?

He spread his hands, helpless.

Apparently he hadn't moved in with Lydia yet, and he'd begun paying rent for his room in Gospel Oak. Barbara seemed to think this was a good sign. There was no need to rush into anything, she cautioned anxiously. Nothing wrong with Alex finding a place to stay, in the interim. — What interim? Christine asked.

— While you all recover from what's happened, Barbara said brightly. — He won't give up your marriage on a whim.

Christine pointed out that people gave up marriages all the time, on whims. — I don't think it's a good sign. I think the reason he hasn't moved in with Lydia is because he's still hoping he can have both of us. He's hovering in between. Hoping he can have his old life and his new life, both at once.

— Now there's Lydia, Alex said. — What's done can't be undone.

Barbara tried to help out sanely. — He was consoling her. They're both so unhappy, they hardly knew what they were doing.

— Oh, consoling! Christine scoffed.

Yet the word stuck to her: perhaps that was what Lydia had done. She had consoled Alex for everything, and Christine had failed to.

It was a relief when school started up again and Alex could take refuge for so many hours of the day inside his performance as Mr Klimec: patient and omniscient, immune inside his dry humour, assertively male and yet sexless and harmless.

Whatever else failed, he didn't have to let down the children in his charge. Lydia tried to give him money for his rent in Gospel Oak but he wouldn't let her. It was just possible for him to afford it and pay the mortgage and still leave enough for Christine. He ate frugally.

He was surprised how much he liked his bedsit room. It had nothing much in it apart from a bed and a table and chair, and looked out onto a back garden whose shrubs had overgrown into trees, and where tenants had dumped curiosities – a broken trailer for pulling a boat, a trampoline with rusty springs. Foxes sauntered through at dusk, their hindquarters insolently drooping, inspecting their terrain. Alex chose carefully the books he brought from home, a few at a time, and liked waking in the room in moonlight – he never drew the curtains against the dark – to see their pale promise solid on his table. He was reading anthropology, thinking that after all this should have been his subject – with its long view, its doubt in relation to human universals, its foundation in the idea of cultural difference.

He marked the children's work and prepared his classes at his table in the window, then walked out among the elongated late summer shadows on Parliament Hill. The trees' darkened foliage hung dully and the grass was trodden hard, or was boggy and yellow in patches; the air was stale and blue, its emptiness limp from all the city crowds who'd been and gone. Stopping for the inevitable pastel view of the city, innocuous and miniature at its safe distance, he was ambushed by how close he felt to his lost boyhood and youth – he'd forgotten this pungent taste of anticipation, this leaping up of his heart in fearful excitement, looking around himself at solitary others dog-walking under the spreading trees in the late light. Then he might drive over to Garret's Lane, perhaps not until midnight. Lydia never came to him in Gospel Oak, he hadn't given her his new address and she didn't question him over where he was or how he spent his time. Images of their intimacy suffused his thoughts, but he wanted for the moment to preserve this distance between them. He had a horror of filling Zachary's place, going out every morning from Garret's Lane to fetch the newspaper for Lydia, or buy milk for her coffee.

Margita turned up unexpectedly to commiserate with Christine. She staggered out of the back of a taxi in her kitten heels, bottle of vodka stowed discreetly in a plastic carrier; the taxi lurched off abruptly the moment she shut the door – she always refused to tip. She was breathless by the time she'd climbed upstairs, and sat balancing rigidly upright on the edge of the sofa, with her hand over her heart, gasping. The mask of Margita's make-up and her stiff hair made her look startled, like an old doll thrown carelessly too often into the toy basket – but actually nothing surprised her. Unclasping her handbag and fishing for cigarettes, Margita found her voice again. — These women are not like us, Chris. We have our own minds. We have education, books, ideas! Some women only think about men all the time, making schemes how to get them.

Christine had never seen Margita reading anything apart

from the *Evening Standard.* — Lydia had a perfectly good education, she demurred in fairness.

Margita screwed her finger, swollen around its rings, expressively against her forehead. — Not interested in the theme of reality versus appearances, too busy wondering if she looks nice.

— I worry, though, that I ought to work harder on my appearance.

— But Chris, why? If you've got a brain!

— We have to remember that she's bereaved. Perhaps she doesn't know what she's doing.

Printing her cigarette thickly with her orange lipstick, Margita flicked at the lighter, then mouthed with certainty around her smoke. — Oh, she knows.

Hannah came to give in her notice and Lydia begged her to stay, apologised for having procrastinated over the gallery's future, offered her a three-year contract and a free hand as Artistic Director. Of course the gallery must be kept open, if it possibly could! — Oh, it's viable, if you can get the right continuity, we really think so, Hannah guardedly said. It must be kept open, Lydia assured her. For Zachary's sake. She would like to be kept informed and involved eventually in a role in management, that was all – and she would be staying on at least for the moment in her home next door. Hannah, who probably knew something about what was going on with Alex, said that she'd think about it for twenty-four hours and then phoned back in two: she wasn't close to Christine anyway, had always liked Alex better. If Lydia really meant it about the free hand she'd be delighted. — So that's settled, Lydia said.

She announced this news to Alex as if she'd done it to please him. And he was pleased, relieved that the gallery would be kept open; although it turned out to be complicated setting up the new arrangements legally, having them approved by the Trustees. As the other executor of the will, Max must be involved at every stage, and was difficult, although – famously oblivious to everyone else's crises – he surely didn't know yet about Alex and Lydia. At weekends Alex sat at Zachary's desk on the mezzanine, working out what Lydia needed from the accountants and her solicitors, filling out the forms for probate, sending emails in her name. Zachary had always done all the practical work in their marriage.

Of all things, Alex and Lydia had this in common – the loss of Zachary; there was some literal, physical sense in which their lovemaking assuaged their loss. Lydia was generous with herself, with her body – Alex took possession of her greedily, overwhelmed by the release and the relief of the sweetness they went seeking in the dark. There had been other women once or twice, in the years since he'd been married to Christine, but he'd backed off from something glib and counterfeit in those affairs. To his relief, Lydia wasn't sexually athletic or competitive. Certain revelations of her character – reserves of her self kept back, like candles saved up to light a cellar or a cave – could only be had, he thought, through this sexual connection with her. He began to see how her intelligence was not wide-ranging but concentrated, and how she was remarkably without illusions, and stubbornly wedded to one or two ideas from her early youth. She was frank with him but never spilled over with self-doubt or asked for reassurance, nor did she want to know his secrets.

He had always been struck by her lack of any ambition for a life lived in public. Now her idleness, which he had once disapproved of, seemed profound to him – like a form of extremity, or a great risk. He thought about the mistresses of bankers and politicians in the past, hidden away behind their flower gardens in villas in St John's Wood, alone all day with their mirrors and their thoughts. But wasn't the stupid servitude of their men more degraded, bound to their wheel of daily work and success, their public banality? Strictly speaking, of course, in the material sense, Lydia was in no danger of becoming a kept woman; it was Alex who must look out, in case he became a kept man. When his car packed up, though, it made sense for him to use Zachary's old plum-coloured Jaguar.

Theatre and concert tickets pinned to the noticeboard had been bought in pairs months ago, when Christine and Alex's married life had seemed to stretch harmlessly ahead of them without interruption. Doggedly, Christine insisted on using up all these tickets. She went alone if Isobel couldn't go with her, nor any of her friends. Wasn't everyone telling her that she should get out, get a life of her own? Sometimes she didn't even ask her friends. These solitary expeditions must look as though she were making an embittered point, but the truth was that she struggled with the problem of how to pass the long hours of her days, and – worse – her evenings. The nights were all right; she slept deeply, without dreaming. Alex had always been so restless beside her, twitching and turning.

The Orchestra of the Age of Enlightenment was playing Lully and Rameau and Handel at the Barbican. In Christine's past life she'd have run upstairs ten minutes before they left, to change her blouse; now she took her time washing and dressing, as if she were going to be exposed on stage herself instead of watching – brushing her hair slowly in front of the mirror, braiding it on her shoulder. Her hair was growing too long because she couldn't face the hairdresser, who would ask how Alex was. She wasn't trying to make herself alluring, she only wanted her outfit to keep her safe, like a nun's habit – black crêpe skirt and cream silk shirt, with a black jacket she'd found among Lydia's things. She still had all those bags of Lydia's possessions. Whenever Alex was coming to the house Christine imagined thrusting them at him, humiliating him by loading him up with women's dresses; then in his actual presence she would change her mind. Sometimes she wanted to violently destroy the clothes, sometimes she fantasised that she could hurt Lydia more by wearing and flaunting them. She had picked out a few treasures: a bronze silk shirt patterned with mauve flowers, a green velvet dress. Once she even got out her sewing machine, altered a skirt to make it fit. The skirts and dresses were mostly too short for her; the shoes fitted but Christine couldn't manage on high heels.

As soon as she was in the Tube on her way to the concert, and then inside the Barbican, she felt less exposed – only dreaded bumping into anyone she knew, who would ask after Alex. Catching sight of herself in the mirror-glass behind the bar, she thought she looked aged and plain but under control, which was good enough; perhaps her suffering even made her interesting. Because she was early she bought a glass of wine, then sat reading her programme, before going into the auditorium to find her seat. She had always in truth preferred going to concerts and films and exhibitions alone, not having to worry about whoever she was with in case they weren't enjoying it – or were enjoying something she hated, so that she had to pretend politely, not wanting to appear too opinionated. Even Alex, so clever and so exacting, had lagged behind her judgement in an art gallery, enthusing about the wrong thing or missing what was original and true.

Already she had an idea about the Lully – stiffly artificial figures moving in fixed patterns around Versailles, pouring into the conventional outward shapes of their music all the liquidity of their repressed passion. At the last moment, as the orchestra began to come on stage, some latecomer made a nuisance of herself, forging along the row so that everyone was annoyed, having to fish for their coats and bags, stand up to let her past. Christine was appalled when this person sat down in Alex's empty seat: then she saw when she looked round, with a dreadful too-thick beat of blood through her heart, that the latecomer was Lydia. Christine must have made some involuntary snarling or repulsing noise, because one or two people turned around to frown at them. Guilty and uneasy, pulling off a cobwebby scarf from around her neck, Lydia dropped her bag into the dark at their feet as if the seat had been saved for her all along, as if they were old friends who'd planned to meet up to enjoy the concert. She leaned across to whisper in Christine's ear. — Please let me sit. I won't be any trouble to you.

— What are you doing here? What's happened?

Lydia shook her head. Nothing had happened. No time now to explain: the guest conductor, hero of the occasion, was making his entrance. If Lydia had come three minutes earlier, Christine would have got up and left, but she was too obediently well trained to make a fuss now that the music was beginning. They sat side by side in a parody of close attention, staring fixedly at the stage, not hearing anything: the first notes the orchestra struck might as well have sounded on another planet. Christine burned with her sense of the trick played on her, and the concert spoiled, and the impossibility of sitting there a moment longer – and then there was the incriminating black jacket. She would have liked to tear it off. How had Lydia known about the concert, and to find her way to the right empty seat? Of course, Alex would have ordered the tickets online, the receipt would have been in his inbox. It was just like Lydia to find out his password and go hunting through his emails.

Making no effort with the music, Christine was surprised when she began to hear it without thinking about it. Inside the space the music opened – as if it pushed back, for all its delicacy, against some melodramatic smash of closing doors – her consciousness rebalanced and calm imposed itself. For who would care about their passion in three hundred years?

Nothing could be more ordinary, after all, than sitting here beside Lydia, whom she had known since they sat together at a school Founders' Commemoration Day. The two women didn't look at each other but, suspended in their proximity as time passed, they became used to each other again. At the edge of her sight in the dimness Christine was aware of Lydia's knee in black tights, and the fluffy sleeve of a cardigan she had shrugged off because she must be hot. So she was mortal still, and not transfigured with her happiness.

When the interval came, Christine stood up at once with everyone else, meaning to go home. Lydia gripped her arm, pulling her back down; people peeled away, going out of the auditorium for drinks, from either side of where they sat. — Chris, wait, just for a moment. Then I'll go, you don't have to.

A rubbery false composure seemed stretched across Christine's face. — So, are you enjoying the concert?

— Alex doesn't know I've come here. It's all my own idea. He'd hate it, obviously.

— They're playing beautifully, aren't they?

Lydia looked at her unhappily. — I just couldn't bear not to have talked to you. It seemed so cowardly. I didn't want to be a coward, just for once.

— But I'm not talking to you.

— I just wanted to tell you some things, so that you knew. Like that I mostly don't know where Alex is. I spend a lot of time waiting for him, afraid he isn't coming back. In case that's gratifying for you. We aren't like a couple, it isn't that sort of thing.

— I'm sure you'll grow into it.

— That jacket suits you, by the way. I'm so glad you're wearing it. And I like your hair longer, it's softer.

Glancing down, Christine pretended to be surprised. — Oh, is this yours?

— I haven't really taken Alex from you, Chris. People aren't available, are they, to be taken out and given back like a library book, date-stamped? He hasn't finished with you, nor you with him, not really, whatever you think. And do you and I have to be enemies? We aren't conventional, are we?

— It turns out I'm quite conventional after all.

— I never complained, did I, when you were so close to Zach for all those years? When he called in so often to see you in the afternoons.

Christine looked at her searchingly, quickly. — You didn't mind it, though!

— Didn't I mind it? Perhaps sometimes I did. When I went looking for him in the gallery and Hannah said he wasn't there, he was with you, again.

— You never said you minded! You should have said. And anyway, we were all happy then, Christine insisted.

— It wasn't anything like this. Everything was balanced differently, there were the four of us. And Zach and I were just talking, those afternoons in the studio. Or he would sit there watching while I worked, that's all: it was about art, that's what we cared about, more than anything. We never hurt anybody, or upset them. It's not the same as breaking the pattern, breaking everything up.

— Though for that matter I loved Alex first, don't forget that. You took him from me, in a way. You've had his life.

— But why do you cling to that old story, Lydia – of things we felt and fantasised when we were more or less children? We're grown-up now, we're growing old! We have children of our own and they're grown-up too. You're such a strange person. Why aren't you like normal people? You should be keeping out of my way, if you were normal.

She saw that Lydia was hurt then: she turned her face away.
— Grace incidentally has announced she's giving up working in stone and wants to paint instead. Because of Zachary, to mark the whole change in her life. I don't know how she is, really. I don't think she's all right. I'm afraid for her.

Christine said crossly that she hoped Grace knew what she was doing, you couldn't just pick up painting on a whim from one day to the next. — How is it that you don't know, Lydia, that this is not a thing normal people would do, to come to this place to find me and try to talk to me?

She shook her head. — I don't know why I don't know.

The bell hadn't rung for the second half of the concert, but people were beginning to take up their seats again. — Alex saved my life, Lydia said. — He saved me.

Christine looked around her with false brightness, said she was looking forward to Handel in the second half. When the light faded and the conductor arrived on stage again both women were relieved, withdrawing into the shelter of the music, recovering from the abrasions of their exchange – only feeling the pain of them belatedly, in the aftermath. Lydia sat forward in her seat, staring as if she were transported by what she heard, and Christine in the dimness saw an actual glassy tear roll down her cheek, luminous against her skin for a moment, reflecting the lights trained on the orchestra, like one of those tricks which show off a painter's virtuosity. Lydia hadn't even cried at the funeral, nor all those years ago at school when their teacher shook her unjustly and cruelly, and Christine had so admired her and taken her part, and had seemed to see in her set pale face something perfected, so brittle and unsentimental.

Grace bought new clothes from a charity shop in the Great West Road, wore them to a party with green high heels: a stiff fitted dress of green and gold brocade, white fake-fur stole, long white kid gloves. She thought she looked like a queen in exile. At first she was jubilant at the party, circulating regally, dancing with abandon – boys kissed her hand, obediently they knelt before her: she was having fun. Then the night performed its bleak new trick of turning inside out, revealing itself as vacant. Other people's pleasures receded to a noise in her ears, the ocean in a shell. Too much drink, too much coke, she told herself sternly: beyond a certain point these ushered in a sobriety more dreadful than anything in the daytime. Letting herself out of the party when no one was looking, she stepped alone into the street, the drenching rain welcome. She was looking for a taxi but the night bus came first. There was almost no one on it – too early for the late all-night crowd – but she took a seat beside a young man whose short hair was shaved raw against a sinewy, unhappy neck. He scalded with colour and stared out the window to avoid her. Putting her head on his shoulder, she asked him to cheer her up; he eased from underneath her, complained that she was soaking him. The fur stole was sodden, ruined. What did she have to be sorry about anyway, he asked, apart from the weather?

— I want to talk like you, she said. — I love your voice. *I cannae do that.* I want to belong to something, somewhere.

He said that talking was easy, in fact it was the only thing he'd ever done well at school. — You see, you're funny, she said. — I want to be funny again, but I've lost my sense of humour. My dad died recently, that's the thing. He was the funny one. We were very close. How would you say that? *We were gey close. He was a guid man. We'll no see his like again.*

He said he knew what she was going through, his dad had died too, when he was a boy. — It's common, I know that, Grace said. — Nothing to make a fuss about. But come home with me, won't you? I'm afraid to be alone, I'm too sad.

Politely regretful, he said that he had to change buses now, he was going all the way to Motherwell. Grace nodded and raised a white-gloved hand in farewell when he got off, exchanging a deep look with the black glass of the window trailed across with silver raindrops. She was too robust, she thought, to think of the river: she wasn't the sort. The bus ran along their street and past the house, the stop was just beyond it. And from the bus window as she passed she saw someone crumpled into their doorway where it was recessed beside the shop, sunk onto the step with his hood pulled over his face – which was turned away out of the rain, against the grubby white PVC of the door. One of the local winos they sometimes invited in and fed? Hurrying back along the street, hunting for her key in her bag, she was glad in any case of the distraction. And when she saw that it was Sandy, asleep, or with his eyes closed at least in some long martyred forbearance, beautiful as a saint, she was weak for a moment with her sense of the blessing she'd have forfeited if she hadn't come home early, or if she'd drowned herself, or brought back the boy from the bus. She hardly dared speak to him, to rouse him.

— Sandy?

The long grey eyes flicked open. — Christ, Gracie, where've you been? This is a shithole. I've been here for fucking hours, since the pubs closed. And the pub was a shithole too.

She helped him up, supporting him as anxiously as if he were lame, unlocking the door and easing him over the threshold: leaning on her heavily on their way upstairs, he stank of beer and whisky. — My darling I'm so sorry, she mourned, pushing the hair back from his fine temple, kissing it. — I forgot to charge my phone, I thought it didn't matter. But what are you doing here?

He groaned. — I needed you.

— If only I'd known! If only you'd told me!

— I have to talk to you. Good god, Grace, what do you look like?

She turned full circle for him on the stained carpet in the sitting room. — Aren't I queenly?

Sandy only flicked his glance once around the room's squalor – sleeping bags, tea mugs, trainers, the landlord's orange furniture, foil trays of half-eaten takeaway: beneath his notice, though his nostrils tightened at the smell. — Drag queenly, maybe.

— Wife at a Masonic Ladies' Night who's had a few too many?

— And fallen into the fishpond. You're soaking, really. Did you swim?

— I can't swim, remember? Grace's laughing face was fresh and pink and blotched with cold, rain was caught in the frizz of her hair. Cheerfully she wrung out a handful of her skirt. — This is just Glasgow, it rains here. I am soaked, aren't I? And so are you. We'd better change out of our wet things; you're shivering. Come into my room, it's nicer. Well, not much nicer.

She kicked off her heels and, as she preceded him down a dank passage, reached up behind her, between her shoulder blades, for her zip; crossing the threshold of her room, switching on a light, she stepped out of the wet dress in one movement, trampling it underfoot, and was naked underneath – her nakedness as frank and unselfconscious, without mystique, as when she and Sandy were children paddling together at the seaside. Only now she wasn't a child – with her lean young breasts like an athlete's, strong goosefleshed haunches, scribble of wiry pubic hair. Visibly Sandy winced.

— Just let's talk, he said. — I want to talk.

— But let's talk in bed, darling. Let's get warm. It's all right: we're like cousins, aren't we? We don't have to do anything.

He hesitated, but the room was disgusting, there was nowhere else for him to sleep. With slow fastidiousness and unsteady fingers, Sandy unbuttoned his shirt, hair hanging forward across his frown, delicately conscious of his exposure as Grace hadn't been of hers. Clutching the pillow, she drank in the glamorous sight of him: he was a god fallen into her room, turning away to tug at his belt, unzip, step out of his trousers, keep on his underpants. He put the lamp out and then they faced each other under the duvet, not touching, in a darkness smudged with light from the street. She asked him lovingly what he wanted to talk about.

— Christ knows, Sandy said gloomily. — I can't remember now. Just everything. The band. Fucking Alex messing up.

— I know, Grace said soothingly. — Everyone's upset.

— I mean, how crass is he? After what happened — how could he do this to you? And Izzy and Christine. He never thinks of anyone else.

— Well, he hasn't strictly speaking done it to me. Because I don't mind.

Grace knew Sandy's eternal resentment of his father: touching his cheekbone with her fingertips, she willed her own calm insight to pass into him, with its capacious forgiveness.

— My mum's always carried a bit of a torch for Alex.

— But it's too awful, at their age.

— When we're that age, we'll probably still want things.

She guessed that Sandy didn't think much about growing old. — You're the wonder, she said. — What you are is so amazing.

— He's never once listened to my music.

— It doesn't matter.

— I'm miserably drunk, Gracie, he said. — But at least I'm

warm. I thought it was the end of the world, waiting outside.
I needed you. I can always talk to you. You're sweet. You're
a good girl.

— You're safe now.

Making some involuntary grunting, assenting noise, he
turned his back on her eventually and fell asleep; fascinated,
Grace kept watch over his absence. Hours passed while rain
washed against the window, cleansing and purifying. Sandy's
intricate, difficult self was in abeyance, his beautiful body
left behind was like her hostage. When the grey dawn came
round, she leaned over his sleeping form to view him in its
sober light, and saw through him for the first time: her en-
chantment had passed, the sexual spell she'd been in thrall
to since before she knew what sex was. That god had slipped
away without any fanfare, out of the mortal guise he'd taken.
When Sandy made love to her in the morning – rather per-
functorily and shamefacedly, as if he owed it to her – although
Grace was eagerly pleased, it didn't make much difference to
anything.

SIX

THEY WERE ALL IN VENICE, but not for the Biennale. Zachary and Lydia would stay on for that, Christine had preferred to come a couple of weeks before it opened – which coincided anyway with the school holidays, for Alex. She'd rather look at the old art, she said, her heart was there. Her feelings about the Biennale were complex: critical, competitive, hostile, excluded. Anyway she wasn't that kind of artist, she worked on a more intimate scale. Nathan Kearney was with them too, for fun, and they had left the girls at home – Isobel was revising for her A levels and being paid to look after Grace, who was fourteen and had refused to join them. Grace was going through a phase of despising all art galleries and museums: she said she was an anarchist, and was contemptuous of the rituals of high culture she'd been brought up on, a cloying diet of too many private views, first nights, award ceremonies. Her critique delighted Zachary and amused Lydia; only Christine felt bruised, though she was also ashamed of this. Grace was only a child, what could her opinion matter? But she felt the danger of Grace's contempt, how it shrivelled her work's meaning.

Grace in her crazy clothes was audacious and stylish, dismissive of tradition and nuance: she might be the future.

In the Campo Ghetto Nuovo the five of them sat drinking Campari in the last warmth of a May evening – the spring's heat was still tentative, hadn't consolidated yet into summer. The women pulled light scarves around their shoulders. The rosy, dusky air was filled with the effervescent spritzing of darting swallows; yeshiva scholars with sidelocks came in and out of lit rooms belonging to some American foundation. Too many tourists drifted through the square, breaking up the picture, disproportionate to the substratum of local life, which nonetheless maintained its steady purposefulness, pretending to be oblivious of them – men heading home swinging briefcases, old ladies gossiping indignantly on the bridges, children's high musical voices glancing in rapid flight, like the swallows, against the water and along the walls of pinkish brick and stucco. A cake shop was open, selling *dolci ebraici*, thin rolls of pastry stuffed with almond paste. They felt the guilt of being tourists, of Venice unravelling at its edges – and for so many decades and centuries now – into something frayed and spoiled. But it was also all exquisite and exalting: they had come from the Madonna dell'Orto full of Tintorettos, and this was the second Campari. Where could one go in the whole world, seriously, and not feel guilty?

— Stay at home, Alex said severely.

The others protested, he was such a puritan. — How can you, Alex? We wouldn't have seen what we've seen, we wouldn't have had today!

Alex said that from the perspective of another age, we

would one day understand that tourism had been as despoiling as the oil industry, or cutting down rainforests.

— Don't preach, Christine complained. — This isn't an assembly.

Nathan argued in favour of mass tourism, small blue eyes animated in his craggy face. — Don't you think it's pious, all this cult of the unspoiled? When was anywhere ever not spoiled, when was anything authentic? In a century's time they'll be writing PhD theses about the sad decline of the traditional British stag party trip to Prague.

— What nonsense you talk, Lydia said to him indulgently. — You just say the opposite of what everyone else thinks. Is that why people think you're so clever?

— I've no interest myself, incidentally, he said, — in travel. Don't see the point of moving from one place to another, seeing things. I'm only here for the drink and because of you nice folk.

Balding, Nathan still wore long what hair he had left, tucked it behind his ears. He had grown bulky over the years, across the shoulders and in the thighs, and now was scoffing more than his share of the potato crisps, dabbing greasy-fingered in the bowl with the oblivious appetite of one who mostly eats alone. Guileless and voluble, transparent in his moods, sometimes he sank deep in himself and needed to be alone for a few hours. And he had turned out unexpectedly in shorts from the first day, as if he'd been informed this was the dress code for holidays – though they were hardly necessary in the mild weather. They'd never seen his shapeless pale knees before. Lydia said she thought things were better when travel was restricted to the upper classes. — At least they had taste and good manners. And there weren't so many of them.

— Now who's being contrary for the sake of it? Christine said.

— It's the downside to the Shelley thing, said Nathan. — Ye are Many, they are Few. Whoops!

— The tourism genie's out of the bottle, said Zachary amiably. — You can't put it back in. We have to make the best of it. I'm the cynical one, I'm finding that reasonably easy, right here and now. Are we going to eat out, or shall we go home to cook veal scaloppini?

Christine protested that she didn't want to move, she was inside the magic of the hour. — I don't ever want to move from here, from this moment right now. All of us here together. I'm so perfectly happy.

— Another Campari all round, in that case?

— Then I'd be inside the magic of alcohol instead. You'd have to carry me home.

— I'm willing.

But Alex was restless and stood up from the table. — You all stay here, he said. — I'm going to walk.

He reproached their inertia, broke up the party. It didn't matter if they changed places anyway, because home was temporarily a rented flat in a palazzo in Cannaregio opposite a convent, overlooking a quiet canal – its rooms furnished in that Continental-archaic style so exotic to British sensibility, antiques mingled with modern horrors, embroidered lace-edged curtains, narrow beds with bolsters, tall locked linen cupboards, austerely functional tiled kitchen and bathrooms.

Leaning on the stone balustrade of the balcony grown over with pink jasmine, they could watch green water chop against the canal walls, its reflections liquid on the stucco, or listen out for the gondolas approaching through the warm peace of the afternoon or evening, or the motor boats carrying cement mixers or crates of bottled water or someone's new fridge. The gondoliers' ritual call, *stogando io,* warning as they neared the corner, was like a message from another age: the past flickered at the edge of vision, as if for an instant a portal opened through to it. Gondoliers stood up in the stern like centaurs, their labour half magnificent – superbly difficult, and ancient, and strange – and half absurd, because of the tourists stuffed self-consciously inside the boat going no-where, taking photographs of each other.

Eighteen months ago, Alex had been made headmaster at his school. Not many men went into primary education, and those who did rose quickly to positions of power. This new role of his at the school seemed like his reconciliation with the world: his friends realised that he was surprised he was good at it, and relieved. It turned out that Alex wasn't only visionary, he was competent: knew how to get money out of the local authority or the Department of Education or high-minded charities, to pay for extra music services, one-to-one support for troubled children, painting the walls of the playground with lines of poetry in fifteen languages. If he couldn't play games with the conditions, then who could? The school would be rated outstanding in inspections; he would get the children to perform well in their SATs. And meanwhile he would also read to them from the *Odyssey* in the school hall every morning, and they would turn its stories into paintings, music, plays for shadow puppets.

Alex and Christine quarrelled that evening in Venice, and with uncharacteristic rancour. At worst, usually, they were a little acerbic in front of other people. The quarrel began with nothing: began in fact, though she would never know it, with Lydia, because she was irritating Alex, and Christine sensed it, and felt defensive on behalf of her friend. Zachary and Christine had dipped the escalopes of veal in egg and bread-crumbs and fried them in olive oil with sage leaves, while Lydia read some crime novel and smoked, stretched out on a spindly sofa upholstered in pink and gold stripes. Nathan and Alex played Scrabble – they were well matched, and too good at it for the others to ever beat them, so that they'd given up trying. These two were locked in vicious competition for the whole holiday, playing game after game whenever they got the chance, bent with ferocity upon victory: although Alex never acknowledged by any look or shout of triumph or defeat that he cared either way. Nathan was less contained. On this occasion, in fact, Alex lost: Nathan got *city* on a triple, and then later added *toxi* in front of it, which reached another triple.

At the table, squeezing lemon on her veal, Lydia said she'd had enough of beauty, she thought she might need a rest from it, tomorrow. — I need to contemplate a tower block or a Jack Vettriano or a Burger King or something, she said. Christine knew that Alex was chafing, too, at the round of churches and art galleries and idle pauses. He looked at the paintings absorbedly, and remembered them as exactly afterwards as Christine did, as well as having a better grasp of the political and social history behind them; when he turned away from looking, though, it was as if he closed a book and didn't want to speak about it. Speaking was crass and everyone's responses were predictable, he winced at them, and despised the guides with their unstoppable bland flow of knowing. Abruptly he'd have seen enough: he'd leave the others to it and wait for them downstairs, or in a cafe. His patience, at the time they took, was ostentatious.

Now he looked at Lydia moodily across the supper table, resenting her voicing what he felt. — You have a lemon pip beside your lip, he said. Lydia dabbed at her face with the kitchen paper they had in lieu of napkins; Alex had dropped his attention to his plate; it was Christine who reassured her that the pip was gone. — What's everyone's plan for tomorrow? Christine said with steely cheerfulness.

Alex objected without looking up. — Do we have to have plans?

— Let's not have plans, Lydia said. — I hate plans. I might just stay here and be lazy.

— Well why don't you? Christine said. — Laziness feels like the right response to Venice. I can always go and soak up more paintings by myself, play the indefatigable tourist.

— Zachary'll go with you, he's indefatigable too.

— I need to get online, Alex said. — I have work to do.

The promised internet connection in the palazzo was a

disappointment – or, Christine insisted, a relief. Alex had a deadline for making a grant application; Nathan, who wrote reviews, was sending off copy which was already late. He stayed up writing it after the others went to bed; they heard the furtive clacking of his keyboard, pausing and resuming, forging his opinion, which occasionally he chuckled at audibly, or groaned over. He and Alex had found a grubby and cramped little internet cafe.

— Alex, that's such a bore for you, said Lydia sympathetically. — Can't it wait?

— Well, no, actually. There's a deadline.

— Because of course, Christine said, — Alex always has to be doing something more important than everyone else.

But her comment wasn't fair, because the grant application really did need to go in: she had reassured him, when they were still in England, that he would be able to submit it from here. She regretted at once, when Alex directed at her a glance of pure dislike, the antagonism she'd unleashed – and the others looked at her in surprise. This was her blunder sometimes, mediating Alex's difficulty for others when actually they didn't mind it, or hadn't even registered it. But she couldn't take back her words, so she might as well unfurl the whole flag of her resentment. — You've noticed how he bestows his presence on us, as if he really ought to be elsewhere, she said, pretending to be teasing. In response Alex was coldly vicious, implacable.

— Chris is always trying to enlist me in her latest scheme for enjoyment. I'm never supposed to enjoy myself in my own way.

— But Alex, do you know how to enjoy yourself? You're always so angry.

Because they had an audience, the temptation of denunciations won out. She said Alex spoiled occasions, like a child, to assert his own power; he said she smothered everyone, fussing over them, subduing them to her good intentions. When they all separated at the end of a soured evening, it was particularly awful because Christine and Alex had twin beds, so had to nurse their outrage separately, lying stiff and inert under the sheets; accidental collisions in a double bed could have helped to heal their breach. Neither could face the deliberate act of crossing the floor between the beds, risking rejection: they didn't want to make friends anyway, they didn't care for each other. In the early morning Christine woke to a bleakness like cold poison: she thought that she hated holidays, hated this ruined place with its beauty tied around its neck like a doom. Heroically, however, in bare feet she crossed the cold space of marble floor and climbed in behind Alex, putting her arms around his chest and pressing against his warm back where she liked to make herself comfortable, suffused in the pungent, sleepy heat of his skin. She did this partly in pragmatic spirit, to save the holiday. Although Alex didn't say anything, he didn't adjust his position away from her, and when they got up they spoke as if nothing had happened. Their antagonism passed. Alex even seemed, from that point onwards, to make efforts to be more sociable.

Nathan was innocently dismayed by his friends' quarrelling. He knew that married happiness wasn't perfect, but only because he'd learned this from films and plays, where its breakdowns were entertaining. Their performance was all the more shaming because Zachary and Lydia were always so pleasant together. Christine knocked sometimes, with puzzled curiosity, upon the smooth surface of the secret of her friends' marriage, trying to test it, find out what it was made of. Who'd ever have thought, considering how selfish Lydia was supposed to be, and how capricious, that she'd make such a compliant and affectionate wife?

Alex and Nathan went off in the morning in search of the internet, and the three of them left behind ate *dolci ebraici* with their coffee on the balcony. The little cakes were disappointing but their vantage point couldn't fail – crisp light, perfumed jasmine, mildly odorous breath of the water slopping across stone steps. Nuns in grey habits and schoolchildren erupted into the quiet, rising and falling over the pure arc of a bridge then passing on the *fondamenta* below. One nun pushed dog's mess into the canal with the point of her grey umbrella. Zachary, who picked up languages so easily – as if they simply all lay dormant in him, rousing in response to suggestion – tried to translate for Lydia and Christine, catching the conversations in snatches.

— Something about a letter, a mother, a kitten, some homework ...

He must be making it up, they exclaimed, it was too perfectly nun-like. Or it was like a passage from a novel by Colette.

— No, really, that's what they're saying, listen!

Zachary had the gift of taking his difficult work lightly, shedding it when he came away, putting himself entirely at the disposal of his friends. Alex would say it wasn't a gift, it was Hannah, who would take care of Zachary's emails for him, manage the gallery in his absence like his second self. Still, there was a kind of genius in how thoroughly, between bursts of his gargantuan energy, Zachary could fall back into relaxation. His presence now, lounging in sunglasses and T-shirt and frayed straw hat on a sagging canvas chair between Lydia and Christine, only shallowly absorbed in one of the novels Lydia had cast off, was palpably whole, not thinned by any lapses of concentration or twinges from elsewhere. Yet in a week or so he would pick up his tasks of networking and negotiation with unflagging enthusiasm. Christine wondered what it meant, to belong so wholeheartedly to the world as Zachary did, have it cast its net of possession so far across yourself, trawling so deep. It must be a virtuous thing: someone had to run the world, and save it. But she couldn't imagine it for herself, couldn't imagine not wanting to keep everything back from the net, or almost everything. Was Zachary cheapened, allowing himself to be made instrumental?

She had her sketchbook out and was drawing him: not Venice, that was impossible, what was there left to see? But she was trying to capture this aspect of her friend, his eagerness to please, in the bold strokes of her charcoal: black scribble of beard, swell of paunch, long lines of the arms flung back in abandon, book half fallen from a lifeless hand. The Art Dealer. Christine had been drawn recently to the work of certain figure-painters of the twenties and thirties – James Cowie, Felice Casorati: they had influenced what she was doing. Not everyone understood or liked her new pictures, narrative art was still suspect. Alex said that they were too explicit – although if she pressed him to explain what he thought they meant, then he couldn't do it, or wouldn't. She had hoped that over the years her works would get bigger – it seemed to be a prerequisite for a career of matching size. But instead they'd shrunk. Not many of them, now, were much larger than a modest TV set.

Lydia looked around with faint irritability at her husband dozing and her friend absorbed in drawing: their absences bored her. She was too alertly vigilant, herself, ever to fall asleep during the day. Because Zachary's consciousness was withdrawn from between them for a moment – he snored, and his mouth fell open – Christine grew to feel something interrogative in how Lydia waited. — I know you think I was horrible to Alex last night, Christine apologised. Only the way Lydia held her head, poised on her neck swan-like, as if she were holding it up above dirty water, expressed any criticism. — You know what he's like, though! He can be so – inexorable.

Lydia blinked thoughtfully, her eyelids painted with blue shadow. — I don't mind him when he's inexorable.

— Well I do. I hated him for it last night. He hated me too, so it was only fair. I can't love him every minute of every day.

— But isn't that what you're meant to do? Lydia said.

— Our married relationships are very different, yours and mine. It's easy to be nice to Zach.

— That's true.

— Isn't it impossible, though, anyway, to love someone all

the time? That's why marriage is a contract. Those awful vows people invent for themselves now: 'I promise to always love the way you rub your nose', or 'I promise that your singing will always make me happy'. But sometimes the way he rubs his nose will make you want to kill him! You stay with him because it's in your contract, it's the deal you agreed. 'In sickness and in health'. That gets you over the tough spot. He stays with you for the same reason. It's more decent.

Lydia didn't laugh, she was in an odd mood: almost reproachful. — But you are happy, aren't you?

— Well, of course I am. I'm so lucky. Christine pressed the end of the charcoal on her page, bending over it, breaking it accidentally, making a jagged mark, seeing her drawing through a blur of emotion. — But how ridiculous, Lydia. You've made me cry. Only it's not about what you think: not Alex. It's Isobel.

— What's wrong with Isobel? Lydia asked patiently, but less interested.

— Nothing's wrong with her. It's only me. I can't bear to imagine our home without her in it, when she goes off to university. Her absence haunts the place already, before she's even gone. When she plays the piano – not very well, I know – I can only think how empty the rooms will be without her music in them. It's sentimental, I'm well aware! But if there's anyone I passionately and irrationally love, in the way you mean, it's my child. Isn't that strange?

— But she'll come back for holidays.

— Something's over, though. I didn't think it would be over so quickly. It felt so monumental and permanent, when it began. You'd think this was something a woman would feel, wouldn't you, who had no life of her own and had invested too much in her children. But there it is.

Alex suggested to Zachary that they go out and walk. The women were washing up after a supper the men had cooked; Nathan was writing on his laptop. Zachary felt the old exhilaration of their friendship, hurrying to keep up with Alex's stride – he walked fast and purposefully, hands thrust in his pockets, even if the purpose were only to lose himself. Diving down narrow passageways, choosing without consultation to cross one bridge rather than another, he hardly seemed to take anything in, never lingering or hesitating. When they crossed a square still restless with knots of visitors – erupting in noisy bursts of partying, made bold by darkness and drink – Alex's glance across the haunting, haunted dusky façades was perfunctory, almost over-familiar. He never let himself be caught out in admiring wonder, which was parochial. If you only marvelled at where you were, you remained apart from it. Rather, it must become a background to your thought, a stage set for it. He was laying out for Zachary's appreciation examples of the absurdities he was up against at school: pulling his hands out of his pockets to wave them expressively, he turned and walked backwards ahead of him, carried away with explaining, with exasperation.

It was a long time since Zachary had seen his friend so animated, so unguarded. Some balance between them was restored, because Alex was caught up in his new role and borne along by it, putting his whole thought to use. When they were at school together, and at university, and for a while afterwards, it had seemed a form of good taste, almost, for Alex to hold back from choosing some work to give his life to: as if he were waiting for the right way to begin, while others chose wrong ones. Then there was the publication of his book. But he had begun to seem behindhand, eventually, in not acting further, in turning in upon himself. It had taken such efforts of tact, in those years, not to draw attention to Alex's not doing anything that mattered; Zachary had had to suppress, to a certain extent, news from his own life. Then he had been disappointed at first when his friend chose teaching, had thought he was walling himself up from the world in a prideful gesture. And had been quite wrong.

They stopped in a small bar in a side street in Dorsoduro – crowded with voluble Venetians, the glass counters heaped with *salumi,* mozzarella, *crostini,* pickles – for a *caffè stretto*: took their drinks outside to stand on the pavement in the warm air. Bats flickered across the canal in knots of darkness. They talked about Sandy, who had dropped out of studying for his degree for the second time; Alex was disappointed in his son. He had waited impatiently for Sandy to enter into an adult understanding of the world and now couldn't bear his ignorance of history, his lack of interest in books. His life was infantile, Alex said. — Lying in bed until the middle of the afternoon, absenting himself from conversation on his headphones, indifferent to ideas. He has no clue that there could be any other kind of life. There's a scene I keep remembering, from one of my father's novels – actually I'm translating this novel at the moment, I work on it at night when I can't sleep. The scene might be from his experience, I don't know, I never asked. I wish I had asked him more things. In this scene a boy watches his own father, a farm-worker like my grandfather, given instructions in a heavy downpour of rain by his master who stands dry under an umbrella: his father's face is blind with the rain.

— Sandy has his music, Zachary insisted. — He's really talented.

— So you keep telling me. But he's lazy.

— You should trust him. Wait and see.

— And I hate that music he plays.

In all honesty, Zachary said, Alex's liking it was not what mattered. Liking it was for the young. Anyway, *he* liked it.

— But then, you're eternally young.

— And you hate too many things, Zachary said affectionately.

They leaned on a stone parapet which gave back to their touch the heat of the day; the night air was balmy with warmth and wine and the water's undertow of rot. Camouflaged among voices raised in Italian, their English speech drew them closer.

— I suppose I do, Alex conceded. — I've always felt that was my task: to be vigilant against liking the wrong things. But it's a mistake, perhaps. I suppose it's what's stopped me writing.

— Do you think? asked Zachary cautiously. Alex never spoke about not writing.

— The heavy hand of the critical law on the scribbler's hunched shoulder. Thou shalt not! Also, this impression that I was living in an aftermath, in the bland time after the real things have happened and the real books have been written. The age of commentary follows the age of making.

— You could have done with a catastrophe, to write about.

— I don't care anyway. I vastly prefer what I do now. It's such a relief to feel myself acting impersonally. And I hadn't expected the classroom's warmth. How interested I am in all of them.

— And now you're translating your dad's books. That's a lovely thing too.

— Well, they're not lovely books. They're brutal. I don't know if there are readers for them in our soft age.

Leaping ahead in his thoughts, Zachary jiggled his tiny coffee cup of thick china, though there was nothing left in it. — Do you think it's a male thing?

— Brutality? History would probably gently nudge us towards that conclusion.

— No, no: that inhibition you talked about, feeling you lived in the aftermath, with nothing left to say. Because in the visual arts, you know, it's occurred to me that women have been exempted from certain forms of self-doubt, which might be gendered.

Alex looked at him vaguely. — Gendered? That's an ugly word.

— Because the pen has been in the male hand and all that, for so long. Now that women have picked up the pen – for writing, for painting, for everything – they may feel all kinds of doubt but not that one. Because they're not belated. As women they're still near the beginning.

— But we all live in the same belated world, we men and women.

Zachary could tell that Alex wasn't interested in his idea. He seemed sometimes to tolerate Zachary's conscientious politics as if they were an occupational hazard, or a temperamental weakness. — Chris's work for instance, Zachary persisted, wanting to persuade his friend in this moment of openness between them. He wanted to open it wider: embrace the women inside their intimacy. — How has she been able to make her art so freely? It's poured out of her, hasn't it? Why hasn't she felt the heavy hand on her shoulder?

Alex looked startled, before a shutter fell across his expression, across some secret. It took him aback, Zachary saw, to have Christine's work invoked in the same scale as anything he, Alex, might have done. Zachary was startled too. He hadn't known that Alex didn't take his wife's work quite seriously: didn't, in their horrible old schoolboy phrase, really rate it. He must have only been kind, and condescending, and keeping a domestic peace, when he had acquiesced for all these years in seeming to rate it. The implications of Alex's mistake – Zachary was sure it was a mistake – seemed for a moment fairly tragic. And the night's happy mutuality deflated, each man was disappointed in the other. — As you say, Alex said drily, but with finality, as if it were the end of any discussion he wanted to have. — It pours out of her.

They all five went on the boat to Torcello, and had lunch in a garden-restaurant beside the path to the cathedral, in the shade of an awning that flapped in a breeze so that patches of brilliance went darting across the white tablecloth. Nightingales sang in the undergrowth in the hot light of day, red wine poured from a glass jug fizzed against the tongue. It was all like Keats on antibiotics, Nathan said.

— So here we are, Lydia said thoughtfully. — Where are we?

— You're going to love this cathedral, Zachary promised. — It's all so simple, so anciently, divinely lucid. In its great fresco: the damned on one side and the saved on the other.

— The trouble with the saved, Christine said, — is that they can't help looking smug. How good are the good, really, if on the Day of Judgement they're enjoying being saved while all their dear sinful friends and relations are shovelled into the burning pit?

— Oh, I'd enjoy it, Lydia said. — Plucking away on my harp, feeling beatified.

— But Lydia, don't disappoint me! Christine said. — Aren't you going to hell? That's where I'm going, because I thought you were!

All wounds seemed grown over in the present moment of pleasure as they talked and ate their pasta and grilled fish. They were flattered by the thick light under the awning, which burnished away marks of ageing in their faces, and they felt themselves significant – as if they were arranged around the table for a photograph, although they forgot to actually take one. The men were concentrations of darker mass, Alex holding something back, Zachary overspilling his place, jumping up and down to order more food, confer with the cook. Even Nathan in his shorts, knees spread wide, wolfing his food, was striking as if he might be famous, or very clever. The women in their summer dresses, Lydia's white and Christine's splashed with blue flowers, were the bright accents in the composition – Christine milky-pale under her sun hat, which flecked her with dancing points of light. And Lydia really did look like one of the blessed, with her long oval face and her hair bleached by the sun, knotted demurely at her neck.

Nathan sank into despondency. They had no idea what it was like to face the future alone, he said: the unmade bed, old VHS recordings of French films, supermarket meals for one. He longed, he said, for the civilising influence of women. His friends were familiar with this phase of his mood, when he let himself fall into the safety net of their sympathy. When Nathan had actually had girlfriends, he'd panicked at the invasion of his privacy – of his den in Shepherd's Bush whose ancient carpet smelled of dog although he'd never had one, and of his idiosyncratic routines: staying up till dawn, sleeping till noon. While everyone else grew out of the sordid spontaneity of youth, it had become his middle-aged fixed habit.

— You could try making your bed, Christine suggested.

Nonetheless the women preened in the light of Nathan's admiration for their married lives, then drifted from wifely maturity into reminiscence of their schooldays. — You can't have forgotten Miss Lowrie, Lydia insisted to Christine. — Creepy and fleshy, with goggle glasses.

— Biology lab?

— Gold watch cutting into her fat wrists. Ghastly malevolent axolotls snapping at rulers when we poked into their tank, and that tall cupboard with rows of jars, foetuses floating in formaldehyde.

— Lyd, they weren't actually foetuses.

— Oh, I'm enjoying the foetuses, Nathan said. — Presumably an endless supply, from disgraced ex-pupils.

What Christine seemed to remember was pairs and threes of schoolgirls in bottle-green uniform, heads bowed in gossip, circling unceasingly around the great cedar in the grounds. The sheer tedium had been its own opaque medium, through which time barely moved. — Because at its root it wasn't morally right, I suppose. Because the whole business of that school was separating people out to think a lot of themselves just because they had more money. Or, for the free-place girls like us, because we were clever in examinations. Entitlement was always in the air, even while they were breaking us cruelly down, in order for us to earn it.

— You exaggerate the cruelty.

Alex had no time for their protests over how hard they'd been made to work. The work was the good bit, he thought, in that kind of school; it was the boarding which was for barbarians. But Lydia insisted: this was her subject and she wouldn't be deflected, even by Alex. — It was worse than she says. What was worse was how the other girls queued up for it. For the entitlement of course: but also, to be broken down. It excited them: being tamed and humiliated and sorted into ranks. Whereas Chris and I, you know, used to read the *Communist Manifesto* in our dinner break.

— Ostentatiously, Christine apologised. — We were awful

show-offs. While the others made daisy chains or played French skipping with knotted elastic bands. And we were terribly bored by the *Manifesto*, couldn't understand a word of it, we preferred historical novels, really. It came from the bookshelves at home: this was when Dad worked for governments in Africa, advising on primary health care. My parents in those days had a sort of mild hopefulness, in relation to communism. They thought things had gone sadly wrong in Russia, but were optimistic for the Third World, as we called it then. They believed that a lot of the bad news we heard was only American propaganda.

— Quaint, said Alex.

That old hopefulness seemed as remote now, she agreed, as believing in phrenology or mesmerism. — They didn't know any better. But innocence has consequences, I know. It isn't really innocent. Like all of us in the West now, having our cake and eating it. And borrowing money against our cake, as if we'll never have to pay for it.

She tipped back and forwards on her wrist a horn bangle she'd bought the day before, from a Senegalese girl selling between cafe tables; when they'd asked the girl if she missed her home, she said she was going back there in three weeks. Afterwards they'd wondered if that was her stock reply. Perhaps it made the tourists more generous, if they weren't afraid of her as a permanent fixture.

— Talking of cake, Zachary said, broaching the question of dessert.

When they'd finished eating and had coffee and paid the bill, they stayed sitting on at their table. — The cathedral's really good you know, Zachary said. — And it does shut at four. But we don't have to move from here, if you don't want to.

They all agreed reluctantly that they must move on, and got up dreamily, eventually, in slow motion and lightly intoxicated, looking around them at the restaurant with regret, as if for something lovely and exceptional that could have been prolonged, but must be given up at last.

On Christine and Alex's last full day, he and Lydia and Nathan caught the train to Vicenza, for a change; Zachary and Christine stayed behind because Zachary had promised to show her the Tiepolo ceiling in the Scuola dei Carmini. The day was overcast, the sky spat flurries of rain, tourists thronging in the narrow passageways were disconsolate. Yet forging her way among them, with Zachary steering, a touch on her shoulder or her elbow – this way, down here, turn left – Christine felt weightless and at ease, as if some effort of performance had fallen away. She was too transparent in her social relations, she thought, allowing the others' moods and perceptions to be reflected in her chaotically, responding in too many directions, making doomed efforts to appease. Now that she let critical awareness drop – like sinking beneath the busily reflective surface of a lake – she was present in the day as quietly and alertly as if she were alone. Zachary, somehow, didn't count; they were dear old companions, they needn't try too hard. They exchanged one significant full smiling look, when the bells tolled from the Carmini church.

They had the Scuola to themselves at first. It took a few

minutes, once they had ducked into the unpropitious entrance and were out of the flow in the streets, for its peace to sift down into consciousness; the sensation of driving forwards beat on noisily inside them while they stood blinking in the dim foyer, eyes adjusting and hearts slowing. They breathed a different stale, cool, motionless air: its ashy aftertaste of incense, layered deeply over centuries of consecration, alien to both their sensibilities and yet powerfully nostalgic. The cold stone itself smelled of it. A woman sold them tickets from behind the usual meagre display of dun postcards. In truth Christine had hardly thought in advance about the art, she was tired of being amazed by things, and Tiepolo anyway wasn't one of her painters. She had thought the Scuola was going to be on a different scale and was pleased by its modest size, which suited her mood; she peered benignly, as if she were actually interested, into cabinets of religious insignia, medals, silverware, certificates of indulgence, embroideries brittle with age. And she was looking forward to finding a characterful little bar afterwards where she and Zachary could stop for coffee, confide their moods, share the latest art gossip.

When finally they were standing beneath the famous ceiling in the Sala, she was exceptionally receptive not because she was prepared, but because she wasn't. It caught her out in her passivity, the blank of apprehension she presented to it. A pale clear light came in through windows composed of rounds of glass like bottle-ends; voices in the street outside were remote as the swallows' shrieking. Dizzily she turned round and round where she stood, staring up, making her neck ache, trying to disentangle individual figures – whose foot is that, whose legs are those? – from the billows of gorgeous drapery, masses of rich form soaring against empty skies. She seemed to experience these colours – sumptuous pinks and gold and pale green – on her skin, the bodies' torsion in her own muscles. Every ordinary day, while their lives went on elsewhere, the Virgin presided in here, a superb queen – and the force of the angels' strong wings was like great birds', so that you felt the updraught of their movement. She was in the presence of what was momentous. And in one corner was an awful darkness – an open grave, bones, brown filth, suffering, two hands emerging from a cloud, forming between fingers and thumbs an O for nothingness.

— Oh, it's … I *love* this, Zach.

He put an arm across her shoulders. — I love it too. They staggered together, craning their heads backwards, gazing up, pointing; then Zachary found mirrors backed with polished wood, put out for visitors to use. Humility with her long eyes, in pink and silver with a crown under her foot, cuddling a lamb, didn't look humble in the least; they both agreed she looked like Lydia. Another couple, French, ascended the staircase, reading aloud from the leaflet; determinedly Christine and Zachary exuded an air of prior possession. By the time the French gave up and left, Christine was sitting on the wooden bench which ran around the base of the wall, looking into the mirror on her lap to take in the whole ceiling. Zachary sat down beside her and leaned over to see what she saw; Christine excitedly met his eyes in the glass, his reflection smiling out at her. — I *love* the past, she said.

— Oh yes, me too, the past.

— But I mean it, I'm serious, listen. Sometimes these days I almost think I can do without the present. The past is enough for me, it's enough for my life. Does that sound insane? I could only say it to you.

— It's not insane.

Watching his eyes in the mirror, she saw him feel with her what she felt. — I'm not saying that the past was good, she went on, — or fair, or better, or anything. But nothing will ever be more beautiful than this, will it? It's surpassingly beautiful. It surpasses anything I could have imagined. It fulfils me, it's enough for me.

Still smiling at her in the mirror, keeping his eyes on her, Zachary took her hand, bent over it, thoughtfully kissed the inside of her wrist. — I'm less original. I hunger for things in the present too.

— Well yes of course. But not in this moment.

— The past makes me more hungry.

— I do love you, you know, she said. — I can always talk to you, Zach, you're my brother.

Then he sighed noisily. — I always seem to be everyone's brother, don't I?

Christine turned her whole gaze, dismayed, away from their reflections onto her friend's actual face: between them in their surprise they almost let the mirror slip – he grabbed at it. She saw him differently: his animated boyish brightness, grey wiry hairs threaded in amongst the black of his beard, darkened anxious skin around his eyes, broken red veins on his nose, alert intelligence looking back at hers. Zachary never usually asked for any attention to himself – his geniality was a gloss, deflecting enquiry. Heavy against her, his body was scented with something nice and he gave off vitality like heat; when he kissed her wrist again she was startled by the tickling soft pressure of his beard. — Zacky, what do you mean? What about Lydia? You're not her brother.

— Aren't I? Or something faintly ignominious like it.

Christine thought that she must tread as delicately among these revelations as if they were jagged glass. — No. I don't know. You're not ignominious anyway.

— Well, that's good.

— Only you two always seem so happy.

— We're happy, it's OK, don't worry.

— I know Lydia can seem oblivious sometimes. She's so imaginative and intelligent but there's something fixed in her. Like Humility on the ceiling. She doesn't change, and that's her greatness – but also she doesn't see you changing. Doesn't see you seeing things.

— I suppose that's about it.

Christine pressed on, disconcerted. — Have you ever had other women, Zach? Since you've been with Lydia. I think you haven't.

— Not ever, no.

— And she's never had other men. I'd know, I'm sure.

— We've both of us been absurdly faithful.

— Oh, and me too! Absurdly!

And Christine was tempted for a moment to ask him, what about Alex, what do you think? Has he been faithful? Then she thought that she and Zachary had talked about Alex too much, they'd been over that old ground too many times. He was still holding onto her hand. Leaning together, each feeling the other's warmth, they sat looking up at the ceiling – just as they might have done in all innocence half an hour ago, except that everything was changed between them, Zachary's dissatisfaction was substantial and discomfiting as a third presence. Christine was less at ease with this new Zachary, who was jaded and more worldly; on the other hand he impressed her more and she had to reckon with his new force, insisting on himself. He hadn't ever been beautiful but his bulk and high colour were suddenly potent like a great merchant-broker's in a portrait. — I find I'm quite ashamed, he said, — of not having sinned, now that we're here in Venice. It seems unworthy. You know, of the art – and of all the incitements to pleasure. The general loveliness. The present company.

She squeezed his hand, he squeezed back tightly. — We could go to the apartment and have it all to ourselves, he said then, murmuring against her hair. — The others won't be back until mid-evening at the earliest. Weren't they going to eat in Vicenza?

— Zach, what are you suggesting?

— You know what I'm suggesting. Why not? It's not as if we haven't done it already. Couldn't that make it all right?

Christine protested, appalled, laughing: he knew it didn't! It could never be all right, not ever.

— Then let's be all wrong. No one need ever know.

She said anyway weren't they too old now? And they weren't the type.

— I find I might be the type after all, he said. — In my old age. What about you?

Carefully she tried to steady her voice, as if she were warning him – or warning herself. — But I so love our London afternoons at home. When you come round and it's raining and I make tea, Alex is at school, we sit and talk. I never even mind that you've interrupted my work: you're the only one, I'm horrible with anyone else who bothers me.

— Well exactly, I love those rainy afternoons too, very much.

— I couldn't want anything like that to change.

— Nothing would have to change. We could go on afterwards just as we did before. We'd never mention it, even to each other: as if it hadn't happened. Except that it would have.

Above them on the ceiling an angel composed of creamy light was about to catch a man falling back with outflung arms from a high scaffold, swooping to scoop him up with such grace and lack of haste, and a long loving look – as if through this act every catastrophe could be held off, everything could be saved.

In the narrow lanes in the rain they hurried home among the tourists in their dripping plastic ponchos: as before he steered her from behind with his hand on her waist or her hip – left here, right there, only each time he touched her now she felt the jolt of their contact, a surge in her veins. They drank something standing up in a bar, for courage, because Christine was afraid their lust would dissipate before they got back, they'd be returned inside their daily selves, too embarrassed to act. But this didn't happen. As soon as they closed the heavy street door behind them, shutting themselves up in the dank dusk-light and earth-smells of the *piano terreno* – along with a disintegrating old gondola and a few unclaimed tenants' letters, brown with damp on a stone shelf – they seized on each other for the first time in twenty years. And they were still good together. She melted against him.

For luck, then, on their way up the stone staircase to their apartment, they both touched in passing the marble lion finial on the bottom step, his head worn blunt and smooth and dog-like from centuries of touching. Inside the apartment Zachary spread out one of the big bath towels on Nathan's bed – by mutual unspoken consent they agreed they couldn't be on either set of marital twins. How easy it somehow was for Christine to undress in front of Zachary, show herself to him: because he'd seen her before, when she was young. They seemed to remember everything, forgave each other everything, it didn't matter if they were hasty or clumsy. When their lovemaking was over and they lay close together on Nathan's narrow bed, the eccentric light-fitting on his ceiling was a revelation: they hadn't noticed it till now. Staring up, they discussed in affectionate detail the twisting metal leaves and rosebuds painted pink and green, the cream glass lampshades shaped like lilies. They swore they would never forget it afterwards, ever. And later, before the others got back, they put the towel in the washing machine along with a few more items waiting to be washed, turned on the machine.

SEVEN

CHRISTINE AND ALEX WERE SITTING together, estranged but familiar, in the darkened room – the same room where she'd brought him the news about Zachary, months before. She was in her usual chair; Alex sat on the sofa, head bowed, hands clasped between his knees. It was the first time since he'd left that they'd been able to talk together reasonably, without recriminations – or, as at that moment, sit without talking. Outside it was autumn: even indoors the air was tangy and dank with leaf mould. The copper beech beyond the window was a tawny purple, sinking into invisibility against the dusk; something outdoors was conscious, rest-less, scratching along the gutter, raking the pavement. Fallen leaves from the plane trees, drifted into heaps, stirred up skittishly in gusts of wind; ragged scraps of blue cloud hunted across livid orange in the west. Christine hadn't put the heating on: there might be a reproach in the distinct chill, she might be making a point about how she was hav-ing to save money, now that her income was so reduced. She was wearing an ancient voluminous seaweed-coloured jumper, grey in the late light, which had belonged to her father – her chin buried for warmth in its deep roll neck, long cuffs pulled down across her hands. Alex's jacket was too thin, he was getting used to the temperatures in Garret's Lane. Lydia kept the heating atrociously high.

Mostly Alex and Christine had talked about Isobel. Neither of them had taken to her new boyfriend – too posh, too serenely assured. Blaise had blinked his light blue eyes at her parents warily, been manifestly unimpressed: as if he had taken it upon himself already to defend Isobel against what was unsound and suspect in their generation. But they agreed he was probably too stuffy to last – although Isobel seemed surprisingly keen. Both parents had observed, separately, deploring it, how pliantly their daughter accommodated herself to a certain inflexibility in Blaise. He was pleasant, well-informed and even amusing, but he didn't adjust to fit in with his company, didn't hold back his opinions – about Afghanistan, say, or about welfare dependency – which were disconcertingly conservative, though not merely conventional or stupid. Isobel darted glances approvingly at him, and was eager not to contradict this man who was not at all like the people she'd grown up with. She was still touchy with her father too. All the old ease had gone from between them and Alex suffered guiltily, though he didn't say so to Christine. He'd forced upon his daughter knowledge of himself as a sexual male, which she'd rather not have had. But that couldn't be helped now, couldn't be undone.

Alex had wanted to communicate to Chris this afternoon how he felt divided between herself and Lydia, and how his desire was to carry on being connected to both of them. But he hadn't been able to bring these words out, because he was afraid of her sarcasm transforming his fragile idea into a travesty, a laughable male offence. He saw Christine more clearly now than when they'd lived pressed up too closely against each other: her eccentricity and awkwardness, her dreamy vagueness, and something liberated in how, reacting to events and people, she came out with her startling pronouncements, her raw pained judgements of value and responsibility. Her character was in her face, worn to the fine bone and dimmed without make-up; her coarse thick hair, which she had cut off recently in a ragged short bob, with her own scissors in front of the mirror, was almost all grey now – in contrast to her eyebrows, smooth strokes of dark pelt. When Christine stood up to switch on the lamps, she offered him tea or a drink and he was grateful.

— Why not? It's dark enough to drink. Shall I do gin and tonics?

She said she would do them, conveyed that he mustn't make himself at home in this flat any longer. Alex was looking around him when she came back from the kitchen with glasses and ice and lemon on a tray. — Is something different?

— I painted the room. Only white again, but it looks nice, doesn't it?

— You did it all yourself?

— I'm perfectly competent, you know. Iz gave me a hand with the glossing. I was sorting out your stuff to give to you, books and CDs, and then I thought, I might as well clear out the whole lot while I'm at it, give it a coat of paint. I enjoyed it. Like the old days: balanced up a ladder in my dungarees with my roller, hair tied in a scarf, listening to Radio Four. I learned all sorts of things. And there's more space in here now, it looks better, not so crowded. I've changed the pictures round. Also I did the alcoves in that yellow.

Christine hoped that Alex felt himself shut out of the attractive room. Painting, she had felt as if she were sealing its walls against him, closing out any return of their past together. She had even given a little dinner party in here for a few friends, and enjoyed the ease of her social relations now that she didn't have to calculate for his severe judgement, his moods. But this afternoon he seemed not to want to leave. They spoke about a play they'd both seen, though not together. For an instant a picture, distinct and materially fleshed out as a hallucination, imposed itself: that one day Lydia might sit in here between them, and their whole history be merely the gaudy backdrop to a new normality. Christine saw her old friend composed and defiantly nonchalant, turning her eyes from one to another while they talked, managing her trick of conveying that she was bored without restlessness, withdrawn inside herself. The idea made Christine nauseous. She hadn't seen Lydia since they sat together at the concert.

Alex went to stand at the tall mirror above the mantelpiece, contemplated himself as if he were thinking about something else.

— Oh Alex, you're not as young as you used to be.

He leaned in to scrutinise more critically. — Do I look older?

— You're starting to look distinguished and senior, not the fiery rebel.

— Senior? Surely not yet, he exclaimed. He tilted his head to look from a different angle, dissatisfied. — You see you can manage very well without me, he said, as if she wounded him. — Lydia's the broken one.

Christine recoiled, the gin bottle jumped in her hand as she poured. When she sat back in her chair she drew her knees up, pulled the baggy jumper down over them; burying her nose in it she breathed in the safe smell of her father, the detached expert Englishman. — Is that how you rationalise it to yourself?

— But don't you think it's true?

— You come off very flatteringly in this version of the story. As Lydia's self-sacrificing saviour.

Alex dropped his gaze from himself, frowning, and played with the *objets* along the mantelpiece, adjusting their position without seeing them. These were lovely exceptional things Christine had found over the years: a small drawing of an interior by one of Sickert's pupils, a glass sculpture like a frozen wave, an eighteenth-century porcelain pink-and-gold cup without its saucer, old type from an Arts and Crafts printing press. He handled them clumsily because she was watching him, as if she were afraid of his dropping something. — The thing happened, anyway, he went on. — So now there's a new set of circumstances. Everything was changed already, because of Zachary. Everything was chaos. Lydia and I ... And aren't we bound to continue, all three of us? Being connected, I mean.

— Alex, you threw all that away!

She carried his gin and tonic to the mirror and uneasily they clinked fizzing glasses. The shock of the first cold mouthful in the chilly room was salutary, they surveyed each other with new gravity. — Of course I know it's complicated, she conceded. — We don't have to fight. But it's difficult for me if you come here. I'd rather you kept away.

It was important for her to say this. And yet whenever Alex announced he was turning up she was excited and roused as if she waited for a lover, a terrible hurtful lover; then while he was in the house she dreaded his leaving as if it would extinguish her. It was easier though, surely, to live without this agitation. Also, his presence forced her to imagine Lydia waiting for him in Garret's Lane, replete with possession of him. Christine said firmly that this wasn't his home any longer. She was well aware, though she didn't mention it, that his name was still on the deeds along with hers, and on the joint mortgage which they were fairly close to paying off. He was still paying the mortgage every month out of his salary, and had given up his place in Gospel Oak because he couldn't afford it, moved in with Lydia. But Alex would never bring up these material considerations to use against her. He didn't even mention money, and she could count on his being generous. His outward behaviour towards her was unfailingly gallant and considerate.

Alex only saw Christine's finished calm; her struggle didn't appear on the surface. He felt that she shut him out, with finality. — How is your work going? he asked, as if he were jealous of it.

She lied, said things were going well and that it was good

to be busy again. In fact the door of her studio was still locked. She was lying about this to everyone, she couldn't speak out loud about the prohibition she still felt within herself, against going back to her art. Her refusal had become a shaming vanity she preferred to dissemble: it wasn't as if she were honouring Zachary's memory or anything so sweet. The fear was paralysing; from day to day she postponed confronting it, and sometimes thought that she might never touch her work again. Only then, what would she do with the rest of her life? — And how's school? she asked Alex cheerfully.

When he'd gone the familiar anguish of loss cut her down like a wielded sabre: she could have sunk to her knees. Now she burned up for him, when it was too late. Oh, Alex! *Lie still, lie still, my breaking heart, My silent heart, lie still and break*. But she knew better than to give way to this. Instead, willing her dead limbs to work, she found her bag and her coat and keys and went out. Even the first gasp of polluted city wind, snatching at her when she opened the front door, blowing her along with scraps of greasy litter, restored her sanity like a slap in the face. She wanted to sew new cushions for the front room; a shop round the corner traded in bright wax-resist printed cottons, made in Holland for the West African market. There was an electric bell to press beside the shop door, and when they let her inside the place was noisy with Nigerians buying up bolts of fabric in quantities to fill their suitcases. By the time she'd puzzled over her choice of colours, she was all right again. This agony of parting came in spasms, it appeared; one had only to endure them, to get beyond them. She was pleased with the joyous pink and mustard-yellow fabric when she got it home, and fetched down her sewing machine right away from the attic storage-space. With no one else to take into consideration, she could order her days according to her own whim, sleep and eat and clean up when she liked.

The cruel truth was, Christine thought, that when she got past the pain and humiliation of their parting, she had no more use for Alex. The pain was a phantom, crying out in longing for something that was no longer part of her. She started and stopped the sewing machine in furious-sounding bursts, snapping off her threads jerkily, measuring for her cushions, calculating. Such ice-cold wisdom: she was half horrified at herself. But it would have been cold wisdom too if she'd taken Alex back – if he'd even wanted it. Once their lives had been full of the hidden meanings each sought out in the other, but that was years ago. And now he'd torn through all those intricate filaments of their coexistence which had bound them, and so she could learn to live without him. He was right: Lydia needed him, and she didn't. There was always the fundamental question – shied away from in imagination even as she sewed – of her work, what to do. But Alex couldn't help with that.

Christine had poured careless slugs of gin, and Alex felt its effects suddenly as he pulled the door of the flat shut behind him: a flare of heightened emotion like a white light in his mind. What if he went back to her? Vividly for a moment he could imagine taking Christine into his arms, comforting her, resuming all the friendly forms of their old life – and he almost turned around, lifted his hand to knock, to appeal to her. He could pretend that he'd forgotten something. Then he remembered the cool self-sufficiency with which she'd said goodbye, that grey glance tinged with mockery. Hadn't she told him he was growing old? Downstairs in the black-and-white-tiled hall, stale with familiarity, lit by its bare energy-saving bulb on a timer, he checked through the mail to see if there was anything for him – but Christine had forwarded it all. The light clicked off.

Outside, a gust of wind came buffeting at him out of the dull light, taking him by surprise; scrappy crows joyriding the turbulence had their feathers disordered. For a while he sat in the car without starting it up. Then when he saw Christine coming out of the front door – on her way, it seemed to him, into her unknown new life – he roused himself and drove, but not home to Lydia. He let the road take him, submitted without even inward protest to the traffic at a near standstill on the North Circular, took an exit at random eventually onto the M40. When he stopped halfway to Oxford to fill the car with petrol, he called Lydia and told her he needed to be by himself for a few days, asked her to ring the school, warned her that he didn't have his charger with him, so wouldn't be able to keep in touch. He said he didn't know where he was going. She mustn't worry.

A couple of things had happened to Alex recently which were almost nothing, yet perturbed and stirred him. One afternoon when he'd been standing on the crowded Tube on his way home – tired from the day's work, aware of pressure from other bodies and the noise rushing in his ears – he had watched a brown-skinned woman, tall and handsome, square-shouldered, her hair dyed bright red and clipped close to her head. He liked the way she held herself abruptly upright, building a little fortress of her own taste around her on her seat, listening imperviously to her music, giveaway white wire snaking from her ear; he had fantasised a whole identity for her – probably she worked in the arts, he thought, but in some skilled, technical capacity. In film, perhaps, as an editor. He had felt himself so invisible that he must have been frankly staring: this young woman was probably Isobel's age.

As she stood up to get out, her eyes met his, and Alex thought she neither repelled his attention nor encouraged it. Squeezing past, she was pressed against him, her coat hanging open – coolly she flicked her gaze beyond him, bumping his knees with her bag. In a moment that was truly mad, full of risk – and he was tired, he only wanted to get home – he followed her out of the train although this was not his stop, and up on the escalator. In the street outside there was a sticky drizzle, there were crowds – he hardly knew where he was, Holborn. The girl's coat was light-coloured – he followed her through the crowd, intent upon her. When she turned into a quieter side street her tall black patent shoes, heavy and punky, clacked on the pavement greasy with wet. She had turned round in the street and challenged him. Was he following her?

— It was stupid of me, I'm sorry, Alex said. — It was an impulse. You're very beautiful. I had no intention except not to lose sight of you for a short while longer.

Christine had said to him once that women dreaded being

called beautiful: it was like cheap perfume, meant either sex or sentimentality – or worse, both together. Yet he thought this stranger was not entirely disgusted, was even curious, receiving the inevitable male tribute with an awkward laugh, her oblique look glancing off him. Perhaps she hadn't closed off altogether the possibility of his pressing home his pursuit, inviting her for a quick drink before they parted. Or perhaps if he'd tried that she'd have pushed him away, shouted out in the street, disgraced him. When he stepped towards her, she had flinched. He had apologised again and turned around, resumed his journey home – and of course never saw her again.

The other episode went further, yet was more ordinary. A teaching assistant had joined his class, she was pretty and flirted with him, and once, when the staff had drinks after school, they kissed lingeringly in the car park. Then he drew back from her, with some relief. After all he had Lydia now. It was both a thirst and a blessing, the late renewal of his erotic life. When he was young he'd been too absorbed in the problem of himself to appreciate possibilities blooming around him everywhere. Now, how long before the women only looked at him with distaste, or pity? He thought that he understood his father at last, how he had accepted this pursuit of women as if it were in lieu of every kind of outward honour. Sex looked like a cheap trick from the outside, but in its moment it burned up the world. You could not have everything: the whole wisdom of life amounted to that. Whatever you had, was instead of something else.

———

Those days when Alex went missing – he was away almost a week – were for Lydia a strange interval of waiting. She didn't know if he was coming back to her. What had he talked about with Christine, that last afternoon before he left? The weather changed, after a first blustery night, to a stretch of mild late Indian summer through all the country: slanting golden light fell tremulously through the windows at Garret's Lane with their old uneven glass, onto the iron spiral staircase and across the warm yellow-brown of the parquet, the rich rugs. On her way to make coffee in the mornings, Lydia paddled with bare feet in warm pools of light and told herself she mustn't be afraid in Alex's absence, must be worthy of him and hold steady. Then she took her coffee back to bed, along with one of the serious books he had recommended. In all that time he was away she hardly went out of the house, though she looked after herself carefully, bathing and washing her hair, eating fruit, taking her vitamin pills daily, keeping away from alcohol. When the cleaner turned up Lydia pretended to be preoccupied, writing business letters at Zachary's desk.

One afternoon she telephoned Grace, and was surprised by how easily they talked together: all their old antagonism seemed to have fallen away and it was suddenly simple to be kind. Grace said she might come back to London, nothing was working out for her in Glasgow, she wasn't happy with having changed from sculpture to painting, she'd lost her way in her art. Lydia encouraged Grace to come home, if that was what she wanted. She could take a year out from her course, or give it up altogether – who cared? When Grace wondered about doing something entirely different with her life, studying to be a nurse, Lydia said it was a beautiful plan. All that mattered, she said, was that Grace was happy. She spoke these words wholeheartedly, and embraced without a qualm the idea of her grown daughter living in Garret's Lane alongside herself and Alex. She wanted to tell her that Alex had gone and she didn't know where he was or whether he would return, but didn't dare speak her doubt aloud in case that made it more dangerous.

Lydia's intelligence was cool and unsentimental, she saw her situation clearly, and knew it was possible that she'd lost everything. She had lived with fatal passivity, she thought, relinquishing her own control over what path she took – this had begun perhaps when she married Zachary, or perhaps long before that. Such cowardice anyway didn't bring good luck. And what would remain of her, if she were left all alone? She might have amounted only to what the others made of her. Bowed under her own judgement – she had spoiled something, and couldn't be forgiven – she imagined Christine at work in her studio, self-sufficient and fulfilled. Lydia had left behind on her friend's wall the painting of her best self, could never have it back. Now the short autumn days of lazy warmth and waiting seemed measured by the ebb and flow of visitors in the gallery next door; at a certain time, when the gallery closed, she was aware of chill emptiness on the far side of the wall. And each night she slept alone underneath the terrible quilt the others had sewn, with its scarlet zed; sometimes in the small hours she woke from nightmares and was afraid to fall asleep again.

She wanted Zachary then, who used to comfort her.

Someone had packed away all his belongings, which had been beside the bed when he died, into the drawer of the bedside table; when Grace and Alex cleared his things out of the house they hadn't thought to check inside this drawer. Alex hadn't disturbed its contents since, although he'd been sleeping on that side of the bed and must have looked in there. Lydia took out the items one by one and held them, then put them in her lap, feeling their cold weight through the thin cloth of her nightdress: his book and his reading glasses, his grandfather's clockwork watch which didn't keep time, his greedy eater's bottle of Gaviscon. His maroon leather slippers, beginning to be brittle from lack of use, were tucked in together neatly down the side of the drawer. She held these against her cheek and smelled the faint leftover odour of his feet, earthy and boggy, with a tang of the eucalyptus he used in the shower.

And in the middle of the night she picked up Alex's books as if they were stepping stones across the darkness, frowning over Clifford Geertz and Alfred Gell, labouring to comprehend them, discipline her thoughts. She never usually read non-fiction; now she couldn't bear novels, which were too much like life. This scaffolding of abstract thought at one remove from experience – describing it rather than enacting it – was a relief, lifted a burden from her. And she began to find her own thought leaping with genuine interest after the leaps of these clever, sympathetic writers; she lifted her head from the page to think, but not of her own life and crisis, or not directly. She copied certain sentences into her notebook. What revelation of the frameworks underpinning things!

Then she wished Alex was with her – not for passion only, but also to question him on this new plane, about these new subjects. She had a fresh lucid vision of possibility for their companionship. Of course, Alex's range was so much greater than hers, he had read everything, understood how it all fitted together. But still, she had her own quick perceptions, her logic and good memory. She had believed in the past that most of her inward intimations were incommunicable: Zachary had been afraid of her thinking too much, had only ever wanted to cherish her and cheer her up. Now for the first time she began to imagine sharing her ideas, even the dark ones. If only Alex would come back.

Christine heard someone unlocking the door to the flat and felt a surge of resentment, sure for a moment that it was Alex. Hadn't she asked him to keep away? She was tidying her bedroom upstairs, sorting out drawers, throwing out a lot of stuff she hadn't worn for years. Then she remembered that Alex didn't have the new keys to the flat. It was Isobel who waited for her in the front room, standing in the sunshine, looking out of the window into the street. — Why aren't you at work, darling? Christine asked anxiously. — How lovely to see you!

— Sorry Mum, I've interrupted you. Were you painting?

— Don't be silly, I don't mind. Are you all right?

Isobel said she'd taken the day off, she was feeling a bit under the weather, that was all, she was fine – and didn't want coffee, only a glass of water. She was looking around

her at the rearranged room with its new paint and cushions.
— It's all lovely in here now, isn't it?

Christine joked that she was depressed by how lovely the
flat looked. Didn't everyone do this as they got older, the ones
anyway that didn't just go to seed? Compensating for their
own decaying looks, they spruced up the outer spaces of their
lives to perfection – then knocked around inside these mini-
palaces like wizened nuts in a shell. Isobel laughed and said
that this was nonsense. Christine's looks weren't decaying
and she wasn't a wizened nut.

— Take off your coat, her mother coaxed, putting an arm
round her shoulders, unwinding the scarf from her neck.
— Tell me what's the matter.

— Nothing's the matter.

But she submitted to Christine's helping her off with her
coat, easing its pink silk lining along her arms hanging down
dejectedly. — Now sit and talk to me.

— I need to go to the bathroom.

She went up to Christine's bathroom in the attic; after a
few minutes, when the toilet had flushed but Isobel didn't
reappear, Christine followed her upstairs and found her lying
on her side on the bed with her face turned away, pressed
into the pillows.

— I'm pregnant of course, Isobel said, muffled. — As if
you couldn't guess.

Christine was overthrown, and shocked at herself because
this hadn't occurred to her. She'd been too distracted, had
thought that perhaps the thing with Blaise had broken up;
hoped for it, even. Pregnant – she couldn't take that in.

Sitting down on the bed beside her, saying everything loving and cautious and sympathetic, she stroked her daughter's downy arms and the brown hair which grew so coarse and strong from the nape of her young neck. Important with her news, Isobel seemed for the first time heavier and more substantial than her mother, the curve of her hip sculptural in her dress – plum coloured wool with a retro paisley pattern, like something Christine might have worn herself when she was young, thirty years ago. Isobel said that she felt like shit – she never normally used bad language, she was never crude. — The condom split. It's the latest in a whole chapter of accidents. Everything goes wrong for us, for me and Blaise. It's just the last thing I wanted. Fucks up my career nicely.

— And what does Blaise say?

Isobel hadn't told him yet. — He hardly knows me, it's all happening too soon. He'll just think I'm a walking disaster area. But I like him, Mum, I really like him. And I suppose he'll want to send his kids to private school, you know there's all that in his background and I'm not giving in to it. I'm keeping this baby anyway, whatever he thinks.

Of course she was, Christine said. With or without Blaise; if Isobel was sure that was what she wanted. Her parents would support her in whatever she chose, Alex would feel just the same. Christine was panicking, though, imagining the reality of a baby – perhaps a baby in this flat. Where else would Isobel live, if Blaise didn't support her? There would be no time for art then, she thought fatalistically. But she calmed down, told herself she should know from past experience not to panic. There was always time for art, you could always make time somehow. Or find the money to buy time, buy childminding if need be – money from Lydia, perhaps. Lydia owed her. And meanwhile her daughter was pregnant, and the fine afternoon darkened into evening beyond the skylight.

— I know I'm the right person for Blaise, Isobel was explaining. — I'll save him from himself, he needs me. We balance out perfectly. Because without me he's in danger of becoming quite stuffy, such an old fogey. With his clocks and first editions.

— Oh, do you think so? Christine said, cautiously.

— I'll be good for him.

After Oxford, Alex had driven west and south in the lovely autumn weather, visited second-hand bookshops, seen four cathedrals, two ruined abbeys and a castle. He who never took time off from work was truanting and aware – not guiltily – of the fixed intervals of school-time passing somewhere, like a clock ticking, behind the wandering formlessness of his days. In the evenings he did what was even more out of character: sat with his drink in the lounges of dull old picturesque hotels, spending money on his credit card, ordering solitary meals, browsing in the books he'd bought. The deadness of his phone muffled him in its silence, like the muffling thick carpets, too-hot central heating, silk-shaded lamps, furniture stiffly uphol-stered. He eavesdropped on the lively, involved interactions and flirtations of the hotel workers – only the guests in these places were discreet, not the staff – but didn't chat to them, as if he was in a foreign land and didn't know their language. The staff were mostly Central and East Europeans, but all spoke in good English.

Alex's first impulse, when he drove off in London, had been rebellious – he had thought that anything could happen next, he could do anything. And he knew it was amusing that his rebellion had been deflected into this utterly innocent thing, a holiday in English beauty spots fit for a blamelessly retired schoolmaster. No opportunities had arisen, anyway, for anything not blameless. Yet it turned out that innocence had its ecstasies too: one early evening, for instance, the façade of a great cathedral was spectral with livid orange light and he had the whole grassy precinct to himself. Pigeons wheeling in their flock, back and forth from the façade with its ranked saints, showed in concert first their dark backs and then their pale undersides, like the flickering play of some spirit around the fixed monument of the Church.

He could have spoken to Lydia – or Christine, for that matter – at any time, from the phone in his hotel room: he considered it. But in the end he never did, and then one afternoon he was suddenly bored by his freedom; the temperature had dropped and the light changed within an hour from clean-washed to louring. Thunder rumbled at the end of the handsome old stone streets of a provincial town whose history seemed to him exhausted, smothered under so much bland cultivation. He paid his hotel bill and headed for home, arrived in Garret's Lane without giving Lydia any warning, let himself in with his keys and hurried through the dusky rooms, full of anticipation. She was on the mezzanine, started up from where she was sitting bent over a book; it was early evening yet she was in her dressing gown, wearing reading glasses which she pulled away from her face as soon as she saw him. She hadn't switched on any lamps apart from the one she'd been reading by. — Alex, I'm so glad to see you.

— Are you ill? Why are you sitting in the dark?

He ran up the last few steps to embrace her, putting his lips to her forehead, anxiously pushing back her hair. Lydia put up her hands to frame his head, holding off their kisses, studying him with intensity. He couldn't imagine why he'd stayed away so long. She reassured him that she was perfectly well. — The day ran away with me. I've showered, I *meant* to get dressed.

She looked older, he thought. There was a new weakness in the flesh around her mouth and her jaw – or perhaps he'd just forgotten this while he was away, made a cult out of his idea of a younger more perfect Lydia. Her weakness disconcerted him, but didn't make him care for her any less; on the contrary, it made him gentler, more considerate. After all, he was growing older too. He touched the blemishes in her soft skin and she offered herself up to his fingers uninhibitedly, without flinching: he saw that she knew what he saw. — Have you been eating enough, Lyddie? You're too thin.

— You should have warned me you were coming. There's nothing in the place for supper. Are you starving?

— I'm starving. We'll go out, but not yet. First things first. Come upstairs with me.

Perhaps because his sensibility was imprinted with the

grave old architecture of abbeys and cathedrals, their love-making on this occasion seemed to Alex ceremonious and poignant, more like leave-taking than homecoming. Draughts stirred the floor-length muslin curtains at the windows, the reflected lights of passing vehicles moved in slow arcs across the ceiling. Afterwards, hidden against him in the near-dark, Lydia tried to talk about the books she'd read. — I had so many ideas! There were so many things I wanted to discuss with you, about religion and history and art. Now they've all gone out of my head.

Alex reassured her that they would come back. It was always like that with reading, he said. It was difficult to translate into speech the density of an argument set out in writing. — I liked the feeling, Lydia said, — that contemplating these big themes saved me from myself. You know, one's insistent self, always so agonised and burdensome.

He was listening carefully and agreed he liked that feeling too.

Lydia didn't want to move from where they were so perfectly mingled together under the duvet. — I suppose we have to go out?

But Alex was hungry. So while he ran a bath she put on the vermilion dress she'd worn on the day of Zachary's vigil, then sat at the dressing table and made her face up boldly, with brilliant lipstick. Across the table in the restaurant she told Alex that she'd come up with a new idea. She thought that they ought to leave the premises at Garret's Lane, find a place of their own. They couldn't sell, because the whole place was tied up in the Trust; but Zachary had purchased another property years ago in Mile End, in Lydia's name, in case the gallery had ever failed. They could sell this, and buy somewhere else – big enough for Grace too, so that they didn't all three have to live too much on top of one another. Perhaps Hannah and Jenny would like to move in above the gallery; any rent from the Garret's Lane premises was Lydia's. She watched Alex push his fish thoughtfully around his plate with his fork. Of course he felt the net of a new ownership dropping over him. And he was wondering whether it would really work out, if Grace came to live with them. Lydia loved the idea of a new relationship with her daughter, but no doubt the daily reality would prove more complex.

— I know I've been feeble, she reassured him, — but I feel better now. I'll be able to do much more, I won't be so helpless. I could be more involved with the Trust, and with the gallery. I've got friends who could surely find a use for me: on one of the art magazines, say.

Alex looked into her face, seeing beyond her words. Following Lydia across the restaurant when they arrived, seeing her swaying on her high heels, poised and buoyant, drawing looks from the other diners, the red fabric of her dress pulled tight across the attractive curves of her behind, he had had some perception of the effort it took to sustain this high performance. He'd been impressed as if with a strained, inward heroism, like an aged actress girding on her costume for the play. — No, you're right of course, he said. — It's a good plan. It's what we ought to do.

Lydia, you will be surprised to get this email from me. It is dawn outside the window. I never usually wake this early –

I've been sleeping well, since I've been sleeping alone. The light in here in the study – which I can't help still thinking of as Alex's study, because I don't really ever do anything like studying these days – is thin, so that I still seem to be inside my dreams. I woke just now to such a lovely sensation, I thought I was somewhere beside the sea. Not just as a memory but the actual thing, real all around me: salty air and waves breaking on a beach, gulls wheeling and calling, rock pools, plastic buckets of seawater, the tide's debris of wet seaweed, white cuttlefish bones. Even as I write down these details the sensation eludes me, it was so delicate – yet overwhelming. I felt very free and unencumbered, like a child on holiday. The long day opening ahead of me, carelessly capacious, ripe with possibilities for pleasure.

One good thing about living alone – of course there are downsides – is that you can act on your impulses, with no one taking any notice. So I got up and came in here. I thought of you. I wanted to tell you something but I don't know what it is. Perhaps it's the same as in my dream – wet seaweed, cuttlefish bones. I had such a luminously clear picture of you, amidst the sensations of my seascape – your crooked wit, your disabusedness. In your school uniform, of all things – which you always wore with consummate stylish wit. That horror of a green felt hat, jammed down on your head like their vain attempt to extinguish you. Don't reply to this, Lydia. I don't want to 'make friends', as the adults say to quarrelling children. Anyway children know that friends can't be made, only found – or lost again. But don't be sorry. Everything's what it is. Your, C. x

The last thing Zachary had arranged for the gallery before he died was an exhibition of late paintings by an American artist, a woman who'd worked in the fifties in Coenties Slip in Manhattan alongside Barnett Newman, Robert Indiana, Lenore Tawney. It was quite a coup because there had recently been a big retrospective of her work at MOMA. — You'll love these, Zachary had enthused to Christine, when he had confirmation it was coming off. — I think they'll speak to you. It's so good that everyone's excited about painting again. And although they're abstracts, and they're big, I see something like your cool sensibility and detailed subtle touch. Even a similar palette.

Now Hannah had finally opened the exhibition. Christine didn't know what to expect, she hadn't seen reproductions and refused to look at anyone's work on the internet, where even numinous masterworks became so many interchangeable Post-it notes. Preparing for her visit to Garret's Lane felt like a kind of pilgrimage, invested with significance, almost dread – and not only because she hadn't been near the place since Alex left. These paintings would surely have a message for her, like a message from Zachary. She checked that she had tissues in her bag because she was afraid that she'd cry if they moved her too much, make a fool of herself. Of course she'd made sure beforehand, through Isobel, that Alex and Lydia were away – in Glasgow as it happened, because they were helping transport all Grace's things back down to London, she was coming home. They hadn't moved out of the Garret's Lane apartments yet, although according to Isobel they had found somewhere to buy. A new member of staff was on duty in the gallery when Christine went in, so she wasn't recognised, there was no embarrassment over her connection with it. Stepping once again into the airy, tranquil exhibition space, with its soaring ribs of pale brick above white walls, she felt as if all her history and future were gathered up there, waiting for her to see it clearly at last. There were only two or three other visitors looking round.

And then after all that fuss of anticipation she didn't much like the paintings. They bored her: that possibility hadn't occurred to her, it really was a surprise. There was no danger of her shedding tears. It wasn't that she thought they were false or pretentious exactly: she could imagine the very authentic journey the artist had made towards these big pale canvases with their silver and grey and wheat colours, their painstaking exact grids and geometries, fine as quilting. In pursuit of some truth of the spirit she had refined away every intrusion of ugly life: all the dirty marks it made, all its aggression and banally literal languages. There were some beautiful effects of paint: Christine liked one work in particular, where the acrylic wash had run between grey stripes into denser forms, like rain clouds. But the end result, nonetheless, seemed to her puritanical, and too wholesome and homespun: even sentimental, in its conviction of the possibility of purity, like a sentimental mysticism. You had to be so vigilant, if you banished all obvious meanings from the front of your art, that they didn't return unobserved by the back door.

By the time she climbed into the upper gallery, and saw

by her quick glance around that there was nothing more to expect, she felt that her own mood of elevated expectation was become something false in itself, because there was nothing on the walls to meet it. She was disappointed – and indignant, too, that Zachary could have thought these works were anything like hers, or these colours. The muted pastels reminded her of the Edinburgh rock of her childhood, sent by distant relatives at Christmas, chalky pink and yellow sticks in a tin, dusted with powdered sugar. Often before, she remembered, she'd been out of sympathy with Zachary's enthusiasms. He was too hopeful, too easily persuaded by others, distracted by clever effects – as of course he had needed to be, if he didn't want empty walls in his gallery. His eye wasn't cruel enough. Christine felt the cooling of something fervid, in her imaginative connection with her dead friend. She began remembering him with a new realism – which left her in a dry parched place, alone.

She bought herself black coffee and sat in the cafe reading through a leaflet advertising local arts events, surprised by how much was always going on, and somehow not at all interested in it. Then Hannah, whom she hadn't seen for months, perhaps not since the funeral, came out through a door which opened into the private apartments beyond the gallery, and was usually kept locked. Looking past her into the room behind – before Hannah saw her and closed the door quickly, as if to shut in a secret – Christine glimpsed the walls denuded of their paintings, the floor without its rugs, shelves bare of books, things packed into piled-up boxes. Hannah and Jenny were going to move in, it all made perfect sense. Hannah came to sit down at the table with Christine, but their conversation was awkward, for no good reason; after all, Hannah wasn't answerable for anything Alex and Lydia had done, and she'd never taken sides. Christine said how much she'd enjoyed the exhibition, made all the required noises about its purity and simplicity. This wasn't merely out of politeness. She was convinced that if she were dismissive of the paintings, Hannah would put it down to sour grapes, see her as the eternally minor artist resenting the achievement of her betters. It wasn't clear to Christine why she felt she had to shield herself so defensively against Hannah's insight, put on this show of charm and enthusiasm.

Inevitably, before they parted, Hannah said that she'd love to know what Christine was working on now, whenever she was ready. And Christine smiled brilliantly, just as if she actually had something good to hide. She lied and said that she'd love to have Hannah take a look, see what she thought, very soon. Only not yet. She wasn't quite ready.

Christine got out of the cab and paid the driver in haste, tipping more than she needed to. She couldn't really afford a cab all the way from Farringdon Road, but she'd been agitated after her encounter with Hannah, and by her whole ambivalent relation to the exhibition. It was good to be home. She didn't belong in that public world of art, she thought, and perhaps now it was closed to her forever. Perhaps her work of lifelikeness and representation and stories was banal, in the face of silver grids and stripes. Alex had said once that she ought to give up her hope of wholeness, of a whole meaning, because it was naïve.

Letting herself into the flat she was glad to be alone. Solitude and silence had begun to be sensuous pleasures for her. It would have been awful in that moment to have to give false explanations to anyone, perform the sociability she did not feel. Instead she slipped off her shoes before she walked around the rooms, as if she didn't want to intrude even her own presence noisily. She made herself a gin and tonic and stretched out on the sofa, listening to music as it grew dark. After a while she lost concentration and her thoughts wandered, but still the music was the essence of the mood of openness and spacious feeling that came upon her. She had been playing with an idea, these last few weeks, for a series of small studies which began with an image of a woman on a bed, beside an open window. On her phone she had photos of Isobel sleeping, pregnant, she could draw from those. When she went into the kitchen to make herself supper, she first lifted down the blue coffee pot from a shelf, took out the key to her studio. Of course it was too dark to do anything in there now. That was what made it safe.

Opening the studio door, she hesitated on the threshold: she could smell rain on the wet autumn garden, mixed up with the studio's particular smell of turps and linseed oil and stale paint rags, and when her eyes adjusted she saw that a sash window had been left open a couple of inches through all these months. She groped for the light switch beside the door but found when she tried it that the bulb had blown.

So she stepped inside the room in the imperfect light from the passage behind her, half feeling her way by touch between the tall armoire with the broken door where she stored her materials, the sink scabbed and filthy with dried paint, the pots of pencils and pots of brushes, her art books, her bags of bits of fabric and plastic. The walls were crowded with pictures obscure in the shadows – her own and a chaos of other art images, as well as things torn from magazines or found in the street. Here among all these substantial tokens of her working life, she felt such promise of relief and happiness that it frightened her. A haze of dust was on her fingertips, and brushing them in the dark across the raised grain of the thick paper on her desk, she thought that now at least she had made the first mark, she had begun something.

With warmest thanks to dear Dan Franklin and Jennifer Barth, Caroline Dawnay and Joy Harris. And thanks to colleagues and friends at Bath Spa University, which is so generous in support of its writers.

ABOUT THE AUTHOR

TESSA HADLEY is the author of six highly acclaimed novels, including *Clever Girl* and *The Past*, as well as three short story collections, the most recent of which, *Bad Dreams*, was a *New York Times Book Review* Notable Book. Her stories appear regularly in the *New Yorker*; in 2016 she was awarded the Windham Campbell Prize and the Hawthornden Prize. She lives in London.

Insights,
Interviews
& More...

About the author

About the book

Read On

An Interview with Tessa Hadley

by Lisa Allardice

66 Long marriages are interesting. You either hang on or you don't. 99

AFTER SECRETLY TURNING HER HAND TO fiction in her forties, Hadley is enjoying widespread acclaim. She talks about happiness, motherhood, and her four failed novels.

Since finishing her latest novel, *Late in the Day*, Tessa Hadley has been "in a real panic." She was worried that the story—about two long-married couples whose seemingly well ordered, beautiful lives become messy after one of the husbands dies—was too sad, "too glum. I thought it was going to be a disaster," she says. But the novel, her seventh, has just received early reviews from the US, including one in the *Washington Post* that begins by hailing her as "one of the greatest stylists alive." We meet the evening before she heads off on a two-week US book tour. Many writers would grumble about this as a necessary evil of modern publishing, but Hadley is looking forward to it, especially her shared events with Irish writer Colm Tóibín, "a genius," and *The New Yorker* critic James Wood. The whole thing is "amazing," she marvels.

Success is all the more gratifying to Hadley "because it came later." After twenty years of struggling to write, *Accidents in the Home*, her first novel, was published when she was forty-six. Much has been made of this late start but, as she points out, it's hardly as if she were Penelope Fitzgerald (who was sixty-one when her first novel was published). In a long printed dress and waistcoat, and with her fine bone structure and expressive manner, Hadley, now in her sixties, could be the elegant, sharply drawn heroine of one of her own books (she is not, she insists, the quietly determined painter Christine in *Late in the Day*, "but I felt very close to her"). She speaks with the flowing, thoughtful intensity of her prose, and says of the impending tour: "I've had my moments of thinking 'wouldn't it have been fun to do this in my thirties? Wouldn't it have been wicked to do this in my thirties!' But then I wouldn't change those strange, anonymous, quiet, private years of feeling quite low sometimes because I so longed to write and I couldn't do it. Feeling like a real person, with friends and family, I wouldn't lose that, that seems part of everything to me. And," she reflects, sinking back into the armchair with her glass of wine, "what a nice compensation for growing older. I'm so lucky."

Reviews of Hadley's work tend to sound like undergraduate reading lists, comparing her to everyone from Elizabeth Bowen to Virginia Woolf. She has a theory that if you mention writers you admire in interviews, your work becomes associated with them, and she is full of recommendations (it's not often Polish poet Zbigniew Herbert comes up in conversation). She is yet to win one of the big literary prizes, perhaps because she is known for "domestic fiction" and is often seen as Britain's answer to Alice Munro or Anne Tyler. *Late in the Day*, with its focus on the enduring conflicts between marriage and freedom (infidelity), motherhood, and art, is hallmark Hadley, although, with its serious, questing characters, it is in some ways more akin to the now rather unfashionable novels of Iris Murdoch or Margaret Drabble.

With this book, she wanted to write about long marriages, in particular, because "they seem immensely interesting and they are ▶

3

kind of new in a way . . . people just live so much longer." She recalls an image from a folktale that appears in the novel of holding on to your lover as he goes through a series of metamorphoses: a fairy, a dragon, a lion. "And it seems to me marriage is a bit like that," she says. "You either hang on or you don't."

Hanging on or not is the starting point for much of Hadley's fiction and she is good on the nagging insistence of desire. "Yeah, I am always writing about the power of that, not in detail, but what a potent thing it is, and yet how hard it still is to talk about." The sex life of one of the couples in the book, Christine and Alex, "is nonexistent and quite inarticulate. You read all those wonderful *Guardian* advice columns, saying: 'You must talk to each other' and they aren't and actually they can't," she says. "There's something about cohabiting that is a little bit numbing. I have a perfectly happy marriage," she adds, laughing.

As Anne Enright noted years ago, "Hadley, for all the felicity of her prose style, is an immensely subversive writer." But, set in the comfortable, self-conscious world of London art dealers, artists, and poets, *Late in the Day* hardly seems radical. In fact, in subject matter, tone, and location, it could be described as a Hampstead novel for Fitbit-wearing fiftysomethings.

Apart from passing mentions of Facebook or Tinder, her fiction has an Austen-like reticence about external events. But Hadley, like her well-meaning, well-heeled characters, is acutely aware of "this dangerous globalized world," reading and worrying about it all the time, wondering: "What am I doing wasting my time on this, when the world is going to hell in a handcart?"

Her characters, like Chekhov's, are burdened by conscience and privilege, angsty and guilt-ridden, but impotent to do anything about it. "All a novelist can do is watch the people thinking that," she says. But instead of the largely upper middle-class groups of the north London novels of yore, she is interested in the overlooked "much-mocked, *Guardian*-reading liberal intelligentsia, who are so characteristic of now, with all their comedy and all their sweetness and goodness".

"Is it drawing to a close, do you think? Our bourgeois sensibility. . . . Our privilege of subtlety and irony is at an end," one character laments, without irony.

"It looks as if we have written about that forever and ever," Hadley agrees. "But we haven't done a catch-up on quite how that feels now." This, she says, is her true subject: "Not a huge one, but here in this little Britain, now. This class of conscientious, flawed, indulgent but self-searching people that is my generation. It is slightly tragic, no, comic, the helplessness of that conscientiousness," she says carefully. "It's a very conscientious moment I think."

Hadley grew up in "a very ordinary bourgeois schoolteacher's household in Bristol." But it was a creative one: her father was also a jazz trumpeter and her "stay at home mum"—"a very beautiful, very sexy, very glamorous woman"—was a dressmaker and artist, and her uncle is the playwright Peter Nichols (best known for *A Day in the Death of Joe Egg*). Although she was "quite clever," she was "no good at formal education," and hated her girls' grammar school in Bristol: "It was like a prison to me . . . the most unhappy time of my life." At fourteen she left to join her brother (now an art historian) at the local comprehensive, where she was much happier, and where an English teacher encouraged her to apply to Cambridge. "Did I enjoy it?" she asks herself. "I felt a bit of a fish out of water. It was a club again. I'd been no good at Brownies. I longed to do ballet. I longed to fit in at grammar school, but somehow I'm not good at it. It was fine at Cambridge. But no, I didn't love it."

AFTER CAMBRIDGE, SHE "HAD NO PLAN, EXCEPT TO LIVE." SHE TRAINED to become a teacher, meeting her future husband, her tutor, Eric Hadley, and thereby fulfilling her mother's prophecy that she would "meet a lovely man, someone older, somebody in authority." And following a brief spell teaching ("I was hopeless"), she "went off and had ▶

babies. . . . What madness. I blame D. H. Lawrence entirely." (She is an unashamedly passionate Lawrentian.)

Over the next ten years she had three sons, and three stepsons, who were "intimately part of our huge family," and was "busy making a life at home and all of that, like my mother had done." But she was seized with a "devouring, painful need to write . . . pushed down with shame when I thought: 'How dare I think of it.'" Her fervent reading only increased her "hunger to do it." Once her boys were at school, she tried more seriously, "in secret, not really making too much of it," finishing four novels. "But my books were no good. That was agony." She was "trying to write other people's books in other people's voices"; Bertolt Brecht inspired one, Nadine Gordimer another, "but in all of them I was faking it in every sentence." She told herself to give up because it was making her so miserable, "but the trouble was, I couldn't." After each rejection letter she would immediately start thinking about "the next novel and that I would get this one right."

In desperation, she enrolled for an MA in creative writing—then quite new in the UK— at Bath College of Higher Education, now Bath Spa University, in her late thirties, despite her misgivings—"Lawrence and Tolstoy didn't do an MA course!" And she loved it so much that she stayed on to do her PhD on Henry James. "I was being my clever self, gradually coming out from disguise," she says. She has taught creative writing there ever since: "a joy to do."

It was while working at the university that she got a call from her newly acquired agent to say *Accidents in the Home* had been bought by Jonathan Cape. In a scene that might come from one of her novels, she called her best friend, who said simply, "'This changes everything.' And it did!" she says, getting a little weepy.

In fact, an excerpt from the novel had already appeared in *The New Yorker*, "one of the miracles in my life. " She tells a good story of how, some years earlier, she had "made a pilgrimage" from Cardiff, where the family lived, to London to meet an agent who had shown interest in her work. They recommended she try placing some short stories. She naively suggested *The New Yorker*, where she was reading Gordimer and Munro. "I saw the agent and her assistant just glance at each other. Aaargh!" But she had the last laugh and is now a regular in the magazine. She credits Munro's stories with giving her "a lovely sense of permission" to write as herself at last and about the world she knew: "I was thinking this is just life. I recognize this, its weave is right, its sensibility."

Today, Hadley writes at a small desk in her bedroom in her London flat, having moved from Cardiff once the boys left home. "I do always feel that if I had a beautiful study lined with books, with an exquisite desk and flowers and a view, I would think: 'Who is that for?' It would feel fraudulent." After all those years writing between the school run and doing the laundry, she doesn't have a strict regime: "The rule is, it's not a rule, it's for pleasure, because I want to. So I write any day I can."

One of the most satisfying aspects of Late in the Day for Hadley is the character of Christine, who, when her marriage falls apart, is sustained by her art. "I was thinking about how I feel about work and its importance, and I was pouring that into writing about her and her painting." She recalls her great heroes, the Elizabeths Bowen and Taylor, who responded to "the gathering despair in western culture" in the mid-twentieth century "by saying 'I'm going to go on describing the everyday life of people getting on with love and parenthood and despair, because I've only just got this. I'm not going to give it up just out of angst and existential despair.'"

So Hadley plans to continue writing about people just getting on with the business of living. She's already at work on her next novel. "It's slightly mad. I suppose it is because I started late or something," she says. "Now I'm loving it, why wouldn't I do it as much as I can?"

Life After Death: A Conversation with Tessa Hadley

by Sarah Boon

LATE IN THE DAY DIFFERS FROM TESSA Hadley's six previous novels in that it features two central male characters, has very little emphasis on children, and follows a much longer story arc. University friends and graduates Lydia and Christine connect with Zachary, another student, and Alex, one of their teachers who is only a few years older than they are. Lydia feels drawn to Alex and Christine naturally connects with Zachary. But at some point they change partners: Christine marries Alex, and Lydia marries Zachary. We first meet them at a breaking point in their long, four-person relationship that spans jobs, moves, group vacations, and children, as the novel opens with Zachary dying. Hadley then moves back and forth between the past and the present to deliver a story that's at once heavy and dark, but ultimately redemptive and freeing at the end.

Tessa Hadley is a UK writer and professor and is the author of seven novels and two short story collections. She has been a regular contributor to *The New Yorker* since 2002. Hadley is a Fellow of the Royal Society of Literature, and has either won or been shortlisted for many prestigious writing prizes. She won the O. Henry Prize for her short stories "The Card Trick" (2005) and "Valentine" (2014), and she was on the Orange Prize longlist twice (*The Master Bedroom* (2008) and *The London Train* (2011)). She also won the Windham-Campbell Literature Prize in 2016 for her novel *The Past*.

I spoke with Ms. Hadley a week before Christmas, successfully connecting with her over the eight-hour time difference between her home in London and mine on the Canadian west coast. We discussed her new novel, the ways in which it differs from her previous ones, and what she's working on next.

Rumpus: How did the story behind *Late in the Day* actually come to you?

Hadley: I wanted to write a novel that covered three or four decades of these people's lives. I wanted to write long marriages, as that seems to me a really, really interesting subject. We are married now longer than ever in the past, not because people divorced in the past, necessarily, but because people died. In the nineteenth century, if you managed to be married to someone for sixty years, you really were against the odds. So there's this formative growth, where two lives begin together in their twenties and then continue through their thirties and forties, and grow around each other's shape.

It's so strange that people stay together so long, because they can change so enormously from what they were when their relationship began. I just think that's such a rich, ripe subject for novels to discuss. And it isn't a subject that's been at the core of the history of the novel. Courtship used to be at the core of the history of the novel, and also adultery, and in a way neither of those things are quite as interesting as they used to be. Courtship because we don't really do it like that anymore, and it isn't so final anymore, and adultery because not quite ▶

so much is at stake. You can have an adulterous affair and then you can leave your first husband and you can go and have another family with the new one and there'll be a lot of heartbreak on the way! It's still a subject, actually it's a subject of my new novel I'm just starting. But it doesn't have the power it once had with Emma Bovary and Anna Karenina.

So here's a new subject, not quite as dramatic as either of those, but nonetheless: the fact of couples enduring through decades. I wanted to write that and I thought, "well, we're going to need some drama to happen, obviously, it can't just be flat." And then I thought, *What if there are two couples, and they're sort of a little bit intertwined, like A is with B and C is with D, and then C is with A,* and you know, what fun to twist them around and play the game differently. And then, one of them dies.

I almost had the shape before I had the people. Also, I thought at first that the death would happen three quarters of the way through, and then before I started writing I knew that would be very hard to write because it would seem wanton or cruel to the readers who'd lived with these people thus far, to suddenly do that, and it would also be hard to make it plausible. It's very hard to write something like that coming out of the blue. I thought the novel had to begin with it, actually. And the minute I thought that the novel had to begin with a death and wind back from there, it seized my imagination and I had that first scene very powerfully, the sweetness of ordinary disregarded daily happiness that we hardly know we're in, until that phone call comes.

Rumpus: I think that was a really good choice to make to start at that part. It's kind of like Joan Didion's *The Year of Magical Thinking*— you're starting at that break point, that point where everything changes.

Hadley: Yes, and of course then everything else is read through it, which is far more powerful than to live through everything else and then suddenly drop this horrible, cruel event. It could have been done; there are ways of doing almost anything. But I think this was right, and I never regretted it. I knew it made things a little bit structurally complicated, that I would have to be coming backwards and forwards between the present and the past. But that was my only fear, and I hope it's worked anyway.

Rumpus: *Late in the Day* feels a lot darker than your other books. The emotions are dark—there's a lot of grief, there's jealousy. The characters are quite serious. Christine works very hard to keep Alex happy, to keep Lydia happy. It seems that the only easygoing character was Zachary and he's gone. And then there's also the heaviness of the past around these characters. Did you intend for the book to be this dark when you first started writing it, or do you even think it's dark?

Hadley: I think it is, and that's been another fear of mine for it, because in a way I sort of love to write a kind of comedy. Not laugh-out-loud comedy, but I do like to write comedy. But how could [*Late in the Day*] be otherwise, really? I don't know why it seized me, but it did. I knew I was embarking on something dark, and I did have my moments when I was writing it that I was worried that it was too dark, that it wasn't enough fun. But there we are—that was the novel as it was and I had to be true to that.

Rumpus: The characters are almost pulling in opposite directions. Lydia wants somebody now that Zachary's gone, Christine's pulling towards her work, Alex is pulling towards his work and also towards Lydia. Do you see this book as a statement on marriage in particular or on long-term relationships in general?

Hadley: I think it's just those particular people and that they have a particular history of being. In a way, the four of them have been a ▶

11

thing for years. And it's sort of what happens in one of those games where you heap up wooden blocks and pull out a piece. What happens when a piece is pulled out? The three who are left are thrown into chaos by the sudden absence, sadness, and grief.

And maybe what you said about how they are fixed in their patterns is why the upheaval seems very cruel when it comes (and I don't mean Zachary's death now, I mean Lydia and Alex getting together). It seems at first like more anguish, but actually I think it's a kind of taking a new breath, and finding new selves to go forwards with. So, probably at the end it should feel not like a happy ending but it also isn't, "Oh dear, something awful happened and what came out of it was more awfulness." It actually feels as if the violence of Lydia and Alex getting together has broken fixed patterns—exactly what you describe. It was quite a fixed marriage between Alex and Christine, it didn't feel very fluid; the pair of them weren't flexibly alive to one another. Which doesn't mean to say that they didn't love each other or that they didn't even respect each other, but it was something hardened.

Rumpus: Ultimately your books are about women. The domesticity, the endless details of family life: looking after the kids, doing the shopping, cleaning house, sharing parenting, etc. All of this is experienced through the eyes of female characters, and it often seems as though the male characters are incidental to the main story. They still affect a woman's character, because of what we talked about earlier that characters don't develop in a vacuum, but in a way, it's as though the men are sort of set apart. Do you consciously structure your books this way?

Hadley: I very much know that I write with women at the center; maybe that is inevitable.

I was really hoping that, in *Late in the Day*, Alex and Zachary would feel more central. I tried to make them not just products of the women's lives or aspects of the women's lives, but men doing their own thing, going after their own thing. And I'm actually much more sympathetic to Alex than a few of the early readers, who really are quite cross with him, though a couple of them were sympathetic. I quite like those rather dangerous men who just won't conform and won't quite buckle down to being nice. It occasionally worries me about women, the pressure upon women to be nice, and their own twisted ways of being nice, so there's something I quite like about men refusing to do that.

Rumpus: I agree with you that Alex and Zachary are more central in _Late in the Day_ then the male characters in your other books.

Hadley: Sarah, you're just saying that because I wanted you to! [Laughter]

Rumpus: No, they are definitely more central! Particularly when you think about Alex, and his lack of respect for Christine's ideas and her art, which we discover through his actions and through his conversations with Zachary. I think that's a huge impact on Christine's life.

Hadley: It is, and it's the worst thing about him, in a way. But there are other things about him in the book that I really hope are very appealing. He's quite gifted for life, in the ways he acts. He's a good teacher, a really good teacher. But I did give him that one cruelty: an obliviousness, in that he's an old-fashioned man and he can't quite grant Christine independence—she's got to slightly be his creature. That felt true to that kind of man, when I wrote it. But I hope it won't be read as the last word on him, that he's just awful. And in fact I'm quite hopeful that he's going to be happier with Lydia actually. They're going to suit each other much better—she's quite old-fashioned as well. ▶

Life After Death: A Conversation with Tessa Hadley *(continued)*

Rumpus: There were two scenes in particular in *Late in the Day* that I thought were a bit odd. The first was when Alex travelled to Glasgow and visited all those little dive flats to find Zachary's daughter. For some reason, I just couldn't picture someone doing that. How did you come up with that scene?

Hadley: Well, I think it's that sense that Alex can't tell Grace, Zachary's daughter, on the phone. This is one of the moments when I'm very admiring of him. The women are a bit collapsed, they don't know what to do, and really Lydia is insufficient at this point but, fair enough, she's stricken, horrified, and shocked. Alex needs to find the girl to tell her because he's sort of her godfather. He can't replace her father, but he's a strong man, and he has a good instinct to act, and he has to find her in person to tell her.

Rumpus: And it also gives him something to do because he needs to act.

Hadley: Yes, that too, yes.

Rumpus: The other scene that I thought was interesting was when Lydia was staying with Christine and Alex, and she climbs in their bed in the middle of the night because she's cold. That struck me as really odd.

Hadley: Well, it is odd, but it's one of those scenes that just came to me as soon as I began—in fact, before I began, I knew that was where that first section ended. Partly it is of course, a sort of symbolic representation, literally acted out in their lives of what's going to happen between them. Not that any of them know that at the time. She climbs in between them, and that is the rest of what's going to happen, like in mime.

I think such strange things do happen under those moments of stress. They fascinate me. I think life is often odder than we tell it, and that weird stuff comes about. Lydia's alone, terrified, terrified of death, terrified of what her life's going to be.

She's in a strange bed, grieving, utterly bewildered and lost. It doesn't seem to me at all impossible that what you would do is climb in between your friends. And then of course it's almost as if the act precipitated the rest of the novel, in which she really will literally climb in between her friends.

Rumpus: Starting the book with Zachary dying, then writing beyond Alex and Lydia getting together, helps you achieve that arc of the instigating event at the beginning of the book, but moving past Lydia and Alex getting together also allows you to show Christine's life changing. Like you said, the violence of Alex and Lydia getting together has broken fixed patterns, so now things have changed for Christine as well. And because you keep writing past that point, we're able to see that more positive story.

Hadley: In a way the moral is there is life after death. It goes on—what happens next doesn't stop. That's good that that's what you took away from it.

This interview first appeared on **TheRumpus.net.** ❧

Have You Read?
More by Tessa Hadley

BAD DREAMS AND OTHER STORIES

In these short stories it's the ordinary things that turn out to be most extraordinary: the history of a length of fabric, say, or a forgotten jacket. Two sisters quarrel over an inheritance and a new baby; a child awake in the night explores the familiar rooms of her home, strange in the dark; a housekeeper caring for a helpless old man uncovers secrets from his past. The first steps into a turning point and a new life are made so easily and carelessly: the stories focus in on crucial moments of transition, often imperceptible to the protagonists.

THE PAST

A novel in which a British family—three sisters and a brother—has assembled at their country house for a summer holiday. Over the course of this seemingly idyllic getaway, the family's stories and silences intertwine, small disturbances build into familial crises, and a way of life—bourgeois, literate, ritualized, Anglican—winds down to its inevitable end.

CLEVER GIRL

A powerful exploration of family relationships and class in modern life, witnessed through the experiences of an English woman named Stella. Unfolding in a series of snapshots, the novel follows Stella from the shallows of childhood, growing up with a single mother in a Bristol bedsit in the 1960s, into the murky waters of middle age.

MARRIED LOVE

A girl haunts the edges of her parents' party; a film director drops dead, leaving his film unfinished and releasing his wife to a new life; an eighteen-year-old insists on marrying her music professor, then finds herself shut out from his secrets; three friends who were intimate as teenagers meet up again after the death of the women who brought them together. This astonishing collection ranges widely across generations and classes, and evoking a world that expands beyond the pages. ▶

THE LONDON TRAIN

Two lives, stretched between two cities, converge in a chance meeting with immediate and far-reaching consequences in this compelling, sophisticated tale. As Paul struggles to reestablish a relationship with his estranged daughter in London, surrendering himself to an underground life of illegal squats and counterculture friendships. Cora has abandoned her home too—escaping her marriage, and the constrictions and disappointments of her life in London, to go back to her hometown of Cardiff. ❧

Discover great authors, exclusive offers, and more at hc.com.